Seaside

Also by Scarlett Thomas

and available from
Kate's Mystery Books/Justin, Charles & Co.

Dead Clever
In Your Face

Seaside

A LILY PASCALE MYSTERY

Scarlett Thomas

Kate's Mystery Books
Justin, Charles & Co., Publishers
Boston

Published in the United States by Kate's Mystery Books,
an imprint of Justin, Charles & Co., Publishers, Boston
www.justincharlesbooks.com

Originally published in the United Kingdom by
Hodder & Stoughton, a division of Hodder Headline

ISBN 1-932112-09-X
ISBN 987-1-032112-09-2

FIRST U.S. EDITION 2005

Library of Congress Cataloging-in-Publication Data is available.

Distributed by National Book Network, Lanham, Maryland
www.nbnbbooks.com

10 9 8 7 6 5 4 3 2 1

PRINTED IN THE UNITED STATES OF AMERICA

FOR LAURA

ACKNOWLEDGMENTS

Thanks to Dina S. Wilner for the ballet information and World Video for supplying the videos. Thanks to all my friends, particularly Jenny, Jane, Alison, Barbara, Kate, Sophie, Quentin, John G., Lee and Chaz.

Other special thanks to yous . . . Tom, for everything. Matt, for being my girlfriend. And Sam Ashurst, as promised, live forever.

gigni de nihillo nihilum, in nihilum nil posse reverti

PROLOGUE

Shadows flicker on the big screen in the dark, cold room. The girl sits on a plush red seat, picking at her fingernails. The blue-black polish is peeling. Her cuticles need trimming.

She is the only person in the back row of the cinema. Her skirt scratches her bare legs. Her black shoes are too tight. It is almost winter, and there is no heating. Only three other people watch as Humphrey Bogart speaks his final line: *This is the stuff that dreams are made of.*

Her heels click on the concrete as she walks slowly, smoking in the cold. No one is out tonight. No one in the alley next to the cinema. No one on the marina. Maybe there was someone down on the pier, there were some sounds. Probably kids smoking dope. If they had seen her they would have been impressed. She is one of the Carter twins: dark, glossy, shoulder-length hair, full red lips and inky black eyes.

Her eyes sting with the cold; the freezing air cuts at her face as she walks.

As she starts up the hill she whispers her plans aloud.

The two small hotels stand next to one another. Each is grey; neither owner can afford paint. Even in the summer each is ever only half full. The seaside is cruel. The winter is cruel. The two businesses fail year by year. Neither can buy the other out; they are waiting to see who goes bankrupt first.

Inside the Tulip Hotel a little girl tries to stay awake. Something is going to happen tonight. She has a secret that she must never tell anyone.

At night a noise sometimes echoes in the long, empty brown corridors. It's a squealing noise, like something that needs oiling. The little girl hears it every night, and sometimes in the day. The sound haunts her, like a bad memory.

On an empty road a car speeds. The driver has been drinking. His wife has been urging him to slow down. A man walks into the road, seeming to come from nowhere. Mr Carter puts on the brakes, but nothing happens. His wife closes her eyes. He swerves. His wife holds her breath. There is a tree. Their bodies shatter.

CHAPTER ONE

In a Solitude of the Sea

It was one of those nights made for curling up with a mug of hot chocolate and a Flake bar to dip in it. Or, at least, the weather was my excuse. I'd signed the lease on my new cottage only a couple of months ago, but tonight was the first night it had been cold enough to light the open fire. So I sat there in front of it in my thickest jumper, sipping from my mug and listening to the crackle and hiss from the pine logs, and the painful groan of the wind outside. My cat, Maude, was draped over the back of the sofa, her tail trailing around my neck.

All night, the weather had been getting worse. Usually at this time there would be a few dog-walkers from the nearby village, out for the last time before bed, their torch-lights bobbing around on the shingle beach or down the small track behind the cottage. But tonight there was no one. This place could get very spooky, but I reminded myself that it was less isolated than it seemed. Situated about half a mile from the nearest village, it was one of three old coastguard cottages in a terrace. But since the other two were holiday rentals, I was almost definitely alone.

My telephone hadn't rung all night, which made me feel even more isolated. Usually somebody rang, even if it was just Mum, who lived a couple of miles down the coast. She didn't seem to realise that, at twenty-six, I didn't need a phone call every day, but I could live without telling her that. Thunder grumbled somewhere in the distance and I wondered if the phone lines were down again. In South Devon this happened quite frequently. Unravelling Maude's tail from my neck, I stood up to check, chucking another log on the fire on my way.

On the floor next to the sofa was a pile of off-white manuscripts waiting to be marked. Stepping over them, and reminding myself that they were due to be handed back to the students tomorrow – and therefore that I should start reading them soon – I walked to the telephone in the corner. I picked it up, and heard the dialling tone hum normally. Strange. Then I remembered. Tonight was Mum's creative writing class. That meant there would be a phone call much later, when the class finished, with details of who had said what to whom, and more praise for the woman who ran the class – Emma Winter.

The rain hit the window hard, and I heard a tumbling noise from outside: probably one of my dustbins being blown down the lane. Then followed a loud clap of thunder, which made Maude jump up and scramble into a corner, scattering some of the essays as she went. The wind pushed more urgently at the windows and the cat-flap creaked backwards and forwards rather eerily. There was a very bright flash and a sharp splintering noise outside. Something had been struck – but luckily not us. Taking a cigarette out of the pack on the coffee table I sat back on the sofa, determined to ignore the storm, and pulled the first essay from the pile.

Then all the lights went out.

Maude looked at me, her small eyes barely visible. The fire was still crackling away, so it wasn't completely dark, but I lit the two candles on the mantelpiece anyway. The room, illuminated only by flames, looked ethereal as shadows danced on the walls and I gave up on the idea of marking for the time being, playing finger-puppet shadows with Maude, who jumped up the walls trying to get the moving 'creatures'. I was trying to cheer us both up. Some people thought I was really tough, but being stuck out here in the middle of nowhere suited me only when the lights actually worked. This was just too spooky.

When I heard the knock at the door I jumped. Who the hell would want to call at this time, in this weather?

'Hang on,' I called, grabbing a candle so I could find my way to the front door. The flame jumped as I walked along the hall, my deformed silhouette hovering around me on the walls and ceiling as I went.

I unbolted and opened the door.

'Hello?' I said, to a woman with blonde, wet hair and a long black raincoat.

'Lily Pascale?'

'Yes?'

'My name's Emma. Emma Winter.' She peered at me through the shadows. 'I can hardly see you. Can I come in?'

'Um, yes, of course.' I held open the door for her. 'It's a bit dark in here, though. We always lose power when there's a storm.'

She took off her raincoat and hung it on the hall-stand. I already knew something of Emma Winter's reputation from local gossip as well as from my mother. She was quite a well-known thriller writer, famous for her double twists, and she had retreated to the countryside a year or two ago. No one knew why. I remembered when I lived in London she'd frequently topped the bestseller lists, but she hadn't published anything new for a long time.

Some rumours suggested that she had gone off the boil; others that she was working on an important secret project. This was the first time I'd actually met her, although I'd seen her once, shopping in Totnes. She must have been in her early forties: far too glamorous for South Devon, with her bottle-blonde hair and heavy makeup. She was a great teacher, though, according to Mum, and I was hoping to acquire her services as a guest lecturer on my first-year creative-writing class. Maybe that was what she'd come to see me about.

'I'm afraid I can't offer you coffee or anything,' I said, as we went into the sitting room. 'Everything's electric here.'

'That's okay. I won't stay long.'

Emma looked a bit vague, as though she was trying to think of the right words for something. She walked over to the fire, where she remained for a few moments, her back to me. She poked at the smouldering logs a couple of times then knelt down, holding out her hands to warm them. Her hair was tangled around her shoulders, wet from the rain. She wore a white shirt, blue jeans and cowboy boots.

She turned to face me. 'I need your help.'

The words *I need your help* never used to bother me, but now the phrase made me uncomfortable. In the last year I'd managed to solve two murder cases, and I was a lecturer in crime fiction at the local university. These things seemed to give people the idea that I felt comfortable with death, and that I was the ideal person to talk to if they had a problem with it. Last time someone asked for my help I ended up being stalked by a psychopath for a week while he tried to decide when and if he should kill me. So Emma's words made me nervous.

'My help?' I said.

'Yes. Your mother told me about your hobby.'

I raised an eyebrow. 'If you're talking about the crime stuff, it's a hobby I'm trying to give up.'

Her dark eyes remained fixed on mine. 'Maybe I can convince you to change your mind.'

'I'm not sure that ...' I began.

Emma's eyes grew cold. 'This could be worth a lot of money,' she said.

I shrugged. 'Maybe I'm not that desperate for money.'

'How about this? I'll explain my problem, then if you don't

want to be involved I'll just leave.' She paused and lit a cigarette.

I passed her the ashtray as she made herself comfortable on an armchair.

'Go on.'

'Okay. This involves identical twins.'

'Names?'

'Alexandra and Laura Carter. Eighteen years old. They live in Torquay. Last night one found the other dead.'

'God.'

'It looked like suicide but the police think it might have been murder. But this is the bit I think you'll be interested in.' She cleared her throat. 'No one knows for sure which twin is dead.'

'Well, I don't mean to sound facetious, but which one's alive?'

'Laura.'

'So if Laura's alive, then the dead one must be ... What was her name?'

'Alex.'

'So where's the mystery?'

'The girl who's alive says she's Laura. But the suicide note was signed "Laura". She can't be both dead and alive.'

I picked up my box of cigarettes and pulled one out. This had me interested. I'd never heard of anything more bizarre.

'Is that why the police think it was murder?' I asked. 'Because of the note?'

'Yeah.'

She nodded. 'Yes. Although it's suspicious enough for them to investigate anyway, because it was an unnatural death. It doesn't take much to make a death suspicious, you know. And faking a suicide is one of the most common things a murderer does.'

I looked at Emma. 'What's your connection to the twins?'

'None,' she said, almost sternly.

'None?'

'That's what I said. And you won't mention my name when you talk to these people either.'

'Hang on a minute. I haven't said—'

'Five thousand.'

'What?' I said, shocked. I'd received a lot of money for solving my first 'case' but I wasn't a professional, and that had been reward money that anyone could have collected. I'd never been *hired* before.—

'Okay, ten,' she said, clearly mistaking my reaction.

'No, no. It's not the amount, it's just—'

'Ten thousand if you find out what happened to the girl. I want to know which twin she is, who killed her and why.'

'It's a lot of money,' I said. 'Are you sure you don't have a connection with these people?'

'Of course I have a connection with them. But I'm paying you enough for you to respect my wishes and not ask what that connection is.'

'Fine,' I said, intrigued by her frankness. 'Except that I haven't agreed to help you, yet.'

'Then I'll be waiting for your call,' she said, handing me a business card and standing up. 'You should think about it. You could have a great holiday on ten grand.'

'I don't actually travel all that well,' I said, smiling, 'but I wouldn't have any trouble finding things to spend the money on.'

'Then what's the problem?'

I frowned. 'This murder stuff. It scares the hell out of me.'

The room is at the end of the corridor; small and dark. At night there are tangerine shadows, cast by the single street lamp outside. It's dark in there now. Do you want to come in? If you come with me I can show you what's in there. It's white. That was her colour.

It's white. The wardrobe, the curtains and the walls. The carpet is white too. But wait. Here, next to the bed, we can see that the carpet is red. And there, on the other side. Red.

There is a noise. We can hear it as we walk round, if we listen carefully enough. It goes like this: pit, pat, pit, pat. Like rain. Listen, can you hear? Look now and see the figure on the bed. It's a girl, slim and beautiful. She is about eighteen, wearing a bra and knickers: both white. She can't see us. Don't be shy — have a good look. See the shoulder-length hair? See it fan out over her shoulders.

Her eyes are open, but she can't see us. She's dead, didn't you realise? Have a good look. Look at her wrists.

The electricity came back at about one in the morning, when I was half-way through the pile of essays. With light and warmth all around, Emma's proposition seemed more attractive. Maybe it would be worth looking into, I thought. Of course I could do with the money — who couldn't?

Emma had an edge: that hardness you see in people sometimes. It was in her eyes, her voice — and in her books, if I remembered them correctly. Her last novel had been described by reviewers as 'beyond *noir*'. Although I didn't really know what that meant, I'd heard rumours of horrifically violent scenes and haunting characters. She'd annoyed me, turning up like that, but I felt sorry for her, too. And her problem intrigued me.

The way I saw it, there were several possibilities. If the surviving twin was really Laura, then the dead one must be Alex. And if the suicide note was signed 'Laura', then it obviously wasn't a genuine suicide note. I wondered what the reason for it would be. Perhaps someone had thought they were murdering Laura, and had left the note as part of a fake suicide. If the surviving twin was in fact Alex, and the suicide note genuine, the question was this: why the hell would she be pretending to be Laura?

The whole thing had me seeing double, like looking into two mirrors at once. If I did accept Emma's proposition, one thing was for certain: I'd have a headache for a lot of the time.

CHAPTER TWO

Vanishing

———————◆———————

The next morning was crisp and clear, like there'd never been a storm. Neither of my bins was anywhere to be seen, and my car windscreen was covered with wet brown leaves, probably the last of autumn. Sticking the box of essays in the boot, I pushed off most of the leaves with my hands and got into the car. It had been purchased with the reward money from my very first case: a silver Saab with all the trimmings. Air-con, CD player, everything. I enjoyed the drive to work much more as a result of it. It cornered like a four-wheel drive and took straight roads as if it had been fired from a cannon. Some part of its spec meant I could overtake virtually anything, at almost no personal risk, which I did, all the way to work.

When I arrived the university was busy. We were still early enough into the academic year for there to be lost-looking students hanging around, occasionally asking directions. You could spot a new student a mile off. In a term or two most of them would have dyed their hair, pierced something or started wearing only black. But, for the time being, most of them still looked as if they were prefects at school.

When I got to my office a group of third-year students was waiting there for me. We knew each other well, since I'd taught them all last year, and they seemed particularly pleased to see me.

'Hi, Lily,' said one of them, a guy called Blake with a scar. 'Have you got our essays?'

'Yep,' I replied. 'But I can't tell you your marks now, you know that.'

'Oh, *please*,' said Heather, a blonde girl with long straggly hair.

'If you do, we'll tell you the latest goss,' said Blake.

I raised an eyebrow. 'Student gossip? Haven't you got anything better to offer me?'

'Ah, but this isn't student gossip,' he said mysteriously.

'What, then?' I said, smiling.

'Your mate Fenn just got called to the hospital. Bronwyn's gone into labour.'

'Oh,' I said, trying not to let my expression change in front of the students.

Once my office door closed behind me, I let the smile drop from my face. Fenn and I had been close friends once, although I hadn't spoken to him since the summer. At one point I'd even thought I loved him. But not any more. He'd chosen the day after he returned from his honeymoon – with someone else – to tell me that he loved me. Talk about bad timing. And this *someone* was Bronwyn, who had been a first-year student at the time of the conception of the baby she was now giving birth to.

On top of that my feet hurt. I kicked off my shoes and climbed up on to the large windowsill, which overlooked the car park. I opened the blind and one of the windows and lit a cigarette. Smoking was strictly forbidden in the building, but rules were there to be broken. And, anyway, I was in a bad mood now. But I resolved not to let it last. Fenn had confused me one too many times before. There was no way, I decided defiantly, that we were going to start all that again.

Some time later, on the way to my class, I ran into Mum in the corridor. She ran the women's studies degree and we often had lunch or a coffee together.

'Lily,' she said, emerging from her office as I walked past with the box of essays. 'Hello, darling. What are you up to?'

'Trying to get to my crime-fiction class. How about you?'

'Waiting for a tutorial student.' She frowned. 'What's wrong? You don't look very happy.'

'I'm fine.'

'Something's the matter.'

I sighed. 'Emma Winter turned up at the cottage last night.'

'Oh, did she? That's good. She said she wanted to speak to you about something. It must have been exciting.'

'It depends on your definition of exciting. It scared the hell out of me, her turning up like that in the middle of the storm and everything.'

'Oh. I did give her your number. She said she'd call first.'

'Mum!'

'What?'

'Well, you can't just give out my address and phone number to strangers.'

'She's not a stranger.'

'She is to me.'

'What did she want, anyway?'

'Nothing,' I snapped. 'Now I've got to go or I'll be late.'

'Goodness, you are in a funny mood,' said Mum. 'This can't all be because Emma called round.'

'Maybe not, but I can't talk now. It's nothing, really, Mum. Sorry.'

When I got home I was surprised to find my bins back behind the house where they were supposed to be. Someone must have rescued them, but I couldn't imagine who. Maybe a dog-walker. There were a couple of answerphone messages for me: one from my younger brother Nat reminding me that I was due to go and see his band, the Immense Standing Timbers, play in some jazz club in Torquay tomorrow night, and one from Emma, asking if I'd made up my mind yet about her offer.

My log basket was almost empty, so before I took off my coat I went out for some logs. While scrabbling around in the shed I thought about Emma and her offer. I really didn't want to accept it, but what else was I going to do? Carry on working at the university and spend my life rotting in academia? No, thanks. Recently this was something I'd been thinking about a lot. I was twenty-six and I still didn't know what I was going to do with my life. Teaching had never really been my thing: it had supposedly been a stop-gap when I'd first come to Devon, and for a while I'd loved it. But now? I wasn't sure. Taking Emma's offer would mean going a step further down this alternative, unlikely path I'd stumbled on. Was I ready to be a private eye? It was hard to be sure what was going to happen next.

Before I went back inside I stopped for a few minutes to breathe in the sea air and gather the last of my thoughts. It was beginning to get cold; my breath was icy and white. The lighthouse flared rhythmically as I stood there – a flash, then nothing, then the same again. Just before I opened the door to go back in I thought I saw some movement over by the next cottage along from mine.

The body is discovered, eventually. The girl, drained all of blood, pale and waxy on the bed; she didn't know what was going on. She had no idea it would turn out like this.

You can stop looking now. Seriously. Stop looking: it's sick.

Be quiet. There's a noise outside. A woman. She's coming in. Hear her as she walks slowly through the lobby of the hotel. Watch as she touches the front desk. It's brown, and has a layer of dust on it. No one is here. No one is ever here.

The room is still dusky: no one thought to turn the light on. In the

corner there is a man. His secret is written in blood; on the carpet and on
the bed. On the knife. He wipes some from his hands. No one must know
what he is doing, and he trusts her not to tell.
  You understand, don't you? This is not as simple as it seems.
Come on, what do you think? Was it suicide, or murder?

The fire didn't take long to build up and light, and once I'd
made a coffee and a sandwich, I sat down to read the paper. It
was hard to concentrate, though. I was still wondering how
long it would take me to earn ten thousand pounds working
part-time at the university. Maybe a year, before tax. Last time
I'd solved a murder it had taken me two weeks. And this might
not even be murder. Knowing I wouldn't rest until I knew what
I was dealing with here, I picked up the phone to call DC Ian
Nagy, to see what he knew about Laura and Alex Carter.

Ian was another friend I'd made last year. After he'd almost
arrested me we had become not exactly close but at least on
regular phone-call terms. Everyone thought he had a thing for
me; I was determined to resist his advances. There had been
rumours of corruption last year, when he'd been found with a
thousand pounds in cash, in a sealed envelope. He'd told me
he'd drawn it out to buy a car, but I'd heard people say he took
bribes from criminals. Whichever it was, he was my only real
contact in the local police so I was determined to be nice to
him.

There was no reply from his home number, so I left a
message asking him to get back to me. Since the questions I
wanted to ask might well compromise him professionally, I
decided not to try him at work. Instead I settled down for a
night in front of the TV, vaguely wondering where my cat was.

By eleven, Maude still hadn't shown up and I was beginning to
get worried. She never liked being outside in the cold, and it

was rare for her not to put in an appearance all evening. I tried opening the back door and calling; then shaking her box of biscuits. Nothing. This was looking bad. That cat had been with me three years, and she was the only secure thing in my life. There was no way I was going to lose her if I could help it.

Outside, it was dark. People who came to rural Devon for the first time often had a problem with just how dark it was. This wasn't city-dark, which was orange. Devon darkness was as black as you could get. You wouldn't want to try to go anywhere without a torch after dark. If you did the night would simply swallow you whole.

With a torch in my hand I locked the door behind me. Calling Maude's name, I walked around the back to the log shed and then up to the lane behind the house. There was a black BMW parked there. I'd never seen it before and wondered who it belonged to. As I walked, the beam from the torch made everything appear to vibrate and cast long, sinewy shadows across the track in front of me. I saw a couple of field mice and a hedgehog. But no cat.

Since there weren't any other options, I decided to try the beach.

The seaside at night bothered me. The seaside in the winter bothered me. Maybe it had something to do with repeated viewings of John Carpenter's *The Fog*, or maybe it was just those horrible sucking noises made by the water. Either way there was something sinister about it. That whole seaside thing got under my skin: those Wurlitzer noises; Punch and Judy. *Oh, I do like to be beside the seaside.* Even that tune was sinister, sung in its high-pitched key.

Still no cat.

It was gone one by the time I got to bed, unsettled by the evening. I didn't sleep very well and I dreamt all night about Bronwyn giving birth to her baby, a strange furry bundle which, when the nurses examined it, turned out to be Maude.

16

CHAPTER THREE

One-dimensional Girl

By seven the next morning I was back on the beach, watching the waves crash against the rough sand. It was very cold. The nightmares had kept me awake and I needed to clear my head.

After walking along to the rocks, I sat on the blanket I'd brought with me and lit a cigarette. There was a lot to think about but, being me, I started with the least important but the most fascinating of my current conundrums: who killed Laura Carter? Or, more interestingly who *was* Laura Carter?

Without intending to, I was being drawn in to all this. I wanted to see this Laura for myself, to see what all the fuss was about. But, of course, I wasn't going to take the case, was I? Maybe I didn't want to be a lecturer any more. Maybe I did. But surely I didn't want to commit myself to a life of crime, even if I was going to be on the right side of it.

My teeth were chattering and I pulled the blanket closer around me. I loved being alone like this, and although the early-morning-on-the-beach routine wasn't really me, I thought I could get used to it. The peace was incredible.

Then, above the noise from the sea, I heard a deep voice. 'Croissant?' it said, stressing the latter part of the word in an unnerving way.

Startled, I looked up and found a very attractive, sandy-haired man looking at me. Without being invited, he sat down next to me, waving some kind of pastry under my nose. 'I said, would you like a croissant?'

My mind processed the possible responses to this. 'Who the hell are you?' was the one I chose.

'I'm your new neighbour.'

Although this didn't mean he was a good-guy, I was hungry.

'Is it poisoned?'

'Uh-uh.' He shook his head.

'You're sure you didn't lace it with arsenic?'

'Yeah. But, hey, if you don't want it, I'll eat it myself.'

'That won't be necessary,' I said, smiling and taking the croissant.

'You're very suspicious. I thought you'd be a regular girl-next-door.'

He was American; his voice was hypnotic.

'I don't think I've ever been described as that before.'

'I guess you probably haven't.'

'Thanks for the croissant.'

'No problem. I called by yesterday to introduce myself, but you weren't in.'

'I'm a busy girl.'

'And do you have a name, busy girl?'

'Lily Pascale. And you are?'

'Jack Tucson. From Tucson, Arizona.'

'How convenient,' I said, smiling.

He grinned back and took out a pack of Marlboros. 'Smoke?'

'Thanks,' I said, taking one. 'So what are you doing on my beach at this time of the morning? Don't people sleep in Tucson?'

'Sure.' He looked at his watch. 'In Tucson they'll be going to sleep right about now. I guess I'm still jetlagged. I only arrived a couple of days ago.'

'I see.'

'And you say this is your beach.'

'Yeah, but I'm stretching the truth for my own ends.'

'A liar as well. You're not shaping up as great girl-next-door material.'

'Yeah, well, I won't cry if you take someone else to the prom.'

'Jeez, and you were my number-one choice. I have to say, though, you have a very cute cat. Maybe I'll have to take her instead.'

'Sorry?'

'The little grey cat? She's very affectionate.'

I raised an eyebrow. 'What do you know about Maude?'

'Maude. Hmm. Pretty name.'

'I said, what do you know about my cat?'

'I know she likes sleeping in suitcases. I haven't been able to unpack yet.'

'Oh, my God! So she's all right?'

'Did you think you'd lost her?'

'Well, I didn't think she'd been *catnapped*.'

'Hey, come on. That's not very fair.'

'Didn't you think she might be missed?'

'I didn't ask her to stick around.'

I got up, pulled the blanket around me and started walking up the sand towards the cottage.

'She loves anchovies,' he called after me.

'Just return the cat,' I called back. 'And maybe I won't kill you.'

As I walked out of earshot I could just about make out him saying something about the cream on top of the milk. Sexy.

My first class of the day was cancelled because the heating system had broken down. Instead I sat in my office shivering, catching up on some paperwork. At lunchtime I had a meeting with the other literature lecturers to attend, which meant walking over to the main building. My feet had turned to ice cubes in my office and I was actually glad to get outside. The university was funny like that: in the winter it was actually colder inside than out, and it would stay that way until the summer, when they would probably fix the heating.

I set off to the main building briskly, but my journey there was cut short by David Andrews, our new head of department. We made no secret of disliking each other, and he was one of the main reasons behind my career rethink. He was into things like management conferences and 'team-building'. I was not.

'Lily,' he said, raising an eyebrow at my cigarette.

'David,' I replied, not slowing down. He fell into step beside me.

'Might have to ban smoking, you know. Looks bad to the students. Very unprofessional.'

'Yeah, right. Why don't you have a meeting about it?'

'Oh dear. Have I caught you at a bad moment?'

I stopped and let the stub of my cigarette fall out of my hands. I ground it into the tarmac with my foot and smiled at him. 'You could say that. It's fucking freezing.'

'And so nearly a senior lecturer as well. This just won't look good.'

'What are you talking about?'

'Didn't you come to the meeting last week?'

I scowled. 'I think I managed about seven meetings last week. Don't tell me I missed an important one.'

'You must have done if you don't know about the new senior-lecturer vacancy. Your name's come up several times, and of course everyone knows you'll be applying. If it wasn't so unprofessional, what with me being on the interview panel, I'd open a book on it. I reckon you'd attract odds of about three to one.'

'Make that a thousand to one.'

'What?'

'I don't want to disappoint you too much, David, but I

think aliens will land on the planet before I apply for a pro-
motion. For one thing, I hate institutions, and for another, I'd
have to go full-time, which would mean getting up early. No,
thanks.'

'It would be a shame if Fenn Baker didn't have any competition.'

'Fenn?' I laughed. 'No. He's into fatherhood at the
moment. I doubt he'd go for it either. I'd say five hundred to
one.'

'Really? Well, I'm afraid the odds won't be that long. He's
given me his word that he's going to apply. Now, I hope I'm
not holding you up?'

'Well ...' I was confused. 'Strangely enough, I've got to be
at a meeting.'

'Maybe you'll think about the position? After all, you're
the one with the MA.'

'Yeah, but Fenn's studying for his Ph.D.'

'Studying. Hmm. Not very concrete, though, is it?'

At five I left the university and drove out of the gates in a
daze. All this corporate university stuff was spinning me out.
It was corrupt in some way, dirty, and made me feel like I
should take a hot shower. I considered the senior lecturer
position. Would they really put a lot of pressure on me to
apply? I hoped not, but then what else could I possibly do? Of
course, it would make sense financially, but so would taking
Emma's offer.

My mobile started ringing just as I was turning for the
road home.

'It's Ian,' said a male voice, when I answered it.

'Ian, hi. How's it going?'

'Good. Long time no see.'

'Yeah. Sorry about that, work's been a bit mad since term
started.'

'I got your message. So, let me guess, you've got theatre tickets, a restaurant booking and no one to accompany you ...'

'Sorry, Ian.' I laughed. 'I could do with a chat, though.'

'It sounds great. Where and when?'

'When are you free?'

'Any time, really.'

'How about now?'

'Now?'

'Yeah. Where are you?'

'Torquay.'

'Are you working?'

'Kind of. I can spare half an hour or so.'

'Great. I'm coming into town to see a gig tonight anyway. Sophie's okay for you?'

'Yeah. See you then.'

CHAPTER FOUR

The White Swan

———————◆———————

DC Ian Nagy was already in the small café when I arrived. Although he didn't wear a uniform, everything about him said *cop*. His suit wasn't quite the right cut for him, and his shirts and ties always looked cheap and slightly thin. He was okay looking, apart from those details.

'So,' he said, after I'd ordered coffee and made a bit of small talk. 'What was this favour you wanted?'

'Laura Carter,' I said. 'What's the story?'

He looked a bit startled. 'What do you know about Laura Carter?'

'Nothing. That's why I'm asking you.'

'Why me?'

'Because you're my only real contact in the police, and you do owe me a favour.'

'How d'you work that out?'

'I helped you solve a murder case, remember?'

He sighed. 'This is *so* off the record, Lily.'

'I understand.'

'Okay. Body found two days ago. Female. Eighteen. Slashed wrists.'

'Nice.'

'There was a note. Fairly straightforward stuff, like, "No one understands me, I can't go on anymore", that kind of thing. The note was signed "Laura". The body was found in Laura's room. But the girl was an identical twin, and the one still alive claims she's Laura.'

This much I knew. But I didn't let on. 'What do you think happened?'

'I think someone was trying to kill Laura and got the wrong twin. Whoever it was made the murder look like a suicide, wrote a lovely note to go with it and everything, just forgot to check they'd got the right girl.'

'Why do you think that?'

'I can smell it.'

'Come on, don't give me all that intuition stuff.' I smiled. 'What have you got?'

He smiled back. 'The dead girl's fingerprints weren't on the note.'

'But there were prints on it?'

He nodded. 'Someone's. But not hers.'

'The sister?'

'I don't think so. Poor thing. She's distraught.'

'Who found the body?'

'She did.'

'I see. And are the twins really that identical?'

'Yep. No one could tell them apart.'

'Any other suspects?'

'We're working with Laura at the moment, making lists of possible enemies and so on.' He shook his head. 'Poor kid. Imagine losing a twin.'

'It must be terrible,' I agreed.

'And she lost her parents recently as well. They died in a car accident.'

I grimaced. This was like some kind of horrible Greek tragedy. I couldn't think of anything to say, so I just shook my head and looked down into my coffee cup.

Ian scowled. 'She has a brother, but that's it. No more family left.'

'Stop it. You're depressing me.'

'That's life, kid.'

'Don't call me that. So is this your case?'

'Yeah. Didn't you know?'

'How could I?' I took a sip of coffee. 'Why haven't I seen anything about this in the papers?'

'We're not releasing any details yet. Since there is a possibility that someone was trying to kill Laura and got Alex instead, we don't want the murderer to realise he got the wrong victim.'

'In case he comes back to have another go?'

'Precisely. We'll put a restriction order on if any journalists get wind of it, but for the time being it's all strictly need-to-know only. Which reminds me. How the hell did you find out about this?'

I looked at my watch. 'Um, I'd love to stay and answer that, Ian, but I've got to get over to Juno's. It's my brother's band's big come-back and everything ...'

He laughed. 'Next time I'll make that question official,' he threatened.

'I'll look forward to that. 'Bye.'

'Yeah. Just remember to keep your mouth shut.'

It's cold outside. The night tastes salty. We walk a long way. Past the seaside. Past all the dead holidays; cold candyfloss that tears in the wind. Up into town, to the cinema. After all, everyone else is already there.

Juno's was a jazz bar with a reputation. This was where Nat's band was due to play, supporting a local jazz funk band called Stoosh, who were currently in the album charts at number forty-one. Nat had been excited about this for weeks – as had most of Torquay, if you believed the local papers. The lead singer of Stoosh was some kind of musical genius called Kurt

Venga, and although the Immense Standing Timbers weren't getting paid for the gig, meeting Kurt would be payment enough for Nat.

Juno's was situated just where a jazz club should be: down a back road called Sole Street next to a crumbling arts cinema. There was only one street-light illuminating the narrow road and it did this in flickering bursts, all its effort effective only in creating its own shadow.

When I got there the road was dark, cold and empty. The air smelt of fried onions and I could hear myself breathing as I walked to the small metal door and confirmed that the club was not yet open. The cinema next door was advertising *Casablanca*. I lit a cigarette and looked at my watch. It was only six o'clock and Nat wouldn't be arriving until just after seven, to prepare for his set at eight. Too early to get in; too late to go home.

After walking up and down for a while, not seeing another soul, I looked into the cinema. There was no one behind the small counter inside the door, but it seemed to be open. It was warm in there, so I walked inside, calling a vague, 'hello,' as I did so. Off to the right was a small door, leading to the single screen in the cinema. Beyond it, I could just hear Humphrey Bogart's voice. I pushed the small red door and looked in. 'Of all the gin joints in all the world,' he started to say.

The place was packed. But no one looked up. The audience was rapt; some were saying the line with Humphrey. 'Of all the gin joints in all the world,' they chorused, 'why'd she have to walk into mine?' Some people giggled. Some younger people looked like they didn't know what all the fuss was about. Since no one had noticed me I thought it would be okay to slip in and watch until the end. As I sat down in the back row, a dark-haired girl frowned at me, but apart from that no one said or did anything.

The atmosphere in the cinema wasn't like it should have been. People were excited; there was a definite buzz in the air. After the film finished people spilled out on to the pavement and lit cigarettes, or blew into their hands. It was freezing. No one seemed to be going anywhere, though, and I soon realised, from listening to a couple talking, that they were all waiting to go into the club. They all wanted to see Stoosh.

Soon Nat's small van pulled up and I walked over. As I approached it I brushed past the dark-haired girl from the cinema. She watched me go and I glanced back at her once. She was stunning. Her shiny hair was pulled into a french pleat, and her short black velvet dress was tight, showing off her slender, fragile-looking body. Her black eyes remained fixed on me as I helped Nat unload the van, but when the doors to Juno's were opened, she disappeared into the crowd.

The bar was small, smoky and dark. Between sets a DJ played jazz and funk classics and some people danced. Most people hung around the bar or the edge of the tiny, dirty stage, smoking and talking. A lot of people here seemed to know one another.

After the Immense Standing Timbers had played, Nat came over to me to see what I'd thought, and we chatted for a while about noise levels and stuff I didn't understand. Everyone was waiting for Stoosh to come out; to see the legendary Kurt Venga play. When he did emerge, the dark-haired girl came out too and kissed him before he went on. Before the band started their first number, he whispered into the microphone, 'Alex baby, this one's for you.'

My eyes went wide and I almost dropped my drink.

'That's Alex Carter, one of the Carter twins,' said Nat reverentially. 'They were at the girls' school. Freaky. I haven't seen either of them for years.'

Alex Carter. Bizarre.

I turned to ask Nat what he meant, and why he was so sure it was Alex, but he'd wandered off towards where his girlfriend was standing. Stoosh played for about half an hour before disappearing off into a back area. I watched Alex follow them through there. She seemed to be saying something urgent to

Kurt. I was about to follow, to try to hear what was being said, when I was startled by an American voice, coming from my left and speaking directly into my ear: 'Hey, girl-next-door.'

'Jack. What the hell are you doing here?'

'*Film noir* season next door.'

'*Film noir*,' I said, raising an eyebrow. 'Don't you have that in Tucson?'

'Lighten up. I saw you in there sniffling as the plane took off.'

'How? I was in the back row.'

'And I was just across the aisle.'

'Oh. Well, *Casablanca* does that to me.'

'Me, too,' he said, smiling.

I smiled back, but I didn't really have time for this now.

'Look, Jack, I have to do something. Can we put this conversation on hold for five minutes?'

'Sure. What are you drinking?'

'Scotch, no ice. I won't be long.'

The music from the DJ was loud. Walking towards the stage I felt a rush as the heavy funk bass line tore through my body. It was distracting, but I was more interested in the dark-haired girl, the one whom Kurt Venga had called Alex, and whom Nat had claimed was Alex Carter. She was standing close to the stage now, having emerged from wherever it was Stoosh had gone. Looking at my watch, I could see that they'd been there for at least ten minutes. I kept my eye on her as she swayed suggestively to the music, cigarette hanging out of her mouth, tops of her stockings beginning to appear as her black dress rode up her thighs.

Without meaning to I walked straight into a man in a dark blue suit.

'Watch out, love,' he said. Then: 'Hey, boys, look what I found.'

All at once I felt myself surrounded by young men; obviously friends with Suit-man. I had no idea who they were, just that they were blocking my view. The DJ changed the record to a tune I recognised. So did everyone else, it seemed, as the dance-floor filled.

'What's your name, love?' asked one of the blokes.

'Do you want to dance?' asked another, putting his hand on my bum.

'Fuck off,' I growled, wriggling away to where Alex had been dancing.

It took me a good three or four minutes to pick my way through the mass of people dancing, and when I got there, Alex had vanished. I checked the toilets and the bar: she wasn't there. It seemed that she wasn't in the club at all. Sticking my head out of the main door, moments later, I was just in time to see a figure in black turn the corner out of Sole Street and walk down towards the harbour. Without thinking, I slipped out of the club and ran in the same direction, stopping at the corner to check she'd definitely headed to the sea then slowing as I caught up with her. She was wearing a short black fur coat over her dress now, but she didn't look quite as glamorous as when I'd first seen her. One of her stockings had come loose, and the other was ripped. She seemed to be pulling at it; probably trying to straighten it out. I kept about fifty yards behind her, not wanting to be seen. All I kept thinking was: is this really Alex?

Confused, I stayed back in the shadows as she made her way around the harbour, past the two piers and up to what seemed a large demolition site, big, hexagonal and bleak, beyond which, down some steps, was the sea. Back down towards the harbour, neon lit up the streets and next to almost every shop was a deserted amusement arcade.

I followed Alex until she went down to the sand, where she stopped and pulled something out of her shoe. It looked like a piece of paper. I hid behind a dead-looking palm tree while she opened it out and read it to herself. Then she took a lighter out of her small handbag and lit the paper. She dropped it on the sand and, after watching it burn for a few seconds, turned and hurried back up towards where I was standing.

I stood still behind the palm tree, watching as she walked up the steps on to the street and then up a hill where, at the very top, two grey buildings stood side by side. One of them said *Tulip Hote* in dull neon lettering. The L had obviously long gone, although I wondered why it hadn't been replaced. The other said nothing at all. I wondered where the girl was going.

As soon as I could safely go down on to the small beach, I did, feeling every hair on my body stand up, because of the cold, and because of the fear I felt. Alex (or Laura, whichever it had been) hadn't seemed bothered by the horrible thin walkway covered in graffiti, or by the seclusion of the seaside below. I moved as quickly as I could to where she had been standing and examined the remains of the burnt piece of paper. Most of it was gone, but a small scrap had become slightly damp on the sand, and hadn't burned properly. In this light I couldn't make out what it said, but I picked it up anyway. I could still see the girl walking slowly up the hill, so I put the piece of paper in my pocket and went after her.

CHAPTER FIVE

The Little Girl

———◆———

The road became narrower the higher it went. At various points there were other, slightly larger roads leading off it, heading for places that were signposted, like the Regency and the Regatta hotels. I'd noticed these grandiose buildings from the harbour below. They seemed big, warm and inviting. Well, they were inviting compared to the grey buildings at the top.

The girl in black was about fifty yards ahead of me, still in sight. She never seemed to look behind her, which was helpful, because where the road narrowed, there was nowhere for me to hide. Down below the neon town glowed like a huge car head-lamp. Up here a single street-light dully illuminated what looked like a winter garden just off to my right. Beyond it was black, and I knew that was where the cliff started, and it was a long, long way down. The view in the day must have been mag-nificent. The two hotels that I was now approaching were obviously not cashing in on any of it, though. It looked like either one might just collapse at any moment and crumble into the sea below.

Alex had entered the Tulip Hotel. I wondered if she was visiting someone. I hoped that something was going to happen, otherwise this long walk would have been for nothing. I needed some clue about who she was. I *had* to know. And I'd thought I was going to turn Emma down? Yeah, right.

Not having many other options, I simply followed her into the hotel, not really knowing what I would say or do once I was in there. The small brown lobby was dimly lit, and a small reception desk sat unattended to my left. To my right there was a rusty cigarette machine. Straight ahead of me were the stairs, above which a red chipped sign said: *Rooms*.

'Can I help you?' said a female voice. I turned to find Alex, still dressed in black, standing behind the reception desk, pen in hand, swaying slightly.

'Do you work here?' I said, kicking myself immediately for being so obvious.

'I own the hotel,' she said, very blasé. 'Do you have a booking?'

Her voice was soft and smooth and she had no accent at all. If you met her you wouldn't know where she was from; if she was rich or poor. If you spoke to her on the phone you'd have no idea how old she was. She didn't seem to recognise me from the cinema or the club, which was a relief. In fact, she didn't really look at me at all, she just flipped the pages of a large hardback book back and forth while I stood there looking at her. Did she really own the hotel? I knew her parents had been killed, and she could have inherited it, but wasn't there a brother? Weird.

Eventually I spoke. 'I'd like a single room for one night, please.'

'Sea view?'

'Whatever.'

'It'll be thirty-five.'

'Sorry?'

'Thirty-five pounds.'

'Oh, right. That's fine,' I said, handing her my Mastercard and watching while she struggled with the manual swiper. Her small arms didn't appear very strong, and her tiny body looked as though it would snap very easily. I didn't know whether I was doing the right thing, but this was obviously where Alex

32

lived, and by staying here, perhaps I would get some sort of insight into what was going on.

'Number twenty,' she said, giving me a large key attached to half a wooden tulip. 'Up the stairs, turn left.'

'Thanks.'

My room was box-sized and cramped. There was no *en-suite* bathroom and the TV set in the far right-hand corner of the room had a sign attached that said, 'BBC 2 only'. I sat on the edge of the bed and lit a cigarette. Then it started.

The first thing that made me pay attention was the sound of something breaking downstairs. Then came the sobbing: a girl, from the sound of it, sobbing her heart out. I moved towards the door, not knowing whether to open it, finding the sound unnerving. Then, for a second, the sounds deadened. Then the words: *'Help me.'*

Opening my door a crack, I peered out. My room was on the first floor, but the sounds were definitely coming from the floor below. I stepped out into the corridor and walked towards the stairs. As I did so, a creaking noise startled me and I jumped, feeling my heart smack in my chest and my breathing almost stop. The sound was like a door being slowly opened; in fact, it *was* a door being slowly opened. It was room number fourteen, right by the stairs. It opened and I was face to face with a very old woman and a very little girl.

'My name's Philippa,' said the girl. 'But you can call me Pippa. What's your name? Are you a new resident?'

Standing completely still, I wasn't sure whether to answer the girl's question, or run for my life. Downstairs, the noise continued, the sobbing and, every so often, the wailing. From the top of the stairs the sound was clearer, and it freaked me out more. The thought that I was stuck up here, on the top of a hill, in a spooky hotel with this going on just didn't make me feel very comfortable. But the girl. She was something else.

She must have been about seven. Her long blonde hair was carefully arranged in two pigtails, which were tied with black ribbons. Her dress was also black and too long for her, covering her feet. This was in direct contrast with the old woman, who was dressed entirely in Adidas sportswear, with a big brown stain all the way down the front of her blue sweatshirt. They looked as if they were wearing each other's clothes; it didn't seem right, somehow. But what I couldn't stop looking at were the little girl's eyes. They bulged out of her head, as if they were too big for her. Unfair though it may seem (after all, she was just a little girl), I found this grotesque. The eyes continued to bulge as I stood there. As she spoke again, she seemed to be staring at some point off beyond the banisters.

'Granny?' she said.

'It's all right, chicken, it's a lass, that's all.' The old woman looked at me. 'She can't see ye, pet. She's got glass eyes.'

'Oh,' I said. Then, ashamed of myself: 'Hello, Pippa, I'm Lily.'

Downstairs a door slammed and a cold breeze tickled my legs as the front door was opened and then closed again.

'Granny,' said the girl, 'who is it? Is it her?'

'Hang on pet.'

The old woman walked into room fourteen and stayed there for a moment, tutting. She must have been looking out of the window.

'It's too dark to see, chick.'

'I know who it was,' said Pippa, mysteriously.

Just at that moment another door slammed below and then there were footsteps, echoing in the almost empty hotel, coming pat-pat-pat down the corridor, and then thump-thump-thump up the stairs.

'Hello, ladies,' said Alex, still in her black dress. 'Out for a snoop?'

'Hello, Laura,' said Pippa.

The twin's face turned stormy for a moment. 'Laura's

34

dead, you little freak.' And then she turned and walked back down the stairs.

The man stands on the edge of the pier now, looking into the water, the dim moon rippling gently on its surface. We can watch from the observation platform at the marina. In the orange light we can see the rain as it starts drizzling around his feet; his moon face as he turns to stare out to sea. What do you think brought him here? He looks like he's waiting for something, or someone. Yes, every two minutes or so he checks his watch. Maybe the person isn't coming. Maybe this was just another trick.

Get inside him: get inside the long, skinny body. Feel what he feels. He is cold. He is alone. He must be scared, standing there alone, but he doesn't seem to be. See him now as he sits down in the wet, dangling his feet over the edge of the pier. That's someone with balls. That's someone who isn't afraid of anything.

Shhh. Can you hear that noise coming up behind him? It's a squeaking, creaking sound. Something maritime, perhaps? A boat noise or a pier noise? He doesn't turn around, but the rusty screech comes closer. It comes rhythmically, every two seconds or so, an industrial noise, like a machine. An unfamiliar noise, like a knife being sharpened on a block. A death noise.

After all that I went back to my room. I wanted to leave the hotel, but felt unable to: that dark hill would have been too terrifying, especially after all the events here tonight. Instead I lay fully clothed in the brown bed, listening as the hotel became silent again, desperately waiting for daybreak. I wasn't sure whether I'd dropped off or not at any point, but at about three in the morning I was aware of some more door-slamming and the sound of taps running, then nothing, except a strange creaking sound, all night.

CHAPTER SIX

Mirror, Mirror

———————◆———————

Since I didn't have any classes on Friday, I thought I should go and see Emma, now that I'd decided to take up her offer. I still had my reservations about chasing murderers around, but that wasn't really what Emma wanted. She just wanted to know what had happened. After all, who would turn down ten grand? And if I got any inkling at all about who the guilty party was, Ian could deal with him – or her.

That stuff last night had freaked me out, but it had also intrigued me. If the twin was so keen to tell the police she was Laura, why was she going around telling everyone she was Alex? Pippa had been convinced the girl in the hall had been Laura, despite not being able to see her, but I had no idea why. And the twin herself had been very clear: *Laura's dead.* What the hell was going on? Why was she lying?

I left the house at about mid-morning, and this time there was no sign of Jack. Poor guy. I hoped he didn't hate me for leaving him stranded last night. I'd left the hotel from hell at daybreak and driven home – fast. I'd intended to go straight to bed and stay there, but haunted by the scrap of paper, I'd spent most of the morning trying to work out what the words were.

There were two parts of words – their beginnings or endings burnt away – one whole word and one whole sentence, all spelled out in blue ink, which had run slightly from the seawater. It seemed that I had got an L-shaped piece of the original document; the rest of it having burnt away. One of the part-words was *lipp*, which didn't make any sense to me. The next one I could see, which must have been part of the next line down, spelled out *Cornel*. The whole word, as far as I could make out, was *Lucky*. Then the sentence: *she looks like the real thing*. What did that mean? Did it refer to one of the twins posing as the other? I didn't really understand what any of these words meant, nor what the piece of paper might have originally been.

It was handwritten, which probably meant it was something personal, like a letter or a piece of diary. Maybe it was just some love letter the twin hadn't felt like keeping. Or maybe it was something more important – after all, she'd gone right out of her way to destroy it in private.

Emma had said we should meet in a bistro in Totnes. When I arrived I found her sitting up at the bar, dressed all in pink, drinking gin. Although it was only midday, I ordered a glass of red wine, and we moved to a small table in the far corner, which seemed private. I lit a cigarette while trying to decide whether I should tell Emma about all the stuff I'd already seen: the twin being identified as Alex by Nat and Kurt, claiming to be Laura with the police, but Alex with the hotel residents; the burning piece of paper; her claim that she owned the hotel; the sobbing and door slamming.

'So,' Emma said, interrupting my thoughts. 'I take it you have some news?'

'Yes. I've decided to accept your offer.'

'Fantastic. What made you change your mind?'

'Alex.'

'Oh?'

'Or Laura. I don't know which one it actually was. Anyway,

this whole swapped-identity thing has me interested. And, of course, I could do with the money.'

'Well, great,' said Emma, looking surprised, but pleased. 'I don't really know how one does this kind of thing. Do I give you half the money now and half later or what?'

'Half now sounds fine.'

'Cheque okay?' she asked, reaching in her bag.

'Wonderful.' I frowned. 'Except what if I don't actually find out what happened?'

'I suppose then I just don't pay you the second half. Don't worry,' she added, seeing my expression. 'I won't ask for this back. And, anyway, you *will* find out what happened. Trust me.'

'I'll do my best,' I said, pocketing the cheque she gave me. Five thousand pounds just like that. Amazing.

'So, shall I give you some background?' Emma said.

'Sure. Everything you know, however insignificant you think it is.'

'Yeah, yeah. I know the drill. Okay. Alex and Laura were adopted by the Carters when they were babies. Real parents unknown to us and also to the twins. Anyway, their adoptive parents own a hotel in Torquay called the Tulip Hotel. It's a bit, um, downmarket. The girls went to school in the town. Neither did particularly well, I don't think. But their big thing is dancing. They've both been doing ballet since they were really young. One of them, I think it's Alex, is – or maybe that should be *was* – very talented.'

'Any other Carters I should know about?' I asked.

'A brother, Tim. Biological son of the Carters. He's been running the hotel since the parents were killed in a car accident recently.'

This was interesting. The girl must have been lying about owning the hotel. Maybe she'd just been trying to show off, but why would she bother?

'Any connection between the car accident and the suicide?' I asked.

'Well, in a simple world there probably would be. If it was really suicide then I would have thought that the death of the parents would have been a contributing factor. Other than that, no. But there was foul play in the car accident, though. The owner of a rival business tampered with Mr Carter's brakes.'

'Do you know any more about it? The accident, I mean.'

She shook her head. 'No. I don't think it really has anything to do with this. I'd suggest that the same person murdered the girl and the parents, but the guy's in prison, so he can't have done it.'

I finished my drink. 'Going back to the suicide. You seem pretty convinced that it was actually murder.'

She nodded. 'Oh, yes. Absolutely. I just don't have a clue who's responsible.'

'None at all?'

'None at all. That's why I've hired you.'

'Do you mind if I ask how you know all this?'

'I'm an interested party.' She smiled, maybe realising she wouldn't be able to fob me off with that stuff for very much longer. 'All right. If I tell you do you promise to keep it a secret?'

'Sure.'

'This is a bit of a long story. Do you want another drink?'

Driving home, I wondered how much of Emma's story I'd believed. It had all started a few months ago, she'd claimed, when she was in Torquay researching her new novel. She had come across the twins then, while they were arguing over a boy in some club, and she'd been so intrigued by them: their beauty, style and anger, that she had decided to follow them and find out what they were really all about. From that day on Emma had kept watch on the twins, becoming fascinated with them, the characters from a book she hadn't yet written.

All of which had sounded like bullshit to me.

When I got home, the black BMW wasn't there. Not that I cared, of course, although Jack would need an apology when he did get home, since I had abandoned him in the club last night. Feeling cold, I went inside and built a fire, which I lit, and then sat next to dreamily, wondering what Emma was hiding. The key problem with her story, as I saw it, was that if her PI skills were that fantastic, what the hell did she need from me?

Outside the wind started picking up; whining outside my windows. Usually Maude would come and purr on my lap with the weather like this, but she was probably still in Jack's suitcase. Fickle cat. It was only about three o'clock, but already it was dark outside — from the rainstorm, and the lack of sun. I switched on a lamp and set about trying to work out what the hell *lipp* was part of, and what *Cornel, Lucky* and *she looks like the real thing* could possibly mean. I was treating the C on *Cornel* and the L on *Lucky* as capitals, since they seemed bigger then the other letters. But I didn't have much to compare them with, so I couldn't be sure.

Half an hour later the phone rang. It was Star, my father's girlfriend, who was also a good friend of mine. Because of a crazed killer, and a combined fascination with the dark side, we'd bonded in the summer and become quite close. She was a criminal psychologist working in London and her most interesting project so far had been a series of in-depth interviews with imprisoned psychopaths.

'How's it going?' I asked her.

'Great,' she said. 'My proposal's just been accepted.'

'Really? Oh, that's wonderful!' The proposal she was talking about was for a research project about criminal profiling. She'd been trying to get a budget for ages.

'Mmm. I can't wait to get started on it.'

I laughed. 'I thought you started it years ago.'

'Yes, well, I mean officially. Anyway. How's the university?'

'Pretty awful. I'm thinking of leaving.'

'No. Really?'

'Well, maybe. I'm going to give it some thought.'

'Gosh. I thought you were so happy there.'

'Not since I got a new boss. Oh, and Bronwyn's had the baby.'

'Right. And you can't face the idea of Fenn and the whole fatherhood thing?'

'Yeah. Especially if it's shoved down my throat all the time.'

'So what are you going to do?'

'I don't know. Probably grit my teeth and stick at it. Or become a PI.'

Star was silent for a moment. 'I thought you'd had enough of life in the fast lane.'

'I had, until this woman offered me ten grand to find out what happened with these twins.'

'Twins? What twins? Why haven't you told me about this?' She sounded excited, which was a bad sign. Last time she'd been excited we'd both almost ended up dead.

'It's literally only just happened,' I said.

'Well?'

While I filled her in on the details as I understood them so far, I was struck by the irony that while other women talked about men, dating and babies, all we ever seemed to talk about was murder. Of course, we did the whole man thing too, but usually only when we were drunk, and since the only man Star had sex with was my father, I wasn't keen for her to share any details with me.

'So you have no idea which twin is dead?' she said, when I'd finished.

'No. Well, at the moment it seems like it's Laura who's dead, but I really have no idea. Unfortunately, I don't even have an intuitive feeling, or anything to go on, except that the girl who is alive isn't very nice.'

'So how are you going to find out which one she is?'

I laughed. 'I have my methods.'

'Sounds intriguing. Any suspects yet?'

'No. But then we don't even know there's been a murder yet. Not for sure.'

'But you do think it was murder, don't you?'

'Mmm. I suppose. The girl's fingerprints weren't on the suicide note, but someone else's were. And the fact that no one actually knows yet which twin is dead makes it all highly suspicious. But the main thing is that the twin who's alive is definitely up to something. In my experience liars are found near murders, not suicides.'

Her voice went up an octave. 'And can I help with anything?'

'I'll let you know. Oh, actually, what do you know about twins?'

'Twins? I thought you'd never ask.' She sounded pleased. 'I assume they're identical twins?'

'As far as I know.'

'If people really can't tell the difference between them they must be.'

'People really can't.'

'Hmm. It's a genetic thing, you see. Fraternal twins can be similar but not usually that similar. I suppose we'll have to assume they're identical.'

'Does it make a difference?'

'Psychologically I think it does. Identical twins are more likely to have identity crises. Fraternal twins seem to find it easier to be themselves, if you know what I mean.'

'Hmm. Remind me what the biological difference actually is?'

'Well, with identical twins, there's only one egg, which splits. With fraternal twins, there are two eggs.'

'What about Siamese twins?'

'That happens when the splitting of the fertilised egg

43

happens late, or when it doesn't happen completely. Also, you can get this thing called mirror-imaging, which is quite interesting.'

'Go on.'

'It's where twins have reversed physical characteristics. Like if one's right-handed, the other will be left-handed, birthmarks will mirror each other and so on. Mirror image twins can have opposite personalities as well.'

'Wow.'

'I treated a psychopath who was a mirror-image twin, once. His brother was a missionary.'

I laughed. 'It spooks me out a bit, all the twins stuff.'

'It is a bit creepy, actually. But do you want to hear the creepiest thing?'

'Probably not, but you're going to tell me anyway, I'm sure.'

'Well, sometimes when doctors do scans on pregnant women, they can see two babies developing, but then the woman only gives birth to one child. Scientists believe that one twin simply gets absorbed into the other, or sometimes the child that is born has a growth, or an extra limb or whatever, and that's the other twin. Trapped in a boil or a cyst or a useless arm that gets amputated or something. Imagine that.'

'Ugh. Stop it. You need to spend more time with people who aren't psychotic, you know. I think it's affecting you.'

'Okay, but I have to tell you just one more thing. Sometimes one twin is born dead.'

'So?'

'Well, sometimes it's not natural causes, if you know what I mean.'

'What do you mean?'

'If it's not natural causes, then the other twin killed it in the womb.'

CHAPTER SEVEN

Ding, Ding

Jack came and knocked on my door at about seven, after I'd
called him to apologise about the previous night and to
demand the return of my cat. When I opened the door I was
very touched to discover him dripping wet and virtually
tipping sideways from the strong wind, with a small lump
stuck protectively under his jacket.

'You'd better come in,' I said, smiling at the sight of him.

'She loves this sweater,' he said, once he was inside, trying
and failing to remove Maude's claws from his black cashmere
jumper. She refused to leave his arms when he sat down,
though, and I thought maybe the jumper was just an excuse.
He was certainly a hit with her, anyway, and the feeling
appeared to be mutual.

'Wine?' I offered, taking a bottle of red into the sitting
room and picking two large glasses from the shelf. I'd decided
it was time to get to know Jack a little bit better and, after all,
who wanted to be alone on such a horrible night?

'Sure,' he said. 'And a towel would be good, if you have
one.'

'So,' I said, once we were settled and Jack had given his hair
a good rub, 'what did you think of Stoosh?'

'They were okay. I've heard much better.'

'I am sorry I left you like that.'

'Hey, I'm a big boy. Don't sweat it.'

I sipped from my wine glass, feeling warm and happy. I had selected an Australian Cabernet Sauvignon, which was slipping down a little too easily.

'So you like *film noir*?' I asked. 'You said there's some film season on?'

'Yeah, that's right. At the little arts cinema.'

'And you're a fan?'

'Yes, I am. But it's also research.'

'For?'

'My second film. I write scripts.'

'What was your first film?'

'It was a fairly small-budget thing when it eventually got made. *Broken*. You probably won't have heard of it.'

I'd heard of it all right. 'You mean the one that won the ...'

'Yeah, um ... Gee.' He looked embarrassed. 'Let's talk about something else.'

Broken was the story of a man who lost everything to a beautiful woman who'd conned him into doing whatever she wanted. It had won a prestigious European award and I'd seen it twice. It had been very stylishly shot, and the dark, shadowy images had been complemented by a great jazz soundtrack. The script was excellent. He seemed embarrassed by the whole thing, which I thought was a bit silly.

'Do you live here permanently?' he asked, changing the subject.

'Yeah, of course. What about you?'

'It's a long vacation. What did the woman call it? "Holiday let." Is that the right expression?'

'Yeah.'

'For six months. It's real cheap in winter.'

'Yeah, isn't everything around here?'

'It's great, though,' he said, finishing his glass of wine. 'And I could sure get used to this part.'

46

Raising my eyebrows, I reached for the wine bottle to give Jack a top-up. But then the phone rang.

It was Ian. 'Lily,' he said breathlessly. It sounded like he was on a mobile.

'Hi,' I said. 'What's the problem? You sound all out of breath.'

'You could say that. It's brass frigging monkeys out here. I've been jumping up and down to keep warm.'

'Where?'

'Torquay harbour. We're just fishing Kurt Venga's body out of the water.'

'Kurt Venga? You don't mean …?'

'Yep.'

'He's *dead*?' I noticed Jack sit up and pay attention when I said that. He frowned, then raised his eyebrows.

'Yeah. Look, you might want to get down here as soon as you can. You stayed in the Tulip Hotel last night, right?'

'Yeah, I did. How did you know that?'

'Never mind that. I just think you'd better get down here.'

'Weird,' I said, replacing the receiver. I looked at Jack. 'I've got to get to Torquay harbour,' I said. 'Sorry to have to cut the evening short and everything.'

'How are you getting there?'

'In my car.'

'After three glasses of wine? I don't think so. I'll drive you in mine.'

'No, Jack, I couldn't ask you to do that.'

'Come on,' he said, pushing Maude off his lap and pulling his keys from his pocket. 'You can complain on the way there.'

We parked in the marina car park and made our way over to a set of rusty iron steps leading from the edge of a pier directly into the sea. All around the dimly lit pier were reporters, police officers and members of the public. Some girls were huddled together in a group, crying. I guessed from what they were saying that they were fans. As we walked past the crowd I was able to see Ian supervising some paramedics as they loaded a body into the back of an ambulance. It seemed like the real action was over.

'That'll be headed for the mortuary,' said Jack, nodding in its direction. He did up his leather jacket. 'It's fucking cold.'

'You don't seem very bothered by all this,' I said, moving my feet up and down and rubbing my hands together.

'Just another homicide,' he said.

'You're strange. Wait here while I go and speak to DC Nagy.'

'Sure. I'm taking notes. This is very *noir*.'

'Whatever you say.'

Jack's blasé attitude was upsetting me. It was hard to tell if he was joking or not. I hoped this was an example of his black humour, rather than something more sinister. I didn't know Kurt, but felt sorry for him nevertheless. When someone's life ended it always made me feel sick.

'Lily,' said Ian Nagy, when I reached him. 'Thanks for coming down.'

'No problem. But you've got me confused. Why did you want to know if I stayed in the hotel last night?'

'Because Laura Carter wants to use you as her alibi. We've checked the guest book and there were three people at the hotel last night. One's blind, the other's about a hundred and fifty. The last seems to have been you. You're the only credible witness available to shed some light on whether or not Laura left the hotel, came down here and killed Kurt Venga.'

'Seriously?'

'Yeah,' he said. Someone came up to him with some kind of clipboard, demanding his attention. 'Look, everything's a bit frenzied here just now. Can we have a chat or something in about half an hour?'

'Sure.'

'That burger place over there does a particularly greasy cup of tea.' He looked at his watch. 'Are you going to hang around?'

'Yeah. Probably. I wouldn't mind knowing what's going on anyway.'

'Hmm.' He looked disapproving. 'I'll give you a shout when I'm ready.'

'Fine.'

As I made my way to the far end of the pier, where Jack was, I turned the previous night over and over in my head. Someone had gone out, certainly, but when the old woman had tried to see out of the window it had been too dark. It couldn't have been Laura because she'd come to see us minutes afterwards – for no reason, but she'd been there. I realised that I was now referring to her as Laura again. But last night she'd been Alex. This was too bizarre.

The pier was long, stretching out into the harbour, past all the boats and steps to a place where you felt like you were standing on the edge of nowhere. The sea made a sloshing sucking noise and from somewhere a tinkling noise kept coming, with the wind. I looked around: the sound was metal on metal, like a tin cup being hit with a spoon, but I couldn't work out what it was. The crowd of police officers and other interested parties was still collected way back near the street. Down here it was lonely and dark. Up above my head there was a string of coloured lightbulbs, which were unlit. When the wind blew they swung back and forth and I realised that they were the origin of the strange noise: ding ding, creak creak.

'Hey,' said Jack. He was standing too close to the edge of the pier, looking at the water, throwing stones in.

'Hi,' I said.

'Freaks you out, doesn't it?'

'What?'

'Death.'

'Yeah. A lot. Is that why you joke about it, because it freaks you out?'

'Who's joking? The saddest thing about it is that it really is just another homicide, just another suicide, just another war, just another missile. Whatever. No one really cares.'

Ding ding. Creak creak.

'That's really cynical,' I said.

'Is it?'

'Yeah. Everyone leaves behind someone who loves them. Someone who keeps their memory alive.'

'You've never been to America, have you?'

'No.'

'I heard a story once of a seven-year-old boy shot dead coming out of a candy store because he was inadvertently wearing gang colours. His parents couldn't get to the funeral because they were too wasted on crack. Like I said, just another homicide.'

'Stop it. You'll make me cry and I'll ruin my image.'

'Who's joking now?' He laughed, and the atmosphere was broken. 'Anyway, what's the story?'

'Are you still taking notes?'

'Sure. I never said working in Hollywood doesn't make you hypocritical.'

Down at the other end of the pier I could see Ian gesturing at me furiously.

'Looks like we're about to find out,' I said. 'Coming for a burger?'

'Sure. This is all very exciting.'

'As well as being so depressing?'

'That's *noir*.'

'Like I said before, you're strange. Come on.'

Beaten to death, the body falls in the water with a cold splash. Hear it. See it. It goes under then bobs to the surface.

The squeaking noise moves away, down the pier, across the street and up the hill.

Where do you think you're going?

We're not going there. We're going next door.

She sits there, the woman with the greasy hair. The blonde woman with the skunk stripe where she hasn't had her roots done. She sits there all alone in front of the TV. It's the middle of the night but she can't sleep. She's watching some chat show, probably: I Stole Your Man *or some crap like that. She heard the screams and the tears and the sobs earlier on. Everyone heard the screams. But she has heard the screams before. She heard them last week, before they found the girl dead.*

In her dreams that's all she hears. Not the girl, though. Her own sobs; her sleepytime tears. She is all alone. There's no one to help her when the pain comes. So let's sit with her for a while and keep her company. She'll tell us the story she always tells, about her husband, and the murder he didn't commit.

The burger bar disturbed me for several reasons. First of all, it was not a chain: a McDonald's or even a Wimpy would have comforted me, but this place simply said 'Burgers' on a dull orange sign outside. There were no other customers except for Ian who, when we walked in, was warming his hands on a chipped mug of tea.

We ordered coffee and cheeseburgers and sat down with him. I made the introductions and, although Ian didn't look too happy about Jack being there, he pressed on regardless.

'So what were you doing at the Tulip Hotel?' he asked.

'Just staying the night,' I replied.

'You went all the way up the hill to stay in that place on purpose? Try again.'

'Okay. I followed Laura and ended up there. But what does it matter, since I haven't done anything wrong?'

'You were following Laura?'

'Yeah,' I said. 'Although then I thought she was Alex.'

Ian raised an eyebrow. 'Can I ask why you followed her?'

'Sure. I'm trying to find out what went on with this suicide business.' Seeing his expression I added quickly, 'But I won't tread on your toes, Ian. You can be sure that if by some miracle I find that someone has killed someone, I'll let you know immediately. I have no desire to meet any more murderers face to face.'

Throughout this exchange, Jack was grinning, looking back and forth at me and Ian like this was the best sideshow he'd ever seen. It must all have seemed pretty weird to him. Because we'd had to leave the house and come down here before we'd really got talking, he didn't even know what I did for a living. God knows what he must have thought.

'And is this just because you get a buzz out of this?' asked Ian, continuing regardless of our audience.

'No! I'm just doing a favour for someone.'

'Name?'

'Sorry. Only if you arrest me.'

Ian looked at Jack. 'And we're supposed to be friends,' he said. Focusing on me again, he continued. 'Right. So you followed Laura up to the Tulip Hotel. Did she seem in a state to you?'

'What kind of a state?'

'Nothing in particular. Did she?'

'Her clothes were a bit dishevelled.'

'In what way?'

'Her stockings seemed ripped and like they were coming off.'

'Nice,' commented Jack, before standing up to go and collect our food, which was waiting on the counter.

'Well, that adds up,' said Ian.

'What? That adds up to her murdering Kurt?'

'Keep your voice down.' Ian let his own voice drop to a whisper. 'This is confidential, okay?'

'Okay.'

'Laura says Kurt raped her last night.'

'Fucking hell. Did he?'

Ian nodded. 'Yeah. There's plenty of evidence.'

'Shit.'

'If you mention this to anyone I will kill you.'

'Yeah, of course. So you think Laura may have killed Kurt because he ...' Jack sat back down.. 'Um, you know ...'

'No, I don't. She's such a sweet kid, so broken-hearted about her family being torn apart like this. I think she went home and cried, felt like her life was over, that kind of thing. But because there's such a strong motive there I'd like to rule her out as soon as possible. Poor kid's been through enough without being a suspect in a murder case.'

'Well, I'd love to be able to help you, Ian, but I can't say for sure that she was in the hotel all night. Do you have a time of death?'

'Not yet. Forensic guy reckons it was around midnight, but could have been some time either side of that.'

'All I can tell you is Laura was definitely in the hotel between about ten and eleven. But after that I can't be sure. I heard the door open and close at about ten thirty, but it wasn't her, because I saw her a few moments later. But as for later on in the night, who knows?'

'Right. You say you heard the door. Do you know who went out?'

'No.' I took a bite from my burger and a sip from my coffee. 'What about the brother?'

'No.' He sounded certain. 'Not the brother.'

'Why not?'

'It just isn't him.'

'Okay.' I shrugged. 'Incidentally what made you so convinced she was Laura? When I saw her at the hotel she said she was Alex.'

'She told us she's Laura.'

'And did you know Kurt called her Alex at the club last night?'

'Oh, my God, you're talking about the dark-haired girl,' said Jack. 'I see her in the cinema all the time.'

'Yeah,' said Ian. 'I'm not really sure what's going on there. I saw her this morning, and she said she told everyone she was Alex last night.'

'Why would she do that?'

He shrugged. 'She's convinced that the person who murdered her sister was really after her. She said it was in her interests to play along and pretend to be Alex. I think she suspected Kurt, and she was pretending to be Alex to try to find out what he knew.'

'Was there something going on between Kurt and Alex, then?'

'Yeah. They were involved. But from what I hear, Kurt was involved with several people – including Laura. But Alex was his official girlfriend. Apparently the day before Alex was killed, Laura had threatened to tell her sister about what went on between them. I think she was trying to give Kurt a wake-up call. Make him choose between them.'

'Interesting. I suppose that makes Kurt a fairly strong suspect for the murder, then.'

'Yeah. Laura says that when he found out she wasn't Alex, that's when he went mad and ... you know.'

'When is this supposed to have happened?'

'Just after Stoosh's set, apparently. In some back room at Juno's.'

I cast my mind back. They had been gone for about ten minutes, maybe slightly longer. There had been plenty of time for a rape to occur.

'You seem more certain that Alex's death was murder, now,' I said.

'Yeah. The fingerprints on the knife don't match the fingerprints of the dead girl, for one thing. Also, there's evidence of a struggle in the room. You know that the girl's fingerprints weren't on the note?'

I nodded.

'Well, it wasn't in her handwriting, either.'

'I see.' So Emma had been right. 'Did you find out whose prints were on it?'

'The brother's are and, it turns out, Laura's too, but that's because when Laura found the body, she showed the note to her brother. There's another set of smudged prints, but we have no idea who they belong to.'

'Could they be Kurt's?'

'Maybe. We're going to check.'

'Hmm,' I said, thinking.

'Anyway, I'd better be getting back. It's a shame you can't help rule Laura out, but if you don't know then you don't know.'

'Why are you so keen to rule her out anyway? Maybe she did do it.'

Ian shook his head and stood up. 'No way. I'd put money on it.'

'Oh, how did Kurt die?'

'Dunno, yet. We'll issue a statement when we do find out.'

'So it wasn't anything obvious, like stabbing or anything?'

'Nope. No blood. But he was dead when he hit the water.'

'How do you know that?'

'Forensic guy said there wasn't any water in his lungs. He floated rather than sank. Also, there was no foam around the mouth or anything. You get that with drowning.'

'Nice.'

'Can I ask a question?' said Jack.

'Fire away,' said Ian, looking at his watch.

'If he was floating around in the water, how come someone didn't see the body sooner?'

'The current takes things out then brings them back in again.'

'Who discovered the body?' I asked.

'A woman who'd gone to the pier to sprinkle her husband's ashes in the sea. She'd just started sprinkling when she heard this bang, bang, bang sound. Turns out it was Kurt's head banging against the wood just below.'

'How horrible.'

'That'll become an urban legend,' Jack said.

'Anyway,' said Ian, turning to leave. 'Give me a call when you want to get together properly.'

'Yeah. I will.'

'So,' said Jack, after Ian had left, 'you seemed pretty friendly.'

'Only when I want something, really.' I smiled. 'I'm a bad friend.'

'Are you? And I thought you were so nice.'

'Depends who you are, I suppose.'

'Hmm. On that subject, I'm quite interested to know who exactly *you* are. You're Little Miss Death-is-wrong one minute, then it turns out you've come down here to talk to some cop about dead bodies and all, which, I might add, you seem to enjoy. What's the story? Are you some kind of private eye?'

'No. I'm just a literature lecturer with an unfortunate bank balance.'

'You'll have to tell me more when we get home.'

'Sounds good. And warm.'

At that moment the wind blew outside and a small metal sign saying 'Amusements' spun round and round. It was freezing when we left the café and by the time we reached the car my hands were almost blue.

CHAPTER EIGHT

The Fall Guy

———◆———

We drove home in silence. Jack seemed caught up in his thoughts, and I was busy going over what Ian had said. Almost everything seemed to tally with what I'd seen that night. Laura had been dishevelled, and I was sure it had been her cries I'd heard in the hotel. But other things didn't fit in. Ian said she'd believed that Kurt murdered her sister. But if that was true, she'd picked a funny way of proving it. Why would she go to Juno's and pretend to be Alex? He was hardly going to confess. I could only think of one plausible explanation for pretending to be Alex at the club that night: to entice Kurt into having sex with her and then say she was really Laura and cry rape. It was possible that was her idea of revenge, and I'd heard of such things happening before.

In any case, it seemed unlikely to me that she had murdered him. After all, if I'd killed someone, I wouldn't go and tell the police the person had raped me. I'd want to keep it really quiet, because all it would tell the police would be that I had a motive for murder. Which implied to me that not only had she not done it, she hadn't even known he'd been murdered.

'Penny for them,' said Jack eventually, when we were about three miles from home.

'Just thinking about all that stuff Ian said. It's all very curious.'

'Do you want to fill me in?'

'Not unless you really want all the gory details.'

'I may as well, since I'm involved now.'

'How do you work that out?'

'I figure that once you've seen a body dragged out of the water, you're going to want to know what happened to it. And when your next-door neighbour is involved because she's been hired to find out something about a couple of twins, one of whom may or may not have murdered the dead jazz musician, and may or may not be posing as her dead sister, well, let's just say my curiosity has got the better of me.'

I smiled. 'I'll tell all when we get back.'

'Does that mean I'm invited in for coffee?'

'Something more alcoholic, but yes. Anyway, I've already asked you about three times. Do you require a written invitation?'

Jack laughed and after a while we lapsed back into silence. There were no other cars on the coast road. Jack's headlights, full beam, reached out into the black, picking out a bat as it dipped in and out of our path. The moon cast a silvery shadow over everything; a mist draped over the sea, clinging to its surface like a cobweb.

It was cold when we got inside. The fire had long since gone out. While I busied myself making a new one, Jack made himself at home and fetched new glasses for the bottle of wine we'd had to abandon before.

'Do you have any chocolate?' he called from the kitchen.

'I think so,' I called back. 'Check the larder. There's probably some Green and Black's in there somewhere.'

For the next few hours we sat chatting, smoking and eating chocolate, and at last I was able to fill him in on exactly who I was. I explained how I'd come to Devon less than a year ago, ostensibly for a holiday after I'd broken up with a boyfriend, and ended up staying. I talked about my mother and father, how they'd split up when I was young, but had remained friends. Without meaning to, I told Jack about Fenn, and our failed romance. At some point we opened another bottle of wine. Later I told him everything I knew about Emma and her offer. The only two things I didn't mention were the amount of money involved, and the rape thing, because I'd promised. I hinted, though, and Jack worked it out for himself.

'Do you think you're going to solve it?' he asked, lighting a Marlboro.

'I don't know. I don't really have any good ideas at the moment.'

'You've done this kind of thing before, right?'

'Yeah.'

'So it shouldn't be a problem.'

'I'm not so sure. It's all very confusing.'

'Mmm.'

'Anyway, apparently you're here for some peace and quiet?'

'Yeah.' He laughed. 'But I'll take whatever comes along. I was real happy to see you on the beach the other morning. Until that moment I hadn't spoken to anyone since I'd gotten off the plane.'

'Really? Don't you know anyone here?'

'I do now.' He grinned. 'I like going to places at random, you know? Someone I worked with on *Broken* raved about this whole area, and I thought I'd come check it out.'

'Wow.'

'Yeah. A lot of people think I'm pretty weird. I guess I'm a loner. I like doing things on my own. And I do need some space to write this next script.'

'What's it about?'

He cast his eyes down. 'I haven't actually started yet.'

'Any ideas?'

'Some. In *Broken* I was trying to subvert that whole *noir* thing where the *femme fatale* always gets killed or put in jail in the end. As you remember, the Charlotte character gets away with it all and leaves the dumb fall guy to take the rap. I loved

59

that idea, but it's hard to know where to go next. Like, what is there left to subvert?'

I looked at my watch. 'I'm sure you'll work it out.'

A bird started to sing in the distance. It was almost dawn.

'I suppose I'd better get going,' said Jack.

'You don't have to,' I said quickly. 'I mean ...'

'It's okay. It's not like I have to travel a great distance.'

'If you're sure.'

'Yeah. Thanks for an interesting evening.'

'Well, thanks for the lift.'

'Any time.'

As I locked the door behind him I yawned. It had been a long night. Maybe Jack was as tired as I was, but I couldn't understand why he hadn't made some kind of pass at me. Wasn't I sexy enough? Bewildered, I turned off all the lights and went to bed, wondering if Jack was thinking about me as much as I was about him. He probably wasn't: after all, he'd made it clear he wasn't interested. I'd looked all over for my cat before bed, with no success. Bitch. Oh, well, at least one of us got our man.

Rather embarrassingly, I slept until two the next afternoon. While asleep, I was vaguely aware of the phone ringing, the cat walking on my head, and at one point I thought I heard a knock at the door. It was Saturday. What was wrong with these people?

When I eventually got up, the first thing I did was make a cup of hot chocolate which I took into the sitting room. Curling up on the sofa, I felt slightly hungover and confused about Jack, but glad we hadn't taken things any further last night. Okay, so he'd made me feel a little undesirable, but I'd been quite drunk, and I might have felt like a bit of a slut this morning if we had slept together.

Once I'd regained my senses, I listened to my answerphone

messages. One was from Nat, telling me Kurt was dead. Another was from Emma, also telling me Kurt was dead and saying she thought it may have some connection with the suicide. Well, they hadn't needed to wake me up. I already knew these things.

Switching on the radio, I waited for a news report. Sure enough, Kurt's death was the headline item. There wasn't any specific mention of the dead twin, but the reporter mentioned that Kurt had been a suspect in a murder case until his fingerprints had ruled him out. Interesting. So it hadn't been his prints on the suicide note. Did that completely rule him out, though? I wasn't sure. And as for who murdered Kurt, I thought that would be an interesting avenue to pursue.

Emma thought so too, when I called her back.

'It has to be connected,' she hissed, rather unnervingly.

'I think so too,' I said. 'But how?'

'That's what you have to find out.'

'Are you adding this to my brief?'

'Yes, I am.'

'What makes you think it's so important?'

'Come on. A girl dies, and then her boyfriend gets murdered? Tell me that's a coincidence.'

'Well, obviously it's not.' I paused. 'But don't you think it means that we might be dealing with something more sinister here?'

'More sinister than what?'

'Well, before last night we were dealing with something that could have been suicide, but was probably murder. A one-off crime, probably done in the heat of the moment. Now it looks like we're dealing with a multiple killer. It was probably the same person who killed Alex and Kurt, especially as it seems that Kurt didn't kill Alex.'

I still hadn't worked out exactly who would want to kill Alex and then go after Kurt – especially as I wasn't even sure it was Alex who was dead. But in my experience, if two people who know each other are killed, it's never a coincidence.

'Are you saying you don't want to be involved any more?' asked Emma.

'No. I just have some reservations.'

'How does an extra five thousand sound?'

'I wasn't trying to negotiate a pay-rise, Emma. I was just pointing out that it's all a bit more heavy now. I've got DC Nagy breathing down my neck, and Laura Carter wanted to use *me* as her alibi to prove she didn't murder Kurt.'

'Which, let's face it, she probably did.'

'The facts don't really add up to that so far,' I pointed out, uncertain. 'What makes you think she did?'

'Just a feeling.'

'A feeling?'

'Just find out who done it, Lily.'

'I'll do my best,' I said, and put down the phone, defeated. At a loss for what to do next, I put on some clothes and walked down to the beach.

The sea was stormy today. I stood just about a foot away from where the heaviest waves were breaking. Towards the cliffs on my left, the sky was completely black. But off to the right, past the lighthouse at Start Point, it was a dreamy blue, with little fluffy white clouds scattered over it. Where the two scenes met, there was a rainbow. It must have rained before I'd got up today.

Emma was doing my head in. I wasn't sure what she'd meant when she'd said that Laura 'probably' murdered Kurt. What did she think, that Laura murdered her sister as well? More and more I wondered what Emma's story really was. She was hiding something, I just didn't know what.

I stretched up my arms towards the sky, feeling more awake now. I wondered if Jack was going to come down and sit with me, maybe bring me another croissant, but there was no sign of him. I couldn't see whether his BMW was parked in the lane or not. Maybe he'd gone out somewhere.

When I got back to the house I sat down with the scrap of paper I'd picked up from the beach. I still didn't get it at all. What was *lipp*? What was *Cornel*? And the other, more complete words: *Lucky* and *she looks like the real thing*. What did they mean? The phrase sounded familiar, but maybe because I'd been thinking it over and over. Of course I really wanted to know what the piece of paper had originally been. Lighting a cigarette, I sat back in my chair and sighed. It looked like I was going to have to go and talk to some people.

But who? Emma wasn't being as helpful as she could be, and Ian wanted me out of his face. Who else would know something? Laura would, of course, but I felt wary of approaching her outright. Something about her frightened me. I wanted to know *about* her, and I believed I'd probably get more information from people other than Laura herself — after all, the girl wasn't completely clear about *who* she was, let alone anything else.

I picked up the phone and called Nat, thinking maybe he would have some insight on the girl he'd thought was Alex, and who she and her sister might have known.

'Did you get my message about Kurt? Isn't it awful?' he said.

'Yeah,' I agreed, not mentioning that I'd been around when the body got carted off in the ambulance. 'Are you okay?'

'Yeah. I'll be fine. What did you call about?'

'Just to check you were okay,' I lied. 'Incidentally, that girl, Alex Carter ...'

'What about her?'

'She was Kurt's girlfriend, right?'

'Yeah. Why do you want to know?'

'I was just interested. She looked familiar. I thought I might know her from somewhere.'

'You don't know her, but you know her brother.'

'Do I?'

'Yeah, of course you do. Tim Carter. You went to college with him.'

'So I did.' Tim had been in the year above me at my sixth-form college. It all suddenly came back. He'd been small for his age, mousy and shy, but he'd been quite popular. At least, he'd been on the fringes of the upper sixth in-crowd. I hadn't thought about him, or any of that lot, for years.

'So, was that all you wanted?' asked Nat. '*Baywatch* is on.' Grief was obviously taking its toll on him.

'Yeah. Cheers, Nat.'

'No problem.'

'Before you go ...'

'What?'

'What were the twins like?'

Nat sighed. 'They were like some kind of town legend. Everyone fancied them. I never really knew them, but I had a couple of friends who did, and they said they were completely wild. They held these parties with just them and a few older blokes. I heard that they were into orgies and stuff. Twin fantasies, that sort of thing. That was before they fell out, of course.'

'Do you know why they fell out?'

'No idea.'

'Is the stuff about the older men rumour, or is any of it true?'

'I think some of it's true. Why are you so interested?'

'No reason.'

'Okay. I'll speak to you soon.'

Not wanting to go up to the creepy hotel again to try to confront Laura, I tried to figure out a way of getting in touch with Tim instead. Maybe he'd seen or heard something significant that night. Maybe he knew something about who killed Alex Carter, or at least what the twins had been like, what enemies and friends they'd had. Trouble was, I hadn't known him well enough then to call him out of the blue now. He would almost certainly have forgotten me, and even if I did pretend I was in the mood for some college-reunion type of thing, I couldn't see him going for it, not with all this stuff going on. He'd lost his parents so recently, and Alex. Poor guy.

Without meaning to, I suddenly started turning that sentence over in my mind. *He'd lost his parents so recently.* Before I knew it, I had come up with a plan that was so vulgar it almost made me feel sick. But it just might work. A few phone calls later I was in my car driving back towards Torquay, the heating full on and the stereo turned up. It was, as Jack had put it yesterday, fucking cold.

The graveyard was in Paignton, about two miles down the coast from Torquay. I drove past acres of housing estate, out-of-town supermarkets and more-brown-than-green palm trees on my way there. I'd never spent that much time in Paignton because it was a weird place. Along the main high street were two pet beauticians, three sex shops and a crumbling hairdresser's, enticingly called Shirley of Croydon. Then, around a couple of corners, I drove slowly past the seaside; the large esplanade hotels, the sports bars advertising karaoke, and down at the end, the quaint candy-coloured beach huts. Maybe it was my odd imagination, or maybe it was just recent experience, but I imagined dead bodies stacked in them, ready to come tumbling out as soon as they were opened for the summer.

I found a parking space right near the seafront and got out of the car, buttoning my brown suede jacket as I did so. I could see my breath harden in the air, and in the distance a man in striped trunks was running out of the water; he was old, blue and obviously quite mad. People said swimming in the sea in winter was invigorating, but they could forget it, I thought, shivering.

The graveyard in which Mr and Mrs Carter were buried was just up the hill and off to the left. It hadn't been difficult to find out where it was: once I'd identified the funeral directors involved I just called them and they told me straight out. After all, I was a relative from overseas, and of course it had been such a shame that I'd missed the funeral. Until I actually spoke to the guy at the funeral place, I'd expected my plan to be a bit of a long shot. But when he pulled out the file on the Carters he was able to share with me a piece of information which made me more optimistic.

'Well, look at that,' he'd commented.

'What?'

'It's the fifteenth today, right?'

'Yeah.'

'Well, it would have been Mrs Carter's birthday today.'

Their graves were side by side, inscribed with nothing except dates: when they'd been born, when they'd married and when they'd died. Oddly, there was no mention of their children. Normally these things said 'beloved mother of ... beloved father of ...' But there was nothing. Maybe it was because the twins had been adopted and Tim hadn't, I thought, remembering that detail from what Emma had told me.

Feeling a bit guilty, I checked the names of the people on the next gravestone and went over to wait on a bench, going over my plan in my head. It was a couple, so I'd be able to say they had been my parents. If it had been just one person, I would have invented some other connection; a grandparent, cousin, or sibling, depending on the age. I placed some tulips on the Carters' graves before I sat down, as a mark of respect and to say sorry for the fact that I was going to try and mislead their son. I sat there, shivering, for half an hour.

Then it started to get dark.

I'd never been particularly thrilled with the idea of grave-yards at any time of the day, but I religiously avoided them at night. When I'd been at school, some kids used to go to grave-yards at night to drink cider and smoke dope, often with the very much bragged-about intention of screwing on some poor person's headstone. This had been the ultimate in cool; at sixteen, the promise of alcohol, drugs, sex and death was about as exciting as it could get.

I was sure no one had actually gone through with it, but I remembered the story of a girl called Michelle who'd gone to the graveyard near our old school, with a guy called Craig. Legend had it that he'd left her there with her knickers around her ankles, while he'd run off screaming into the night, claiming he'd seen 'something' coming up behind her. No one ever found out what it was he'd seen, and he never talked about it again. They'd broken up after that.

So what was I doing sitting here, in the dark, surrounded by dead bodies? The thought of all the rotting flesh, the teeth and gristle and bones beneath the ground was just too creepy. And to cause me even more concern, not so far away from me there was a faint squealing sound, like a rusty bicycle. It was animal, though, not mechanical. *Please, not rats*, I willed, pulling up my legs under me. But the sound got closer and closer and soon I was able to see its origin: two flappy bats, in and out of the tree above my head. Great.

An hour later, cold, terrified and hungry, I was about to abort this mission, feeling silly and as if I'd gone a tangent too far. Then I heard a cough. More squeaking. I stood up and moved into the shadows behind the tree, feeling that I might be sick with fear, then I relaxed a little. It was Tim, or at least, it looked like Tim.

In some ways he hadn't changed much over the years. He'd grown a small, fair, goatee beard, but apart from that he was the same: small, wiry and weak-looking. He wore jogging bottoms, a bomber jacket and white plimsolls. But the detail I hadn't been expecting, and the one that made me gasp as I crouched behind the tree, was the big grey wheelchair in which he was sitting. It looked old and well-worn; some of the wheel spokes were rusted and the two steel foot-rests seemed precarious, wobbling every so often with the pressure of his feet. He certainly hadn't been in that when I'd known him.

Not noticing me, he moved towards his parents' graves, pushing his large penny-farthing-style wheels with both hands. Getting the contraption through the mud here seemed to take all his strength, but he manoeuvred to the position he wanted and stopped, wringing his hands in the half-light. I stood still and listened as he began talking.

'Hi, Mum. Happy birthday. Hi, Dad. I hope you're okay. That sounds stupid, doesn't it? I just don't know what to say. It's not easy, trying to talk to you like this, not knowing if you're really there or not. I hope you're listening, because I'm so sorry about everything, so sorry you had to go like that. I suppose Laura's there with you? I hope she hasn't told you everything, because I want to be the first to do that. I've let you down so badly. We both did, but mainly me. And, Laura, if you're listening ... Please forgive me. Please. I'm so sorry I didn't listen to you. I'm so sorry about everything.' He started to cry.

'Alex misses you as well. She's been in such a state since you died, Laura. She wants you to forgive her for everything. I know you didn't get on towards the end, but she's sorry. I'll tell her you are, too. I suppose you'll be buried here soon, when the coroner has finished whatever it is they do. I'll visit you every day, I promise, to make up for everything.

Tim finished talking. Feeling like a really bad person, I continued with my plan. Slipping out from the shadows, I walked to the neighbouring grave as if I had just arrived, knelt down by it and pretended to pray. Actually, I wasn't pretending: I was praying to God to forgive me for what I was about to do.

'Are they your parents?' asked Tim, noticing me at last.

I nodded numbly.

'Same here,' he said. 'Other people don't understand, do they?'

'No,' I murmured. 'No, they don't.'

Before coming into Tim's view I'd hastily constructed my 'disguise' in case he recognised me from college. I'd put my hair in two long plaits, and put on a pair of old wire reading glasses, which changed my appearance dramatically, and hid my mismatched blue and green eyes a little.

Unfortunately, the glasses also changed the appearance of everything else, since they'd been misprescribed when I was about seventeen. The headstone in front of me vibrated and wobbled, and when I turned to look at Tim, there were four wheelchairs spinning around his head like something out of seventies Indian cinema.

'I feel so alone,' I said.

'Would you like to go for a drink?' he offered.

Bingo.

CHAPTER NINE

Bitch

———◆———

The first pub we found was running its weekly quiz. This was a fairly recent thing and had almost reached craze status around here. I imagined myself trying to explain it to Jack or someone from another country. It wasn't that hard to understand, really, just difficult to comprehend. The basic concept was that someone called out questions over a PA system and people who wanted to participate tried to answer them on an answer sheet.

This was a problem, though, if you were trying to have a serious conversation.

'How did your parents die?' asked Tim, after ten minutes of small-talk.

'In what month was President J. F. Kennedy assassinated?' said the PA system.

'Car accident,' I said. 'What about yours?'

'Same.'

'I know how awful it is. The worst thing for me is that I'm an only child, so I don't even have anyone to share it with.'

'That must be hard,' he said.

'What is Madonna's surname?'

'What about you? Any brothers or sisters?'

He looked down. 'One sister.'

'What's her name?'

'Alex.' As he said this his hands started to shake. 'I had another sister, but she's dead.'

'Was she in the same accident as your parents?'

'No. She killed herself.'

'God, that's dreadful,' I said, looking down at the table. 'You poor thing.'

'Yeah. Me and my other sister Alex discovered her body. It was so horrible, you know? I still have nightmares about it. My fiancée, Christine, is very supportive, but I don't know how much more of this she can take.' A single tear slipped down his cheek.

'Who was the first man on the moon?'

I was struggling to keep up with two thought explosions. The first was that I was doing a bad thing: guilt cubed, reaching to the depths of my mind. The other involved the implications of what Tim was saying. It seemed to be the opposite of what the police and Emma thought. Tim believed the dead twin was Laura; it had been suicide. Interesting. And, after all, he should know, particularly if he had discovered the body. And Tim was adamant that he had been with Alex, not Laura, at the time. I wondered what he'd told the police, and why they were still convinced 'Laura' was telling the truth.

I thought about everything else I'd found out; that it was more likely to have been murder than suicide, that the dead girl's fingerprints hadn't been on the note or the knife ... Surely Tim knew about all that? So why did he still think it had been suicide? And if it really had been Alex in the club that night, what would have made her go to the police and say that she was Laura and that she'd been raped? Indeed, why would she be posing as Laura at all?

'Do you live in Paignton?' I asked Tim, trying to keep the conversation going while my thoughts buzzed in my head. I knew where he lived, but I wanted to see how accurate his version would be. Maybe I was testing his credibility as a witness. Perhaps he'd get these details wrong, too, and then I'd be able to discount his version of events on that night.

He shook his head. 'I live in Torquay. In a hotel.'

'Do you work there?' I asked.

'I own it. Well, since our parents died I half own it with my sister Alex. I want to sell up really and move on, but she's intent on keeping it. It's hard to know what to do. I think she wants to stay surrounded by memories, but I'd rather forget.'

'I understand,' I said. So he wasn't living in a fantasy world at all. Damn.

He looked at his watch. 'I'm going to have to be going, I'm afraid.'

'Yes, of course. Well, thanks for the company.'

'No problem. Oh, I didn't catch your name.'

'Daisy,' I said instantly, picking the name I would have been given had my mother not discovered what she thought was a more appropriate flower.

'You look slightly familiar,' he said. 'I think it's your eyes. I knew someone with eyes like that, once.'

'Did you?' I said nonchalantly.

'Anyway, if you need to talk any more, I live at the Tulip Hotel, Torquay. We're in the book.'

'Thanks,' I said, and watched him push himself out of the pub.

On the way home I thought more about the twins. Maybe the surviving twin was the one living in a fantasy world: genuinely believing herself to be Alex one minute and Laura the next. That would explain a lot. I thought it would be possible to be that deluded and screwed up if you'd just lost your parents and a sister. In that case no one would be lying, which would make my job less complicated. But somehow I knew that wouldn't be it.

*

73

She unzips his trousers, pretending to be her sister.

*   'Are you sure about this?' he says.*

*   'She did it to you.'*

*   'Yes.'*

*   'Pretend I'm her.'*

*   'I can't.'*

*   'Just close your eyes.'*

*   Look at how excited he's getting He doesn't mean to. He doesn't want to pretend.*

*   She takes it out. Pulls it out of his jeans. It catches on his zip.*

*   'I'm sorry,' she says, and moves her head towards it.*

*   Now this is more like it. This is what he's used to. It might as well be her.*

*   'Suck it, bitch. Suck it.'*

*   The familiar words.*

*   'Suck it suck it suck it suck it suck it suck it.'*

*   His voice is as rhythmical as her movements; the pale face moving up and down on him. Her action is very familiar.*

*   Now he comes to think of it, she is remarkably like her sister.*

*   'Bitch,' he says, as he comes in her mouth.*

When I got in it was almost half past ten. There was a message on the answerphone from someone called Tony Bryce, whom I had never heard of. He asked me to call him back and left a number, which sounded like a mobile. The code was 0467. Definitely a mobile. When I tried the number, the phone was switched off so I made a mental note to call him back tomorrow. I still felt cold, inside as well as out, after my experience in the graveyard, so I ran myself a really hot bath. While it was filling I lit some candles in the bathroom. Five minutes later, after applying a St Ives clay face pack, I got in and let the hot water soothe and warm me.

    The doorbell went about ten minutes after that.

    'You're blue,' observed Fenn, when I opened the door. He

looked sheepish. Also, he looked as though he hadn't slept for at least a week. His dark, shoulder-length hair was greasy and his shirt was wrinkled. A button was missing from his button-down collar, which had the effect of making him seem curiously lopsided, since the other one was done up.

'Oh,' I said, realising I couldn't talk properly, because my face was completely set. 'My face pack. Wait here for a moment.'

'Can I come in?'

'Of course. Make yourself at home. I'll be five minutes.'

So we were speaking again. As I rinsed my face and put on some clothes I wondered what had made him turn up out of nowhere like this. Well, it seemed I was about to find out.

'I made some coffee,' he said, when I walked into the sitting room. 'I hope you don't mind.'

'No. Thanks. Did you find everything all right?'

'Yeah. I had a bit of a wander around. Checked everything out.'

He was sitting in the armchair I usually favoured. I settled on the couch with the coffee. He hadn't put any sugar in it and the bitterness came as a shock. Surely he would remember that I had sugar? Even Jack knew I took sugar. I didn't say anything, though, I just stuck the cup on the coffee table and lit a cigarette. Fenn did the same.

'I thought you'd given up,' I said, remembering that I'd overheard him telling David that he wouldn't be smoking any more once the baby arrived.

'Yeah, well. I've got to have something to keep me going.' He smiled; it looked forced. 'How are you, Lily?'

'Me? I'm fine,' I said breezily.

'I've missed you.'

'Have you? I thought you'd be a bit busy to think about me.'

'Don't be fucking ridiculous. I think about you every minute.'

75

His tone took me by surprise. 'Oh,' was all I said.

He sat in silence for a few minutes, looking around at everything. His breathing was heavy and his eyes were dull. From somewhere I could smell alcohol. Then I realised it must be him. He'd been drinking.

'I like the cottage,' he said.

'Oh, this is the first time you've been, isn't it?'

'Yeah. You didn't get round to inviting me.'

'Come on, Fenn. You're married to a woman who hates me. It wouldn't have been very appropriate.' I looked down at the floor. 'Where does she think you are now?'

'At David's, talking about work.'

'Isn't it a bit late for that?' The clock said almost eleven.

'It is now. I've been driving round and round, trying to summon up the courage to come and see you.'

'Why?'

'What do you mean, *why*?'

'Why have you come to see me?'

'Because I miss you. Because you know how I feel about you.'

'You're drunk, Fenn.'

'Maybe.'

'You shouldn't have come.'

'Great. Make me feel welcome.'

'No, seriously. I stopped talking to you for a reason, you know. I'm not usually wrong about people, but I was totally wrong about you. I used to think you were nice. I thought you were my friend. I respected you and, yes, I was jealous when you married Bronwyn. Maybe at one point I thought I was in love with you. But I just don't feel any of those things any more. Like I've said before, it really is all over. And I don't particularly want to be friends, either, not after the way you've treated me, pushing me to the background whenever it suited you. You're too selfish for me, and too weak.'

'And you're a bitch, but I still love you.' He laughed, not

76

taking this seriously. 'Come on, Lily, you need me, too. This is what you wanted, isn't it?'

'You're just not listening, are you?' I said, pushing him away as he came over and tried to put his arm around me. He persisted, so I stood up, leaving him lying back on the sofa, still grinning drunkenly at me.

I raised my voice without meaning to. 'I'm not playing games, Fenn. So you're unhappy? Well, I told you so. Big fucking deal. I don't even care any more. And if you think that you can lie to Bronwyn, come round here and have me play out some pathetic little mistress fantasy with you then you are just so wrong. I think you'd better go.'

My cigarette had burnt down to the tip while I was shouting. Ash fell in a heap on the floor as Fenn sat up, his grin now gone. He picked up the coffee cup I'd discarded, and looked at it for a moment before throwing it across the room, where it shattered and fell, leaving a wet, black stain where it had hit the wall. I jumped, shocked. What was going on here? All of a sudden I was really afraid: his eyes looked stormy. As he stood up to face me, I didn't know what he might do next.

At that moment I heard the back door open, and the sound of someone walking quickly.

'Okay, what's going on in here?' demanded Jack. Thank God. He must have heard the coffee cup smash, and the shouting.

'Who the fuck's this?' said Fenn.

'Is this guy giving you any trouble, Lily?'

I nodded weakly.

'Right. I think it's time for you to be leaving,' Jack said to Fenn.

'What? Are you the new boyfriend?'

'No. I'm just a friendly neighbour. Now leave.'

'Yeah. I'm going.'

As he went, Fenn kicked a chair, and the table. All of a

sudden I felt really sorry for Bronwyn. He claimed to love me, and this was what I got. What must her life be like?

'Are you okay?' asked Jack, once the door had finally slammed, and Fenn's car had pulled away.

'I'll live.'

'I guess that was Fenn, right?'

'How did you know?'

'I didn't like him when you described him to me. I imagined him like that.'

'Well, I suppose that makes me the stupid one.'

'How come?'

'I just went off at him, calling him a weak, pathetic man. I really lost it.'

'And then he lost it, too, I guess,' said Jack gently.

'Yeah.'

'Did you have any idea he'd react that way?'

'None.'

'Yeah, well, it's not your fault he's such a dickhead.'

'He should be able to take it, really. After all, he's said worse to me in the past.'

'Really?'

'Well, in that very *nice* way, you know?'

'In California they call that passive-aggressive.'

'Sounds about right.'

'Anyway, you look like you could use a drink.'

'Yeah. Could you get the bottle of Scotch from the kitchen?'

'Sure. And two glasses?'

I smiled. 'Yeah. Two glasses. And bring a cloth for that wall.'

'Sure.'

Ten minutes later we were happily curled up on the couch in front of the fire. Trying to forget about Fenn, I told Jack about my evening at the graveyard and waited for him to look shocked.

'So you actually pretended your parents were dead?'

'No. I just pretended I was the daughter of the people in the next-door graves.'

'Is there a difference?'

'Of course there is. Anyway, are you disapproving?'

He raised his eyebrows. 'What's to disapprove?'

I laughed. 'Good.'

The Macallan that had been in my kitchen for weeks was slipping down very easily. The taste was clean, warm and smooth. I'd already had one top-up, and I was becoming a bit loose-limbed and smiley. This was good. If I'd been on my own and sober, I would have been shaking still after what had happened before.

'I feel a bit embarrassed,' I confided to Jack, the drink helping my thoughts leak out of my mouth.

'Embarrassed? Why?'

'About last night.'

'Last night. Hmm. I don't recall you doing anything very embarrassing.'

'When I asked you to stay. I must have seemed a bit forward.'

'Oh, that. I was incredibly flattered. Are you embarrassed because I said no?'

'Not as much as I am now. Let's talk about something else.'

'Don't you want to know why I said no?'

'Probably not, but you'd better spit it out.'

'I like you too much.'

'And that's a reason?'

'Sure. Now, how about a nice game of chess?'

'Um, okay.'

The rest of the evening consisted of me being checkmated time and again by Jack. I'd never been that great at chess, particularly not with good-looking men. Poker was a different story, of course, but you really needed three for that.

When it was time for bed, I didn't ask and he didn't offer. In a rerun of last night, I let him out and went to bed on my own. This time I'd be waiting for him to ask *me*. And if he liked me that much, maybe I wouldn't have to wait too long. A goodbye kiss would have been nice, but I thought he was probably a bit shy. As I pulled the covers over my head in an attempt to get warm, I decided that was definitely it. How could he refuse my charms? Because he was shy. And I'd just have to thaw him out slowly.

CHAPTER TEN

Pitter Patter

It was Jack's idea to go to Torquay the next day.

We drove there in a two-car convoy because he had something to do later, which he said he had to do alone. I had no idea what this might be, but it didn't seem appropriate to ask. I'd spent the morning in bed, and most of the afternoon in front of the TV, watching a video of *The Maltese Falcon*, which Jack had recommended. I'd tried to call the mysterious Tony Bryce, but there had still been no reply from the number he'd given. At about five Jack had knocked at the door and I was ready for a trip into the outside world.

It was raining hard as we set off. I could barely see his BMW in my rear-view mirror, but I felt glad he was there. When we drove into the town, the sky was almost black. Over the sea I could see lightning; the raindrops pounding the surface of the alternately bright orange and deep black water. We parked in the main area of the town, which was deserted. All around, puddles reflected the neon of the shops, amusements and street lamps.

'Do you want to go up to the hotel?' asked Jack, when we met up beside my car.

'No. Tim might recognise me.'

'So what do you want to do?'

'Come on,' I said, an idea forming. 'I'll show you.'

Ten minutes later we were standing outside Juno's. The club was shut and the street empty. Bins overflowed, and the rain bounced off some plastic sheeting lying in the middle of the road.

'Right,' I said. 'You can be Kurt.'

'Gee, thanks. Role-play. Who are you going to be?'

'The murderer.'

'I thought you were supposed to be finding out who killed Alex Carter.'

'Yeah. Although I think that might be Laura, now.'

'Whatever.'

'And Emma's added this to my brief, so I have to do it.'

'Oh, yeah. I forgot. Anyway, so I'm Kurt.'

'Yeah. You come out of the club after your set.'

'Okay,' he said, moving to the doors. 'So I light a cigarette and think about ...'

'What?'

'Alex, I suppose. I might wonder where she went.'

'Although if you'd just raped her you wouldn't care.'

'Maybe I'd want to make sure the little bitch kept her mouth shut.'

I smiled at his active role-playing. 'In which case you'd want to find her.'

'So I'd go to the hotel.'

'Which is past the harbour where you got killed.'

'Do we know how I got killed yet?'

'No. I must call Ian, actually, and find out.'

The rain intensified suddenly, as if a cloud had just split its seam above our heads. 'Hmm. This role-playing's gotten kind of wet,' said Jack, trying to shield himself.

'Don't worry. You'll live. I'm just thinking about what else would have taken Kurt down to the harbour.'

'Maybe he was scoring drugs?'

'No. I think someone like Kurt would have had better connections than the "meet me down the harbour" sort. Anyway, there would have been drugs in the club.'

'So definitely a woman, then?'

'Maybe. Perhaps he just wanted to be on his own,' I suggested.

Jack laughed. 'Yeah, right. When did you last see a pop star alone? They hate it. You can guarantee that if a pop star goes somewhere on his own it's because he has something to hide.'

I laughed. 'Interesting theory.'

'I thought so.'

'So. What would Kurt Venga have to hide?'

'His talent?'

'Very funny. Come on, this is serious.'

'Sorry.'

'Right. You're Kurt, remember. You walk down to the harbour. Did you tell anyone where you were going?'

'I probably told the rest of the band. Although if I told them they'd want to know what I was doing, or come with me or something. So I guess if I really wanted to be there alone, for whatever reason, I probably didn't tell anyone.'

'So if you didn't tell anyone, the murderer must have followed you.'

'I guess.'

'And unless he or she picked you up randomly, your last-known whereabouts were right here. So, logically, the killer must have come here first.'

We started walking down Sole Street towards the harbour, following the same route I'd taken when I was tracking Alex the other night. Jack walked in front of me, while I played murderer still, trying not to be seen.

'You're being very obvious,' he called back to me, as we came out of Sole Street and walked down the main road.

'Am I?'

'Sure. I can hear your footsteps.'

'Hmm.' This was interesting. It was about as deserted now

as it would have been that night. Alex hadn't heard me following her because I'd been wearing Converse trainers. Jack heard me now because I was wearing hard-soled loafers. Alex had been wearing high heels, though, and I remembered the way they'd sounded: sharp and echoey, stabbing into the pavement. If she'd been following Kurt, she would have needed to change her shoes first. And since I'd seen her go up to the hotel she would have had to get all the way back down to the club in order to follow him down here. Which would have been almost impossible, and pretty pointless.

Of course, I had no idea what time Kurt had left the club. Maybe Alex had known; perhaps he'd told her, or called her or something. Maybe she'd taken a phone call from him, but I hadn't heard any phones ring in the hotel.

'Maybe we're doing this all wrong,' I called out to Jack when he was half-way up the pier.

'How do you figure that?'

'Maybe no one followed him. Maybe the killer arranged to meet him.'

'Interesting,' said Jack, stopping and lighting a cigarette.

It was dark already. In the distance, the lights of the marina glowed. Beyond that was the Princess Theatre, grubby and grey. I walked up to where Jack was and stood beside him.

'It's freezing here,' he said.

'Mmm. And scary. Would you be frightened standing here on your own in the middle of the night?'

'You bet.'

'Why did he do it, then?'

'Maybe he didn't. Maybe he was killed somewhere else and then dumped in the harbour.'

'Yeah, but you can't get a car anywhere near the water. Could one person carry his body all the way down here by themselves?'

'A girl couldn't.'

'But maybe a man could.'

84

'Maybe.'

This was taking us nowhere.

'Are you hungry?' I asked.

'Sure.'

'Burger?'

'Why not?'

Although I had no real inclination to revisit the burger bar, it made sense, because from it we could get a clear view of the pier. And I wanted to think a bit more about all this, even though the more I thought, the more confusing it got.

'I definitely think he was lured to the pier and killed there,' said Jack, after a quarter-pounder, a banana milkshake and a cigarette.

'Why?'

'Well, you know this area. If you'd killed someone and wanted to dump the body, where would you go to do it?'

'Somewhere secluded. Probably where the current would take them out a lot further. Probably off a cliff. Or maybe a river, like somewhere along the river Dart. Now you come to mention it, the harbour is the last place I'd choose.'

'Exactly. Unless the opportunity was there in front of you.'

'Actually,' I said thoughtfully, 'just outside the Tulip Hotel would be a great spot for a murder.'

'We've stopped that hypothetical thing now.'

'No, seriously, think about it. If I was Alex, and I wanted to get rid of Kurt, where better than just outside the hotel? There are cliffs there – it's a long way down. Even better, she could have claimed that it had been suicide, or an accident. All she would have had to do would be get him up there and, bingo, there would be a thousand ways of getting him to just slip off the edge. Which also makes me rethink the other death – Laura. If someone wanted to play pretend suicide, who would seriously choose slashed wrists when you've got that fall as an option?'

'Sounds like Murder Central up there.'

'Well, it should be, if you think about it.'

'Hmm. Does this mean Alex is becoming less of a suspect?'

'Yeah. Although Emma seems to think she had something to do with it. But it doesn't make sense in any case. There are two possibilities here: either Kurt did rape her and she's telling the truth, or he didn't and she's lying. If Kurt really *did* rape her, he'd hardly agree to meet her on the end of a lonely pier. Like you said before, she could have been followed by him – maybe he wanted to finish the job – but I can't see them both ending up at the pier, particularly when I saw her go all the way up to the hotel. So that scenario seems unlikely.'

'I'm with you so far.'

'Well, if Kurt *didn't* rape her, and she just made it all up to get him into trouble, why would she go and murder him? I mean, it would be easy enough for her to lure him to the pier, but after that it doesn't make sense.'

'Maybe she didn't think the rape story was punishment enough.'

'Yeah, but then why still go to the police with it the next day if she'd chosen murder instead?'

'Maybe she's really, really stupid.'

'She'd have to be.'

Jack looked at his watch. 'Well, I'm afraid I have to be out of here.'

'Your secret mission?'

'It's not a secret, it's just not that interesting. Will you be okay here?'

'Yeah. There are still a couple of things I want to do.'

'Are you sure you don't want me to walk you back to the car? It's not very safe here on your own.'

'Aha! So you do care.'

'You know I do.'

'Don't worry. I'll be fine.'

'Okay. I'll see you later.'

'Yeah.'

As soon as Jack had left I started feeling a little insecure. Suddenly the burger bar seemed desolate and lonely; the only sound coming from chip-fat dancing in the fryer behind the counter. I looked out down the pier. No one was there. But someone had been there on Thursday night, and they had murdered Kurt. Maybe that person had hung around and was still in the area somewhere, looking for their next victim. I lit a cigarette and picked up my mobile. I needed to hear a human voice, and since I needed to speak to Ian, he'd have to do.

'Lily,' he said. 'Not in any trouble, I hope.'

'Not yet.'

'What can I do for you?'

'Just wondering if you knew any more about how Kurt was killed.'

'I thought you would be.'

'So, don't keep me in suspense ...'

'Well, it looks like he was hit on the head with something.'

'What kind of something?'

'A blunt object.'

'Is that all you know?'

'Mmm-hmm. For the time being. The pathologist is working on it. He's very intrigued by the shape of the impact area.'

'What do you mean?'

'That the blunt object was a funny shape, kind of long, thin and square, if that makes any sense. Pathology think that it was made of hard metal.'

I frowned. 'Interesting.'

'Yeah. Whatever it is, it doesn't sound like the kind of thing Mr Average would be carrying around on a dark night.'

'So you don't have any clue what it is yet?'

'None. We need to work it out, though. It's such an odd kind of injury that, if we found the object that made it, it might tell us something about the killer. Anyway, how are you getting on?'

'Okay.'

'Any information you want to share with me?'

'Can't think of anything.'

'Come on, Lily. I've scratched your back.'

'What's that supposed to mean?'

'Well, if I do you favours I expect some in return.'

'If I knew anything, I'd tell you.'

'Yeah, of course you would.'

'I would!' I said indignantly.

'How's the new boyfriend?'

'Which one?'

'Are there several?'

'There aren't any, actually. Who did you mean?'

'The American who was following you around like a puppy the other night.'

'He isn't my boyfriend. And he wasn't following me around.'

'No?'

'No.' I looked at my watch. It was getting on for eight. 'Anyway, Ian, I've got to get going. Thanks for the info.'

'No problem. Nothing I've told you is any big secret, anyway.'

'Well, thanks all the same.'

There was no one on the street outside the burger place: no one down on the pier. As I walked slowly up the road, past the amusements arcade and the boarded-up fish-and-chip shop I thought about the metal object. What could it have been? A gun? Some other kind of metallic weapon? But why hit him with those things? Why take the chance that he'd fight back?

Suddenly I remembered the strange demolition site I'd seen when I'd followed Alex on Thursday night. Presumably all number of metal objects would be lying around there. Without really thinking what I was doing, I wandered up the hill, past the yacht club and down the dark alley.

It was too dark to see properly, so I flicked on my lighter. The grey concrete beneath my feet was damp and cracked; the white boards to my right large and imposing. There was graffiti scribbled on some of the boards, and someone had written 'Lily' in large pink letters. So there was another Lily in Torquay somewhere; probably about seventeen and desperate to be famous. I remembered myself at that age, still hanging out for my first kiss. Either I'd been really naïve, or the world had changed, but I bet the Lily who'd written on this wall had gone way beyond first kisses.

As I walked, my hair caught on something: a prickly bush hanging over from the road. I shivered and continued. I knew I could go no further when I could hear lapping, sucking noises at my feet. The sea. I'd come slightly too far. Turning off towards my right, I found the entry to the demolition site and scrambled up to it. This place had fascinated me when I'd seen it before. It was on four levels, and covered the area of at least ten tennis courts. The bottom storey was the largest. The light was slightly better here, and the whole place was illuminated by two dull street-lamps and a flickering strip-light over a noticeboard explaining what was going to happen to the site.

As I walked across I almost tripped over a lifebuoy left carelessly in the middle of the concrete square. All around were small doors, leading to little cabins, warehouses and old boat-building sheds. The next level up was some kind of platform: a steel rail ran around it, stopping you from falling into the sea at one end, and on to the bare concrete at the other. The next level was small and muddy, and went up to the top section, a hexagonal waste ground that led directly to the pier.

Could the murderer have come this way? It would have made sense to use this route and not be seen, although that meant that they had not come from the town, and that they had not followed Kurt. Of course, after my 'game' with Jack, I was beginning to think this was quite likely – at least, that the murderer hadn't followed Kurt. It seemed more likely, as we had worked out, that Kurt had been lured here. But why? And by whom?

From the top level of the site I could see all around: lights from Paignton across the harbour and sweeping around into Torquay. Straight across from me, at the marina, the lights fuzzed halo-like; every edge of every building redrawn in the night sky. Could there have been someone over there on Thursday night, watching? Alex had been down on the beach, just beyond the demolition site. But she had gone up to the hotel and I'd followed her. Who else had been here? Who else could have come?

I only walked part way down on to the pier, finding the experience too disturbing on my own. I had been looking all over for metal objects, but hadn't found any. The police would have been here too, of course, but there could have been something they hadn't seen. I'd had in mind one of those square-edged metal bars. But the thing about the demolition site was that everything like that had long gone. All there had been was concrete, dirt and those wooden doors. The only metal there had been the railings.

I didn't hear the footsteps as they came up behind me.

'Lily Pascale?' said a gruff male voice.

I turned quickly and found a tall, blond man standing there. He looked like he hadn't shaved for a few days and his thinning hair was all windswept and ruffled on his head. He'd taken me by surprise, and I had no idea who he was, so my voice came out almost as a whisper. 'Who are you?' I said.

'Tony Bryce. I called you.'

'And I tried to call you back. Do we know each other?'

'Not yet.' He smirked. 'Why were you staying in the Tulip Hotel on Thursday night?'

I shrugged. 'Why do you want to know?'

'I'm trying to find out what happened there. Who killed Alex Carter?'

'*Alex* Carter. How would I know?'

'Because you seem to be trying to find out.'

'What do you mean by that?'

'I've been watching you.'

'Stop it. I don't know who you are and you're frightening me.'

'Why are you snooping around?'

'I'm an interested party.'

'Like hell you are.'

'Okay, I'm an uninterested party if that makes you any happier.'

'So why were you at the hotel?'

'I was staying there because I was too drunk to drive home.'

He laughed. 'Fucking hell. Did someone actually hire you?'

'I have to go.'

He grabbed my arm as I tried to push past him.

'You are going to tell me everything.'

I wrenched my arm away. 'Sorry. I don't think so.'

'You're cute, you know?'

I started to walk away. 'Leave me alone.'

'I bet you're a really good fuck,' he called after me.

'Piss off.'

'This is only going to get worse.'

'Is that some sort of threat?'

'Read all about it, Lily.'

Feeling like I'd been abused in some way, I continued walking until I was back on to the street then I ran down round the harbour to my car. I could still see Jack's BMW parked where he had left it. So he was still in Torquay. Shame he hadn't been around to protect me from Tony Bryce, whoever the hell he was. As soon as I got into the car I locked the doors and started the engine, driving as fast as I could out of Torquay. Tony Bryce had frightened me more than I'd let on and I just wanted to forget about him.

*

SEASIDE

The little girl sits on the edge of the bed. Everything has changed. The hotel doesn't feel the same. Even the noise, the squeaking sound, has gone. Now the place vibrates with silence: it's overbearing. Tears slip from behind her false eyes. She takes them out and puts them in her lap.

The old woman has something on her lap; something to cheer her grand-daughter up. It's a photo album, filled with pictures of a small Jack Russell terrier. See him there, jumping for a bone: see him asleep in his basket. The old woman tries to describe all the pictures, but her heart isn't in it.

The little girl can't see. But she hears everything. She hears about how fluffy his tail is, how he once saved her from drowning when she was only a baby. Lucky, that was. Of course the dog is dead. He died of old age. But the little girl likes collecting memories: they are new to her. The old woman, though, she has too many.

CHAPTER ELEVEN

Ballet Shoes

———◆———

Jack didn't appear for the rest of the night. When I left for work the next morning the BMW was back in its place on the lane. I wondered where he'd gone last night, and what he'd been doing. I felt like I was becoming close to him, and wished he felt the same about me. But all that mysterious mission stuff made him seem distant, like I was just fooling myself that we were becoming good friends.

Usually, I never stopped on the way to work: I just drove straight there, as fast as possible, wishing I was going somewhere else. But this morning I'd been too strung-out to have breakfast. I'd been worrying about Jack and also about the previous evening. Who was Tony Bryce, and what did he want from me?

It didn't take me long to find out. There was a corner shop not far from the university where I stopped to buy a bar of chocolate. And there I saw it: a tabloid newspaper, red, grey and grubby-looking with the following headline: 'Well, Can YOU Tell Which Is Which?'

Underneath the headline was a picture of the twins. It could have been the same picture repeated twice (from what I knew of tabloid reporting, it probably was). They were absolutely identical. In a daze, I picked up the paper and, forgetting my chocolate, walked to the counter to pay for it. As

I did so I noticed the byline: Tony Bryce. So that was who he was.

The story was sensational. Over-sensational. It talked about these 'stunning brunettes' and the fact that one of them had been 'brutally' killed. *But which one?* it kept asking. Tony Bryce had clearly managed a bit of research apart from trying to get me to spill what I knew to him. And someone had obviously talked. There were details about the hotel, how it was now run by the twins' brother, Tim; and about Kurt Venga and the way that he had been found in the harbour just after seeing one of the twins in the club.

The report speculated about who could have killed whom. All the usual suspects had been rounded up: Laura, Alex, Kurt; the three of them jumbled up even more badly than I was managing in my head. The paper said that the dead twin was almost certainly Laura, but because the twins were so identical, the police were investigating the possibility of the suicide note being a forgery. It didn't mention that the twin who was alive had been masquerading as both of them. Ian was going to love this. No one was supposed to know about the suicide note, or about the possibility that the murderer could have got the wrong twin. I was glad I hadn't let something slip out when I spoke to Tony, or this would have been all my fault. But it changed things: it put the pressure on.

To put me in a worse mood, the first person I saw when I walked into the Samuel Beckett Building was Fenn, on his way down the corridor towards the main office. I didn't want to speak to him, so I walked past him quickly. He looked me up and down as I did so, but didn't attempt to apologise or anything. Like Jack had said, he was a dickhead anyway. It was even colder than usual in the building today, and there didn't seem to be any students around either.

When I reached my office I found a note pinned to my door from David. It said that the students had been told not to come in again because of the heating problem and also that

since David was out of the university for the day, on some
kind of strange management conference, he'd left me in
charge. This didn't mean I had to do anything particularly,
just that I would be the one people would come crying to if
there were any problems. And then I would tell them to wait
until tomorrow when David was back. It all seemed a bit
pointless, really, and it pissed me off, because instead of going
home after lunch like I usually did on a Monday, it meant I
would have to stay in this hole all day. Shit. And there was so
much I had to do.

For the next couple of hours I did some paperwork, feeling
cold and slightly bored. By lunchtime I was beginning to wish
that someone would have a problem for me to deal with, but
apart from everyone complaining that it was too cold, and
walking around in their coats, nothing seemed to be going
wrong. I wondered what point there was in us all being here,
since there were no students, but what did I know?

At about one David rang to see how everything was going.
I told him it was too cold. He chuckled and told me how
lovely and warm he was at his conference. Then he went
through a list of things he'd forgotten to tell me to do, which
included filling in about ten equipment forms, checking all
the attendance records and booking some dance teacher to
guest lecture on the theatre and performing arts course. I
hated David.

Outside the winter sun shone low in the sky, and the halls
of residence were coated in a cold light. I really didn't want to
be here today. I wanted to be at home, walking along the
beach, thinking about other things, like, what had killed Kurt
Venga?

Or even more important: who, if anyone, had killed Laura
Carter? Was it Laura? Tim had thought so, and he was the
most reliable witness so far. But if it was Laura who was dead,
why was Alex telling the police she was Laura? Of course, in
theory, the living twin should be the most reliable person, but

she still didn't seem to be clear who she was. I could just about accept that she'd lied on that night at Juno's and said she was Alex to fool Kurt, but it seemed as though she'd been fooling her own brother as well. Unless she really was Alex, I didn't know why she would want to do that.

Because of Tony Bryce and his half-arsed reporting, there was going to be trouble — I could feel it. While I did the equipment forms I thought through everything. It was clear I needed some kind of new lead and I could do without being stuck in the university all day. I decided I needed a break.

The coffee machine in the hall spewed out dark, super-boiling liquid while I stood there trying to look unapproachable, in case anyone had any more problems. I drank my coffee outside with a cigarette. It was already almost three, and I still had all the attendance forms to do and this dance person to find. With my cigarette only half smoked, and my coffee only half drunk, I walked back to my office and sat down with the *Yellow Pages*, to see whom I could rustle up.

The section for Dance Schools and Teaching covered about a page. Sticking my finger at the top, I scanned downwards, looking for entries that seemed local and accessible. They all had weird names, made even weirder by the fact that my finger covered the last couple of letters of each one. There were such delights as the All-Star School of Music and Da, Arabesq, Balleri and then — my heart stopped — Cornel.

Moving my finger away, I looked at the whole entry. 'Ballet, tap and modern. For professionals and promising beginners only. Call Cornelia on ...' Was this the Cornel from the note? It had to be. Emma had said the twins were training as dancers. Without thinking any more, I picked up the phone and dialled the Torquay number.

The line crackled, but I could make out a woman's voice saying: 'Hello?'

'Hello. Is that Cornelia's?'

'This is Cornelia Page speaking. Can I help you?'

She sounded about sixty and very middle-class. Her words were clipped in such a way that you felt she was doing you a great favour in speaking to you at all. Her voice instantly scared me: she sounded like she might literally bite my head off.

My voice sounded small and weak compared with hers.

'I was phoning about the Carter twins,' I said.

'I'm not taking any bookings any more. The twins are unavailable.'

So she did know them.

'Bookings?'

'Isn't that what you wanted?'

'No, not at all. I'm a ... I'm an investigator trying to find out what happened to Laura.'

'Laura?' Her voice grew sterner. 'Has something happened to Laura as well?'

'You've lost me.'

'As I'm sure you know, Alex was killed. Are you saying something's happened to Laura as well?'

'I thought it was Laura who was dead.'

'No. We must have our wires crossed, young lady. *Alex* is the one who is dead.'

'I must have made a mistake,' I said, not wanting to argue.

'You say you're an investigator,' she said, sounding intrigued. 'I take it you're not with the police?'

'No. I'm working for a friend of the family.'

'Which friend?' she asked instantly.

'Emma ...' I stopped myself revealing Emma's full identity since she'd asked me not to. 'I can't remember her surname. I think she's quite an old friend.'

'Must be. I've never heard of her. And you are?'

'Lily Pascale.'

'What a fantastic name. Do you dance?'

'Not if I can help it.'

'So, how can I help you, Miss Pascale?'

'I'd like to come and see you, if it's at all convenient.'
'This evening is the earliest I can manage.'
'That's perfect. About six?'
'Fine.'

The rest of the day passed without too many more problems. I booked someone from the Arabesque dance school in the city in the end, since they were the most expensive and David would have to justify the expense. Luckily, no one cried or lost anything for the rest of the day and I managed to get away just after five, having composed a memo to David outlining all the loose ends he would have to tie up tomorrow when he returned.

The phone rang just before I left. It was Ian, and he sounded very pissed off.

'What's wrong?' I asked.

'Have you spoken to any reporters lately?' he asked.

'No, but I've seen the story.'

'Don't speak to him.'

'Who?'

'Tony Bryce.'

'I never speak to strange men anyway,' I said coquettishly, trying to cheer him up.

'I can't believe that someone's done this,' he spat. 'We couldn't even get in a restraining order because it was too late, and now every bastard out there knows that Laura might not be dead. We've had two arseholes confess to the murder already. Both nutters, but I've had to question them because there's always a chance they might not be lying, and I've had the rest of the fucking national news on my back all day. I'm in trouble with my boss, because he thinks *I* might have let something slip. And there's a murderer out there who I can't get close to because of all the dickheads trying to get a piece of me, and he's probably going to try and get to Laura now he realises he fucked up killing her the first time. Tell me you've found something, please?'

'Sorry, Ian. Sounds like you're having a bad day.'

'Yeah, well. It's all part of the job.'

'Yeah.'

Half an hour later I was back in Torquay. The street that Cornelia's dance studio was on had seemed very small on the map, so I'd parked in the centre of town and decided to search for it on foot. It was dark already, and cold; so much colder on the coast than in the city. Thinking about the blazing fire I would have later I walked up through the shopping precinct, my head down in the freezing wind, trying not to bump into all the people milling around.

Torquay town centre looked as though it had been planned by a spider: every so often a tiny roundabout appeared with two or three roads coming off it, each leading in a different direction, up, down, towards the sea or away from it. When I came to such a junction I had to take a very small road up and then a smaller one away from the sea. I could still see people down below, but up here it was still and quiet. There were a couple of houses, an old watchmaker's and a set of steps going up to the street on the next level. I walked up the concrete steps slowly, hoping I'd come the right way and that the dance studio would be somewhere at the top.

Cornelia's was about three doors along when I reached the top of the steps. It was a pink terraced cottage, with cast-iron stairs leading up one side of it. There didn't seem to be any other way in, so I walked up the staircase and knocked at the door there. A few moments later a woman answered. She was slightly younger-looking than she had sounded on the phone; probably in her mid-fifties. Her clothes were loose and expensive-looking and her hair was dyed blonde and worn in a classic bob. She was thin and supported herself on a walking-stick.

'You must be Lily Pascale,' she said. 'Do come in.'

Inside the door lay what was obviously the dance studio. Along the left-hand side the wall was entirely mirrored, and a silver *barre* ran along it. In the far right-hand corner was a stack of old folding chairs and a stereo system sitting haphazardly on the floor. An upright piano stood against the wall, and between it and the pile of chairs sat a girl of about ten, wearing a pink tutu. Her legs looked as if they were made of pipe-cleaners, and were stretched into an impossible-looking arrangement. Her face was wet, though, and her back was hunched. Every so often there was a sniff and then a sob.

'Come along, Lulu,' said Cornelia. 'It's not the end of the world.'

'It *is* the end of the world,' said the little girl brattishly. 'It's so unfair.'

Outside a car pulled up. 'That will be your mother,' said Cornelia to Lulu. 'Hurry up, now.'

The little girl walked past us and down the steps, sniffing as she went and tugging at her tutu. Once she was gone, Cornelia led me through the studio to a door at the back which led off into a hallway, through which we walked to a large sitting room.

'Poor thing,' commented Cornelia.

'Who?'

'Louise Rivers. The little girl. She just failed another audition.'

'What for?'

'*Sleeping Beauty*. It wasn't a major role, but it would have been good for her.'

'Oh dear.'

'Yes. Anyway, can I get you a tea or something?'

'A glass of water would be good.'

While Cornelia was out of the room I took the opportunity to look around. The mantelpiece was covered with little cups and trophies, some in the shape of ballet shoes, others in the shape of a ballerina. In a presentation case on the substantial shelves was a tiny pair of *pointe* shoes, pink and worn-looking. In the corner stood three other walking sticks. The far wall was covered with framed photographs. Most of them were of young girls in tutus with flowers in their arms, or taking a bow on stage. But in the middle was someone I recognised.

'Is that Alex?' I asked, when Cornelia walked back into the room.

'Good heavens, no,' she said, offering me my seat again and giving me a glass of water.

I sat down and took a sip. It was fizzy.

'No,' she said again. 'That, of course, is Laura, taking the lead in *Swan Lake*.'

'Someone told me that it was Alex who was into dancing,' I said. 'I suppose I've got mixed up again.'

'No, no. Alex *was* very passionate about her dancing. Much more so than Laura. But it didn't matter how much Alex wanted it, or, for that matter how much Laura didn't, it was Laura who had the gift.'

'The gift?'

'Once in your career someone comes along who has that kind of talent. She was just wonderful. I've never seen anyone dance like she did. She could have taken it all the way. Royal Ballet, anything.'

'God, I had no idea.'

'Hmm.' Cornelia looked down; something was bothering her.

'What's wrong?'

'Well, she gave it all up. I'll never understand it. That little girl Lulu who was here before would have given her right arm even to speak to Laura Carter. Every little girl who comes in here wants to be her. It's so tragic. Such a waste. She wouldn't even come and discuss it with me.'

'Cornelia, I suppose you know that there is some ambiguity around the identity of the dead girl.'

'Yes, of course.'

'How do you know about all of this, by the way? The police say they haven't released details of the murder.'

'They came to interview me. I told them what I'm telling you. Alex is dead.'

'Why are you so sure that it was Alex?'

'Because if Alex was alive she would have been here by now. She and I were very close. Laura never wanted to put much time into her dancing, but Alex was here every day, practising, helping the little ones, trying desperately to become as good as her sister.'

'Are you sure?'

'Absolutely.'

'Why didn't Laura like dancing?'

Cornelia shook her head. 'I have no idea. I think she liked it well enough, but she wasn't driven by it in the way you have to be to be professional. She took the lead in a lot of shows a couple of years ago. Alex, of course, was her understudy each time.'

'What do you mean, *of course*?'

'Well, you can't have two identical girls in the same show. It would distract attention from the lead, and it would cause all sorts of mix-ups with lifts and routines. It just isn't done at all. They could have done it with *Swan Lake*, since Odette and Odile are supposed to be identical, but to be honest, Alex wasn't up to either role. It's a very difficult ballet.'

'Poor Alex. Did she mind?'

'Yes, I'm sure she did, but she never did anything about it. If I'd been her I would probably have pushed Laura down the stairs or something and got myself on stage. But not Alex. Of course, Laura rubbed her nose in it the whole time. She isn't the most sensitive girl in the world. Do you know, I don't think she would have even carried her dancing as far as she did if Alex hadn't been so passionate about it.'

'What do you mean?'

'Well, she did it to spite her. She wanted Alex to know that she, Laura, was the dominant twin, that she was the success-ful one, the one who could get whatever she wanted.'

'Sounds very unpleasant.'

'Oh, it was. In public they were all smiles and so on, but in private they had bitter rows.'

'Really?'

'Oh, yes.'

'Murderous ones?'

'What? Do you mean did Laura murder Alex?'

This was what Emma had suggested. It was worth a try.

I swallowed, and then said, 'Yes.'

'But why bother? She had already eclipsed her sister com-pletely. It wasn't as if she would have had anything to gain from it. And who would she compete with if her sister was dead?'

'I see your point.'

She paused. 'Is that what the police think?'

'What?'

'That Laura murdered Alex?'

'No. Not at all. In fact, the police seem to be under the impression that Laura is a dear sweet little thing incapable of hurting anybody.'

'Oh, that old routine. They should ask me about Laura — I could put them straight. We've all seen that act before.'

'Didn't they ask you about the twins?'

'Not really. Since they are in agreement with me — that Alex is dead — we didn't discuss the identity problem in any depth. I just explained where I was on the night in question and told them I had no idea who would want to kill Alex.'

'Really? What about people who would want to kill Laura?'

'They didn't ask me that.'

'No, but I'm asking you now.'

She sighed. 'Now that's a different question altogether. Alex, possibly. Kurt Venga. Probably countless ex-lovers and their wives.'

'Their wives?'

'Oh, yes. Laura loves older men.' Cornelia looked at her watch.

'Sorry if I'm keeping you,' I said.

'No, it's all right. I'm being picked up at seven, that's all. I'll have to go and get ready in a few moments.'

'Right. Look, do you know anything about what the twins did when they weren't dancing?'

'All Alex did was dance. She earned a bit of money working up at her parents' hotel and tutoring some of the younger girls here. Laura worked in the cinema.'

'The little arts cinema?'

'Yes, that's right.'

'I see. Oh, incidentally, does the word Lucky mean anything to you?'

She shook her head. 'No. I don't think so. In what context?'

'As a name, maybe?'

'No.'

'What about this phrase?' I repeated the words: *she looks like the real thing* and even tried my luck with the part-word: *lipp*. But Cornelia just looked confused. She'd been referred to on the note, but the other words just didn't seem to mean anything to her at all. I pressed her, but although she obviously tried hard to come up with something, she couldn't.

'By the way,' I said, getting up to leave, 'where were you on the night the girl was killed?'

'At the theatre,' she said, smiling.

As I left I was lost in thought about the implications of it all. Maybe Laura hadn't felt the need to murder Alex, I thought, but what if Alex had murdered Laura? From what Cornelia said, it appeared that she would have had a strong motive.

Why all the pretending-to-be-Laura business, though? It didn't make sense. This whole thing was so confusing. Which twin *was* actually which? I now had two trustworthy accounts of the twins – one from their brother and one from Cornelia – but the problem was that Tim thought Laura was dead, and Cornelia thought it was Alex. Presumably they both had good reason for this, and there was only one possible conclusion to be drawn from it: for whatever reason – and I had no idea what that might be – the surviving twin was trying to play tricks on people.

The first thing I did when I got in was phone Ian.

'Lily. Sorry about before,' he said. 'I needed to let off steam.'

'That's okay. Did you sort it all out?'

'No.' He laughed sardonically. 'But that's life.'

'Ian, look, I've been wondering about this whole identity thing.'

'Yes?'

'Do you know for sure which twin is dead yet?'

'Nope. Just like the paper said.'

'But you were convinced that Laura was telling the truth.'

'Yep. But my superiors aren't so sure now.'

'Why not?'

'The brother says she's Alex.'

'Oh,' I said, not telling him I already knew this.

'And I wasn't supposed to take her word for it in the first place.'

'Whoops,' I said kindly. 'So, how are you planning to find out for sure?'

'No idea.'

'Isn't there some DNA test you can do or something?'

'Nope.'

'Dental records?'

'Nope. They both had perfect teeth.'

He sounded pissed off again.

'What's wrong?' I asked.

'Nothing. I've just had this conversation with my chief superintendent. He seems to think there's more we could be doing.'

'Is there?'

'Not really. The one thing we would usually do if there is any question over the identity of a dead body is take their fingerprints.'

'What if the person didn't have a criminal record? What would you have to compare them with?'

'Surfaces in their house, books, toilet seat, whatever. That's how we'd usually do it. Trouble with this case is that we can't seem to find anything that one twin would have touched that the other couldn't possibly have done.'

'Are twins' fingerprints different, then?'

'Oh, yes. Just like you and me. It's the only bloody thing that is different, though.'

'Hmm.'

'So if you think of anything do let us know.'

'Something one twin would have touched that the other wouldn't?'

'Yep.'

'I'll try.'

'Okay, cheers,' he said, and rang off.

The next thing I did before settling down for the evening was check my answerphone messages. There were two hang-ups then a message from Mum inviting me for dinner on Wednesday night with, horror of horrors, Emma. Great. I rang her to confirm and asked if I could bring 'someone'. I didn't mention Jack by name because I wasn't in the mood for questions; I still got them, though. I wasn't entirely sure that Jack would be desperate to come in any case, but I thought he would probably be interested to meet Emma and, of course, the family.

All evening I half expected a knock on the door from Jack, but it didn't come. I hoped I didn't seem desperate – I really wasn't. Perhaps it was just the novelty of having such a sexy neighbour, or perhaps I just liked the idea of being warm on such cold nights. I wondered if Jack was staying away because he didn't want to seem too forward, or whether he just didn't find me that interesting. Perhaps he was just working really hard on his script. Yeah, that could be it.

There didn't seem to be much on TV tonight, but I ended up engrossed in a rerun episode of *The X-Files* in which two little twin girls murder their parents, then everyone around them. It unnerved me, but fascinated me. Why *were* twins so spooky? I blamed Stephen King. While I watched TV, I kept thinking about Ian's conundrum: what would only one girl have touched? But I couldn't think of anything. At a loss, I rang Star.

'Lily,' she yawned, 'I was just on my way up to bed.'

'Yeah, but you're going to love this.'

'What?'

'I've got a riddle for you.'

'A riddle? Now I'm interested.'

'Well, it's not exactly a riddle but it's right up your street.'

'Come on, then, the suspense is killing me.'

In the distance I could hear my father Henri calling out in his French accent: 'Who is it?'

'It's Lily,' Star called back. 'She says she'll talk to you at the weekend.'

'You liar! I didn't say that!' I said, astonished.

'Yes, well. I want to hear the riddle.'

'You are awful. Anyway, we're still on this which-twin-is-which thing.'

'Goodness. You haven't got very far, have you?'

'Well, the living twin isn't being that helpful. She's still claiming to be both of them. Anyway, my detective constable friend was telling me that there is only one way of finding out which is which.'

'What's that?'

'Fingerprints. If they can find something that *only* Alex or *only* Laura would have touched, they can compare the fingerprints on it with the fingerprints of the dead girl. So the riddle is: what is that thing?'

'That only one of them would have touched?'

'Uh-huh.'

'God. Toothbrush?'

'Not conclusive enough. Like, if the living twin wanted to keep pretending she could just say she touched it as well.'

'Um ... Something at the boyfriend's house?'

'No. Both twins were connected with him. Did I tell you, by the way, that he's dead too?'

'No! Lily, you're not keeping me up to date properly at all.'

I filled her in on the details as I knew them, and what Jack and I had already deduced.

'So they have to be connected, I suppose,' said Star thoughtfully.

'Mmm. But how?'

'Well, you're the super-sleuth.'

'I don't feel like one now.'

'This Cornelia woman. Did you believe everything she said?'

'Yeah. I think so.'

'Strange that she and Tim have such opposite views on which twin is alive.'

'That's what I thought. I bet it turns out to be significant somehow.'

'Yes, I do too. I can't think how, though.'

'No,' I said, thinking.

'What about somewhere Alex or Laura worked?' said Star.

'Sorry?'

'For the fingerprints.'

'No. The only places Alex worked, Laura went as well, like the dance studio and the hotel. Laura worked in the cinema, but the girl who is alive was there on Thursday night in any case, so if it was Alex pretending to be Laura pretending to be Alex, she would have had every opportunity to touch everything.'

Star laughed. 'Alex pretending to be Laura pretending to be Alex. Is that a triple bluff?'

'I don't know but it's giving me a headache.'

'Well, let me know when you have a breakthrough.'

'If it ever happens.'

'It will.'

Just before I went to bed the phone rang. But when I answered it there was no one there. Or that was what I'd first thought. Just as I was about to replace the receiver the breathing started. It wasn't the kind of normal breathing you would get from someone just being on the phone and not speaking. Instead this was fast, insistent breathing like the person was almost out of breath, panting down the phone. Frightened and confused I replaced the receiver, then took it off the hook.

It was three o'clock in the morning when I woke up, disturbed by a sound I couldn't place. I hadn't been sleeping that well anyway, feeling confused by this case, and scared by the breathing on the phone. Feeling thirsty and weird I got up and went downstairs to the kitchen for a drink. The moon was full and I could see the sand, the cliffs, the sea and the lighthouse through the window, all the moon-shadows as black as the sky. The light from a full moon was different from any other kind: clear but dark, the kind of contrast impossible in the day. I stood there for about five minutes, smoking a cigarette and watching as the waves crashed on to the beach, frothy and silent.

Then I saw the figure of a man, hunched on the sand, his knees brought up to touch his body. If he hadn't moved his arm I may have thought he was a rock, or a shadow, but it was a man.

It was Jack.

CHAPTER TWELVE

Killing Your Brain

———◆———

'Hi,' I said, walking over to him.

He didn't respond. He was wearing blue jeans and an unbuttoned shirt that flapped in the wind. He must have been freezing. I placed the blanket I'd brought down for me around his shoulders. He pulled it close to himself, but he didn't look up.

'Jack?'

Nothing. I wondered if he had sleepwalked down here. It didn't seem very likely, but why wasn't he responding?

'Jack? If you need me I'll be up at the cottage.'

He gave the smallest of nods then went back to watching the waves. Weird. I turned and walked back, grateful of the heat when I let myself into the house.

David phoned the next morning and said that the university was going to be closed for the rest of the week while they sorted out the heating problems. So no freezing building today. Thank God.

After that I went back to bed and slept until about eleven. When I woke up for the second time I felt more rested. After seeing Jack on the beach like that last night, I hadn't been able to sleep properly. What thing was it that made him so inaccessible? What made him warm and friendly one day then moody and distant the next?

It was colder than ever and the light was dim outside. I ate breakfast slowly and thoughtfully, knowing that I was going to have to take advantage of the university being closed and try to get somewhere with this investigation this week. Emma was obviously thinking along similar lines, because when the phone rang a few minutes later, it was her.

'So, when do I get my report?' she asked.

'Report?'

'Isn't that what you do?'

'No. I told you before I'm not a professional.'

'Oh.' She sounded disappointed. 'Okay. So how are you getting on?'

'Fine. I'm up against a couple of brick walls, but I'm going to try to do something about that situation today.'

'Good.'

'Emma?'

'What?'

'Which twin do you think is dead?'

'I have no idea. That's why I hired you.'

'Yes, but what does your intuition tell you?'

'That someone's lying.'

'Who?'

'I don't know.'

This wasn't getting me anywhere. I tried another route. 'When you first told me about this, you said Laura was still alive.'

'I also told you that Laura was dead.'

'Yes, I suppose you did.'

'You have to find out which one is which, Lily.'

'I'm trying my best. Incidentally, do you know which twin was born first?'

She remained silent for a few seconds. 'Why would you want to know that?'

'I don't know. Could be relevant, I suppose.'

'I'm paying you to have better ideas than that,' she snapped.

'Calm down, Emma. I just think it might give me an insight into who they were.'

'Well, I can go and look it up for you, but I really don't see what difference it will make.'

'If you wouldn't mind,' I said, puzzled as usual by her reactions.

'It was Laura,' she said, when she got back on the line. 'Laura was born first.'

'Thank you,' I said.

While I got dressed I thought about the whole birth-order thing. It didn't surprise me that Laura had been born first. It certainly confirmed Cornelia's story about Laura being the dominant twin. It still didn't tell me which one was dead, but today I was determined to try to get some more insight into Alex and Laura Carter, to see if there was any detail about them: anything that might have made someone want to kill one of them.

The roads were icy driving into Torquay. When I arrived, I parked the car in a multi-storey car park near the marina. It was grey and concrete inside: scary, but at least the car wouldn't ice up too badly. I made sure I locked it securely and walked towards the exit. A young mother with a double pushchair was struggling to get the door open so I rushed over and held it for her. When she turned to thank me I could see her face covered in purple acne. She must have been about nineteen.

Out on the street the icy wind whistled up from the sea. My body trembled and I wished I owned a pair of gloves. Cold lights flickered in the shops along the high street and as people came out of their doors you could almost see the heat leave their bodies in a kind of fog.

Sole Street was quiet again, being an evening kind of a place. I'd noted from the local paper that the cinema did matinées, though, so I was hoping to find someone inside who might tell me something about Laura.

The door of the cinema swung open when I pushed it, but

there was no one inside. In a repeat of Thursday night I found myself walking inside calling, 'Hello.' In the daylight, such as it was, the inside of the lobby looked old and dusty. The small ticket booth was grubby and the black covering on its small counter was almost entirely peeled off, revealing chipboard underneath. Yellowing posters advertised last summer's main events: a James Bond Weekender and *Tetsuo*: The Whole Experience.

By the ticket booth a montage of posters advertised the event which was still ongoing: the *film noir* season. Each poster showed a dark, glamorous scene. Many had women hiding in the shadows, holding small revolvers or beaded purses. I noted the films shown so far: *The Maltese Falcon, Double Indemnity, Dark Passage, Out of the Past* and *Casablanca*. The rest of the season, finishing in the New Year, included more recent takes on the genre: *Devil in a Blue Dress, Chinatown, LA Confidential, The Last Seduction, Romeo is Bleeding* and, interestingly, Jack's film, *Broken*.

I was about to leave when an old man came walking out of the door leading to the screen. He was thin and tall and dressed in a lemon yellow suit, with faint pinstripes. 'Can I help you?' he asked, his voice higher-pitched than it should have been, and with the last remains of what must once have been a strong East London accent.

'Are you the manager here?'

He chuckled. 'Who wants to know?'

'Lily Pascale,' I said, holding out my hand, which he took limply and kissed. 'I hope you don't mind me just walking in. The door was open.'

'Not at all. What can I do for you?'

'Do you have a few minutes you could spare?'

'That depends if you're anything to do with the Inland Revenue.'

'I can assure you I'm not.'

'Well, you'd better come with me, then.'

He led me into a little room with two chairs, a kettle and a sink with rust all around the edges. It smelt of cheap perfume, deodorant and stale cigarettes. He plugged in the kettle and switched it on, creating some sparks as he did so.

'Bleeding thing,' he mumbled, fishing around in a red and white checked container, which said 'Tea' on the front.

'You've just caught me on my break,' he said. 'Can I get you anything?'

'No, thanks, I'm fine, Mr ...'

'Harry. Harry Duckling.'

I tried not to laugh. 'Can I call you Harry?'

'By all means.'

'I'm an old friend of Laura's. Laura Carter? Does she work here?'

He looked down at his feet. 'She did, of course. Before ...'

'Before what?'

'She died, love. Police reckon it might have been murder. I'm not supposed to tell anyone that,' he added.

'I didn't know,' I lied. 'God. That's awful.'

'It was a nasty business,' he said, getting up and pouring boiling water into his mug. 'She was like a granddaughter to me. She loved this little cinema. It's going to be so different without her ...'

'How dreadful.'

'She made me smile. Now nothing does.'

'Have the police been to see you?'

'Yes. They asked me what time she left the cinema that night and where I was when it happened.'

'Where were you?'

'At home.'

'I see. So they told you exactly what happened?'

'Not really. Her sister came to speak to me, though. The twin.'

'Alex?'

'Yep, that's right. She told me that her sister had been killed, and that the killer had set it up to look like suicide. There was no way Laura would have killed herself, you know. No way at all. She was the strongest, most upfront person I've

115

ever met. She wouldn't have chosen the coward's way out. Although, if you're an old friend, you don't need me to tell you that. She made me very happy, you know. I'm really going to miss her.'

'You poor thing.'

'Don't worry about me. I'm not long for this world, now.'

'Did, um, Alex give you any more details?'

He looked uncomfortable. 'Maybe you should ask her.'

'Come on,' I prompted him gently. 'You can tell me.'

'Someone slashed her wrists, and made it look like she'd done it herself.'

He stopped abruptly, clearly shocked by the memory of what he'd been told. It was the same story that I knew already, though. There were no new insights here. Seeing tears form in his weak blue eyes, I got up to leave, patting him on the shoulder. I didn't ask him about the words from the piece of paper, but how could I? The poor guy had obviously been through enough.

The air outside seemed fresh and clean. Lighting a cigarette, I thought about where I should go next. Hungry and cold, I decided that Bella Pasta would be the best option for the time being.

I was the only person in the large restaurant. The waiter seated me in the smoking section and brought me a glass of red wine. I needed it to warm up, and to try to oil my brain, which felt as if it had seized up in the cold and the confusion. Seeing Harry had just made things more muddled, of course. How could it be that he was so sure Laura was dead, when Cornelia had been so clear that it was definitely Alex? But Tim: Tim had thought it was Laura as well. So that was two votes for Laura, and only one so far for Alex. Make that two for Alex — the little girl had been sure she was talking to Laura on the stairs the other night. But if Laura was alive, what possible reason would there be for her to go and tell her boss that she was dead? There had to be better ways to resign from a job than that.

'Another lovely day in Torquay,' commented the waiter, coming to take my order.

'Mmm,' I agreed.

'What can I get you?'

'One of these, please,' I said, pointing to the *quatri formaggi* pizza on the menu.

'Okay,' he said, scribbling on his pad.

'With extra olives,' I said.

'Olives ...'

'And anchovies.'

'Uh-huh.'

'How many cinemas are there in Torquay?' I asked him, when he'd finished writing.

'Just one, the Odeon,' he said. 'Oh, and Harry's. There aren't any multiplexes around here, you know.'

Suddenly I realised that he must have thought I was a tourist, perhaps from somewhere distant and exciting, like London or Manchester. It pissed me off that it was still seen as something odd when a woman ate in a restaurant by herself. That must have been why he'd assumed I wasn't local: people like him imagined that local people wouldn't do this.

Instead of voicing my thoughts, I smiled flirtatiously and said, 'What's Harry's?'

He laughed. 'Harry's? It's like an arts cinema round the back of town. They do loads of student-night type things in there. All the trendy stuff. Harry, the guy who runs it, is completely mad. Lets you in for free if he likes the look of you.'

'Sounds fun.'

'Yeah. Shit films, though. All in black and white.'

My pizza was good and warmed me up inside. I looked the other way when the waiter brought things over, hoping he wouldn't start another conversation with me. Afterwards, sipping the last of my wine and smoking a cigarette, I thought about where I should go next. The twins' old school seemed like a good choice, but in a way I was dreading what I might find out there. More facts that didn't add up; more skewed perspectives. I was confused enough as it was, and the questions I was asking people just didn't seem to be getting me anywhere.

Once back in the car, I tried to work out some way of approaching the head-teacher of the school. In my experience, just saying I was a private detective and hoping she'd spare me some time wouldn't be enough to swing it. But what could I say? After a few minutes' hard thinking, a plan came to me. Quite cunning, I thought. I picked up my mobile and, once I'd obtained the number I needed from directory enquiries, I dialled.

'Torbay Girls' High,' said a voice.

'Hello, could you tell me how long the current head has been at the school?'

'Fifteen years.'

'Right. Could I speak with her, please?'

'Who shall I say is calling?'

'Lily Pascale,' I said, seeing no need to make up an alternative.

'Dr Ravine,' came a harsh voice presently.

'Dr Ravine, I wonder if you can help me ...'

I told her that I was a student at the university researching twins and education and that I was calling to enquire whether she'd had any experience of twins, and whether she would be prepared to be interviewed. She asked lots of questions about who was supervising my research, and other details before admitting that, yes, they'd had several sets of twins at the school, and that she would be able to see me – but not until tomorrow. It was a good thing the university was closed: I certainly didn't want her ringing my alleged 'tutor' (I'd said it was David) to check me out.

All I hoped was that she would have some better insights into the Carter twins – *what* a good case study – than I'd met so far. Everything conflicted too much; nothing made sense.

You would have thought that by now there would be some way at least of telling which was alive but, of course, that was made difficult when the survivor was so keen to mislead everyone. At some point I would need to speak to her directly, but I wanted to gather information first, something that might trip her up, a detail she might get wrong.

On the way home I thought again about everything Cornelia had said, since she seemed to have been the most useful contact so far. I was tempted by the hypothesis that Alex had murdered Laura for being such a bitch, but wouldn't it take more than that to make you actually murder your own sibling? After all, all sisters could be bitches at times. I should know: I was one.

When I arrived home I found a note had been slipped under my door. I threw it on the kitchen table while I collected logs for the fire and put the kettle on to make coffee. Once everything was organised, and the first flames were dancing in the fireplace, I sat down with my coffee and opened it. It was from Jack: a simple request. Have dinner with me tonight?

What a change from last night. Maybe he really had been sleepwalking.

A couple of minutes later, the phone rang. It was Jack. 'Did you get my note?' he asked.

'Yes.'

'Is that yes you got the note—'

'Yes, I would love to have dinner with you tonight.'

'I'll pick you up at eight,' he said, and rang off.

Jack was in a good mood as we set off for Paignton. This hadn't been my first choice of places to have dinner, but Jack had assured me that the little seafood place we were headed for had been recommended by a friend.

All the way there, he chatted about his new script, and about how cold it was outside, and about how gorgeous I looked in my black dress. He didn't mention the incident last night, so I chose not to either, chatting instead about my day: what I'd done and how little I thought I'd achieved. I was still talking about all this as we parked the car and walked into the restaurant.

'What do you think killed Kurt?' asked Jack, after I'd explained about the metallic object.

I shook my head. 'I don't know. Any ideas?'

'No. Sounds like a gun, though.'

'I thought that. But, really, if you were murdering Kurt and you had a gun, wouldn't you just fire it at him?'

'Yeah. *I* would. But maybe the murderer lost their nerve.'

'Maybe they were worried someone would hear the shot.'

'Maybe.'

'Mind you, if you were Kurt, standing there—'

'I was, if you recall.'

'Yeah. Thanks for that. Anyway, if you were standing there, at that precise spot, and someone pointed a gun at you, what would you do?'

'I guess I would jump in the water.'

'Exactly.'

'Interesting. I suppose it would help if you knew what had happened to the girl.'

'Yeah. Or even which one she was.'

'Do you think the twins are really that identical?' he asked.

'Hmm?'

'I knew a set of twins in Tucson. They were called Ladle and Spoon.'

'You're not serious?'

'Uh-huh. Anyway, they were identical, except Ladle had a mole on his face.'

'Maybe there is some detail we don't know about,' I said, when I'd finished laughing.

'There must be. No set of twins is that similar, I'm sure.'

'Probably. Anyway, let's not talk about that tonight. It's creeping me out a bit.'

'Really?'

'Yeah. It's like that feeling you get when people start telling you ghost stories.'

'I know the one.'

'Anyway, tell me more about you,' I said.

The waiter came over.

'Saved,' said Jack, and proceeded to order lobster for both of us.

'I usually hate it when people do that,' I said.

'Do what?'

'Order for me.'

'I don't usually do it, I just figured you'd want lobster.'

'I'll let you off this time, then.' I smiled. 'Anyway, you were telling me about your fascinating childhood.'

'There's not much to tell. I was an only child. My parents split when I was ten and my dad went to live in Boston.'

'Do you ever see him?'

'No. He hates me.'

'What's your mother like?'

'Fucked up. She drinks.'

'So you haven't had a very happy time, then.'

'It's been okay.'

'How did you get into writing film scripts?'

'I guess it was something I always wanted to do.'

'Like a lifetime ambition?'

'Yeah, I guess. I never made the soccer team at school. Never dated cheerleaders or anything like that. I was the geeky kid who always did his homework and wrote poetry in his bedroom while the other kids were having sodas down at the mall.'

'Wow.'

'Yeah. I was really into my books and all. I guess it paid off.'

'Yeah, right. I bet all the other kids have got about ten children each by now.'

'Yeah.' He smiled. 'It was kind of a small town.'

The waiter brought our food which was, as Jack had promised on the way over, wonderful. The lobster was sweet and moist and I ate mine much too quickly, listening to Jack telling me about all the other places he'd travelled to. Somehow he'd got me off the subject of his family life. He didn't seem that comfortable talking about it, and I wasn't going to force the issue.

Since Jack was driving, I seemed to drink most of the wine. When it was time to leave he paid, ignoring my insistence that I should pay half, and walked me to the car, his arm protectively around me.

'Thank you for dinner,' I said.

'Thank you for coming.'

We sat in the car for a few moments before Jack pulled away.

'Do you know which way to go?' I asked him.

'Sure. It's just ... How would you like a drive around the harbour?'

'Torquay harbour?'

'Sure.'

'Okay,' I said, puzzled by why he would want to go there.

He parked just outside the theatre and we got out. He'd claimed he wanted to check something out, and since he was being so mysterious I'd given up quizzing him on what that something might be. It was cold, frosty and dark. I shivered and Jack put his arm around me again, without saying anything.

We walked past the theatre and across the winter gardens, past the fountain to a walkway. It was on two levels: the top section was a semicircle that you could walk on to get across the water from the theatre to the marina. The bottom level was the same thing, but it was dark and enclosed: concrete turrets supporting the top layer; holes in the wall to see outside. On our right, as we walked through it, railings separated us from the harbour. I could hear the water sucking beneath us and I shivered. Jack drew me closer.

'Where are we going?' I asked him.

'Back to the pier.'

'Then why are we coming this way?'

He suddenly stopped and pulled me around to face him. Taking me completely by surprise he touched my cold face gently and ran his fingers across my cheek. His hand moved behind my head to grasp my hair as he pulled me towards him and kissed me hard. We stayed like that, in the dark tunnel, for about five minutes. I'd ached for him for so long that I felt myself melt into him as he pulled me closer and our bodies pressed together. I wanted him right there and then, but just as I was getting warmed up, he pulled away and grinned at me.

'We came this way so I could do that,' he said.

'I see,' I said, bewildered.

When we got to the pier, I was so excited by Jack that I didn't even feel cold any more. We walked right to the end, to where Kurt must have been killed; where Jack and I had stood together on Friday night. There were a few wreaths and dead-looking flowers here, left by fans. I bent down and looked at the card on a bunch of tulips: 'We'll always love you, Kurt', it said.

'Right,' said Jack. 'Stay here.'

'And where are you going?'

'I'm conducting an experiment. I won't be far off and you won't be in any danger.'

'Fine.'

'Are you cold?'

'A bit. It is fucking freezing, but you warmed me up nicely on the way here.'

'Good,' he said, and strode off back the way we had come.

Once he was out of sight I began to feel strange standing here by myself. It was very cold, and as my blood was no longer pumping as hard as it had been when Jack had got me so excited, it soon seemed even colder. The air slashed at my face, making me wish I had a hat. In my whole life I had never been as frozen as this.

Five minutes passed, then ten. I had a cigarette, but I could barely feel it between my fingers and in my lips as I smoked it. As the wind blew I was forced to lower my head to protect myself. As I did so, I realised that the lower down I stooped, the less abrasive the cold air became. Another five minutes passed, and still no sign of Jack. In desperation I lowered myself completely and sat on the edge of the pier, dangling my legs. It was still cold, but I wasn't such a target for the wind now. I smoked another cigarette and clapped my hands together to try to warm them up. I thought about Jack kissing me, and raised my temperature a few degrees that way.

Then, from nowhere, I felt a hand grab me around the waist and pull me back on to the pier. Any words I might have had froze in my mouth. I was too scared to speak. As the person pulled me back further I tried to scream, but nothing happened. Irrationally, all I kept thinking was, *I'm so cold, I'm so cold. Don't kill me, get me a blanket.* The only word I managed to say in the end was, '*Jack.*'

'It's okay,' he whispered back. 'It's me.'

'Jack?'

'Shhh.'

I pulled myself to my feet slowly and turned to face him. By now the adrenaline had thawed me out a bit and I was spoiling for a big fight.

'You sick ... *bastard.* What the hell do you think you were doing?'

'Proving a point.'

'What point? That you're a fucking psychopath?'

'Calm, down, Lily.'

'I am calm. Take me home, please.'

We walked to the car in silence. So my dream man was a psycho? Fantastic. All the way there Jack kept trying to justify himself, saying there had been a reason for all this, that he'd had to grab me to stop me throwing myself in the water. I wasn't ready to listen yet. Why the hell did he think I would have thrown myself in the water in the first place? Like I wasn't freezing enough as it was? Get real.

Inside the car, with the heating full on, I began to feel slightly better. Jack had become silent eventually, having got no response from me all the way back to Paignton. But once we'd passed the beach huts and the cemetery, I was ready to listen.

'Right,' I said, my voice sounding too loud in the so-far silent car.

'Sorry?' said Jack.

'I will listen to your explanation for that ridiculous stunt and then I'll make a decision about whether I'm ever going to speak to you again.'

'Lily, I—'

'Start explaining.'

'Okay. Look, first of all, I'm so sorry. I was calling to you as I walked towards you, but you couldn't hear me. I had to grab you because if I'd just touched you on the shoulder or something I may have startled you and you may have fallen in the harbour.'

'You say you were shouting at me?'

'Uh-huh. In that sense my plan worked too well. But it proved everything I wanted it to.'

'You're confusing me. Start at the beginning.'

'Okay. This time you were Kurt.'

'Gee, thanks.'

'Well, I couldn't have been Kurt this time because the key thing was that you didn't know what to expect.'

'You can say that again.'

'Okay. First of all, why did you sit there for so long waiting for me?'

'Because you said you were coming back.'

'And you trust me, right?'

'Well, not any more, but I did then.'

'*Touché.* Anyway. Would you have sat there for so long if your boss had asked you to?'

'No way.'

'Ian?'

'Definitely not.'

'You must really like me.'

'I do. Well, I did. Anyway, where is this leading?'

'I just think that in that cold wind, out on the edge of that cold harbour, Kurt would only have stood there for any length of time if the thing he was waiting for was something he really wanted.'

I shook my head, smiling. 'Remind me never to get you interested in role-play again.'

'Aha, you see. My role-play is better than yours.'

'Is it?'

'Oh, yes.'

'Well, I can exclusively reveal, Sherlock, that Kurt wouldn't have been standing there waiting for anyone.'

'Say what?'

'He would have sat down like I did. There's no way you could actually stand up there in that wind for very long. It's too cold.'

'So it did work. We have new information.'

'Maybe. How come I didn't hear you when you shouted at me?'

'Your ears were too cold by that point.'

'So?'

'Well, when your ears get cold you go a little deaf. It happens to me when I'm jogging. Also, the wind blows the sound away and drowns things out.'

'I never knew that,' I said. 'I avoid the cold wherever possible.'

'I'm sorry I grabbed you. But you just couldn't hear me shouting.'

'So if you'd walked up behind me and hit me around the head with a blunt object ...'

'You wouldn't have known anything about it. Those were the two things I wanted to prove, really. That Kurt could only have been lured there by someone he really liked, and that by the time that person came to hit him, he would have been too fucking cold to notice.'

'And he would have been sitting down, which would have made him an easy target.'

'Exactly.'

'So a girl could quite easily have done it.'

'Mmm-hmm.'

'In fact, it's more than likely it was a girl, if he really wanted to see her.'

'Yep.'

'Interesting. Okay, you're forgiven.'

'Any conditions?'

'Oh, yes. If you ever, ever do anything like that to me again I'll kill you.'

'Deal.'

We drove the rest of the way home warm and considerably happier. When Jack pulled up behind the cottages, I considered asking him in, but I thought I'd better wait until he invited himself. He was constantly blowing hot and cold on me, and I didn't think I could stomach another rejection.

We got out of the car and walked to the front of the cottages. I still half expected Jack just to say goodnight and leave me standing there, but instead he drew me towards him, just as he had in the tunnel, and kissed me.

'Can I come in for a while?' he asked.

I smiled, and unlocked the door. He went to fetch logs for the fire.

While the kettle boiled and I fussed around filling the cafetière, Jack hovered behind me, touching my hair and kissing my neck. I felt warm inside while he was doing this, and incredibly turned on. I was trying to remember the last time a man had driven me this wild with the hard-to-get routine. I couldn't. But, finally, it looked as though I was going to get him, and it felt delicious.

When the coffee was made we sat together drinking it on the sofa in the sitting room. My legs were pulled up underneath me, and my head was resting on Jack's shoulder. The fire was blazing with the logs he had brought in before and I'd put a CD on the stereo.

'This is lovely,' he said eventually.

'Mmmm.'

'I mean it, Lily. You really are something.'

'Am I?'

'Uh-huh. You really are.'

'Are you going to kiss me again?'

'Probably,' he said, beginning to stroke my head.

'And when do you think this event might take place?'

'Any second now.'

'And what location will we be using?'

'Right here.'

'Are you sure you wouldn't prefer the bedroom?'

'Just come here.'

Kissing him again, I ached for him. Our hands fumbled all over one another and I could feel his palms start to sweat as he pushed me down on to my back on the sofa. He pulled himself on top of me and kissed me more passionately. There was something slightly awkward about this position, though. I tried to wrap my legs around him and found I couldn't, because the back of the sofa was in the way. He didn't seem to notice, kissing me harder and harder.

'Jack?'

'Shhh.'

He reached his hand down inside my dress, but didn't touch my breasts. He seemed to move around them deliberately, touching my sides, and down to my stomach. I strained towards him, wanting more, but he removed his hand and used it instead as a prop behind my back, pushing me closer to him.

I sat up, forcing him to do the same, so we were facing one another. The music had reached a kind of crescendo, and the fire was hot. I was also still a little drunk from dinner. It was a combination of these things that made me pull my dress over my head and throw it on the floor, now facing him in my underwear and stockings.

He looked at me, his eyes wide.

'You're beautiful,' he said.

'And you're coming with me,' I said, taking his hand and standing up.

He stood up too, and rubbed his eyes.

'Where are we going?' he said.

'The bedroom.'

'I'm sorry, I can't.'

'You what?'

'I'm really sorry, Lily. I want you more than anything else, but—'

'What?'

'I can't explain. Not now.'

'Are you married?'

'No.'

'Are you gay?'

'No!'

'Then what?'

He stood silently, his eyes cast down to the floor. Feeling conspicuous and a bit humiliated standing there in my black lace underwear I reached over and picked up my dress, which I slipped back on over my head. All my passion now gone, I reached across to the table and found a cigarette, which I lit with a shaking hand. This was just too embarrassing.

'I think I'd better go,' he said. I didn't reply. After all, what could I say? Obviously I'd been right the first time. He just didn't find me attractive. Feeling rejected, I listened to the door slam when he eventually found his jacket and left. I sat there smoking, watching the fire begin to die.

After having a hot shower and changing into my fluffiest pyjamas I managed to compose myself. At about five I went to bed, and, for once knowing when she was needed, Maude came and slept in the crook of my neck until I got up the next day.

CHAPTER THIRTEEN

The Same

———————◆———————

Star rang at about ten, just as I was about to leave for the school to talk to Dr Ravine.

'Lily,' she said, sounding cheerful.

I grunted.

'What's wrong?' she said, instantly concerned.

'I have never been so humiliated—' I began.

'What have you done?'

I cringed, and laughed with embarrassment. 'I can hardly bear to say.'

'Come on. Out with it.'

'Well, I stripped off in front of someone who I thought wanted to take things further, then he went all strange, said he couldn't do it, and left.'

'Ouch. Is he gay?'

'He says not.'

'Married?'

'Ditto.'

'Weird.'

'Yeah, I guess I'm not as irresistible as I thought.'

'You're sounding a bit transatlantic recently,' she observed.

'Yeah, well, that's a habit I want to drop. Men. I hate them all. Especially Americans.'

'You poor thing.'

'Anyway, enough about my failed love life. What did you ring for?'

'Well, your father is going off to some conference in Spain at the end of the week and since one of the psychopaths from the research project is in love with me and threatening to break out of prison to come and "devour" me I thought I should have a few days in the country.'

'In the country? Do you mean ... ?'

'Yep. I thought a day or so in Devon would do me the world of good. What do you think? Can I come and stay with you?'

'I think it's a wonderful idea,' I said, feeling a bit more cheerful. 'Maybe you can help take my mind off everything.'

'Mmm. And if we get lucky we can catch a murderer.'

'That,' I said, 'is looking more and more unlikely. But we'll have fun.'

'Great. Well, I'll call you when I know what time I'll be arriving. It'll be Friday.'

'Great.'

It was bright outside. As I drove to the girls' school in Torquay I noted the way that the world expanded on a clear day. Usually you could see maybe one hill in the distance; the next village or town. But on a very clear day there were hills for ever. And in between them sat countless little villages, shrouded in fuzzy light and smoke from open fires. In between the villages were fields, green, yellow and brown, punctuated with sheep. The winter sun only managed to stroke the tops of the hills with its low light. Some glowed yellow with its touch and others, out of the direct rays, seemed black.

The school was easy to find. It was not in central Torquay but out towards Marychurch, up a very long, winding road. I knew where it was, because it faced Nat's old school, the boys' grammar. That, of course, was how he had known about the

twins. Boys and girls from both schools mixed so freely that I
didn't really know why they were separated at all. Of course,
the boys' school was a grammar school and therefore free. The
girls' school was private and fee-paying. I wondered how Mr
and Mrs Carter had been able to afford that, when it seemed
that they couldn't even afford to replace the L on their hotel
sign.

Dr Ravine was still in some meeting when I arrived, on the
dot of eleven. I sat outside her office, feeling like I was waiting
for a telling-off: one of those oh-my-God-I'm-in-trouble
moments that I still remembered with great clarity from my
own schooldays.

When she appeared I was startled by her massive, obese
form. For some reason I had expected a thin, birdlike woman:
the voice on the phone had certainly sounded as though it had
come from someone small. But she was massive. Her hair was
completely white – she must have been at least sixty – and sat
on her head in tiny little curls. Her eyes were bright blue,
though, and sparkled when she introduced herself to me. She
was dressed all in blue as well: long loose blouse; long loose
pleated skirt. On top of all this she wore an ankle length
sleeveless navy cardigan and lots of silver jewellery, including
a cat brooch with a dangling silver mouse, which she wore
pinned just above her left breast.

'Lily Pascale, I presume,' she said, in her no-nonsense
voice.

'Dr Ravine,' I said, holding out my hand, which she shook
vigorously. 'Pleased to meet you.'

'Come on through,' she said, and led me into her study.

The room was big and square. On the right-hand side sat
her large desk. Catching no light from the window, it looked
dark and imposing. On the far side of it was a big chair
covered in leather. On the side nearest the door was a smaller
chair: where pupils and teachers sat to get their tellings-off, I
imagined. Directly facing the door was a large bay window

overlooking what seemed to be an orchard. On my left there was a panelled wall in front of which stood several large bookcases, with volumes bound in leather. I felt as though I had stepped into the past.

'What a lovely room,' I said politely.

'Yes. I like these character buildings,' she said.

I took the telling-off chair, while Dr Ravine tucked herself into her large leather chair behind the desk. She moved a stack of papers from in front of her and I noticed her fingernails. They were very thick, very ridged and painted dark blue.

'So,' she said, looking straight at me. 'You are researching twins and ...'

'Education. That's right.' I pulled my notebook out of my bag and scrabbled for a pen.

'And you are on which degree course?'

'Cultural Studies,' I said, thinking quickly.

'Cultural Studies. Interesting.'

'So how many sets of twins have you had here?'

'Sets of twins,' she repeated, sounding slightly suspicious, 'I think we've had about twelve sets since I've been here. Of course, three of those are in the current first year. As I'm sure you have discovered in your research, twins are a far more common phenomenon now, with all the fertility treatments and so on.'

'Yes. I did read that. How many sets were identical?'

'Three. The Carter twins, the Davies girls and the Barton-Clarkes.'

'I was interested in the effects of that. You know, mix-ups with which girl was which and so on.'

'We try to be very sensitive here. Obviously at school the issues around identical twins are more significant, because all the girls are encouraged to look the same by wearing uniform. It was fairly easy with the Davies twins, because they were complete opposites in every way. Janet was very studious and her sister Tamsin was very wild. Tamsin dyed her hair red in the second form and, although I wouldn't usually approve, it made it easier to tell them apart. The Barton-Clarkes were quite similar, although their friends could tell them apart, and the teachers could after a while. They had different expressions, and Dominique's nose was slightly more turned up than Isobel's — if you cared to look that hard. They played a couple of tricks on us all when they were in the first year, but the novelty wore off after that, and they didn't seem to be gaining anything from it anyway.'

'What would they gain?'

'You sometimes get cases where twins make a deal that one will concentrate on one subject, and the other focuses on something different. In the school where I used to work as Latin mistress there were identical twins who had made a pact to do exactly that kind of thing. They sat exams for one another and so on. They were expelled.'

'You haven't mentioned the third set of twins you had here, yet,' I prompted.

'Yes, I was coming to them. Laura and Alexandra Carter. Now, they are a case-study if ever there was one. First of all, they were the most identical twins I have ever seen in my life.'

'Really?'

'Absolutely. I knew them for five years and by the end I still couldn't tell the difference between them.'

'They must have been very similar.'

'They were. Exactly the same hairstyle, exactly the same facial expressions. Their voices were different, and some of their mannerisms, but they both did very good imitations of one another, so you could never be completely sure which one you were dealing with.'

'What did they look like?'

'Very pale skin, dark hair and black eyes. They were very beautiful. Lots of boyfriends. They were both very graceful — they were training as ballet dancers, you see.'

'Were they different as people?'

'Yes. Laura was very dominant, assertive and so on. She was very good at maths, if I recall. Alexandra was the more timid of the two. She spoke more softly and did well at English. Apparently outside school they dressed quite differently, so people could tell the difference.'

'In what way did they dress differently?'

'Laura always wore white, and Alex always wore black.'

'That's a bit dramatic.'

'It was all completely in character. They were a very dramatic pair.'

'So they must have played a few tricks on you, I would imagine.'

'Not on us, no.'

'Sorry?'

'They didn't get on. The only tricks they played were on each other.'

'I don't understand.'

'They spent their whole time here trying to damage each other. That black and white gimmick only made things worse. They were always meeting boys after school and more than once, if one had to stay behind, the other would go and pretend to be her sister. Laura would wear black, or Alex would wear white. It lost them a lot of friends, and I'm not even clear why they did it. It seemed to be the case that whatever one of them had the other wanted.'

'Why were they like that?'

'I have no idea. All the other twins I've known were delightful. They were all very close to one another and in most cases seemed to be best friends as well as sisters. You must have found that in your research so far.'

'Yes,' I improvised. 'Most twins are very close.'

'Well, these two hated one another.'

'Do you think they really did?'

'Who knows? I never knew the reason in any case.'

'Were they popular with the other pupils?'

'Yes. Although for the time they were at this school, the whole place was divided. There were Alex's friends and allies, and Laura's. The two groups didn't mix.'

'Must have been difficult.'

'Yes. Especially in games. They would never play on the same team, of course, and they spent the duration of any netball or hockey match trying to dupe the opposite team members into passing the ball to them.'

I laughed. 'Sounds quite entertaining.'

'Very tiresome after the first few times, I can tell you.'

Dr Ravine looked troubled. For a moment she didn't say anything, but looked around the room, squashing her hands together as though she was nervous.

'Is there something wrong?' I asked.

'Sorry?'

'You seem bothered by something.'

'Yes.' She looked at me hard. 'Could you excuse me for a moment?'

'Sure.'

Dr Ravine left the room and was gone for about three or four minutes. When she came back, she was shaking her head and looking at me peculiarly.

'You know, there is no Cultural Studies at the university any more,' she said, standing by her desk. 'I've just phoned to find out.'

'I don't understand.'

'Cultural Studies? The degree you're supposed to be on.'

I looked down. 'Oh.'

'So are you going to tell me exactly why you've been wasting my time?'

'I'm an investigator, trying to find out what happened with the Carter twin murder.'

'I see. So you lied to me.'

'Yes. I'm very sorry, but you wouldn't have seen me otherwise.'

137

'No. I don't suppose I would.'

'I'm really sorry.'

She coughed. 'Have I been useful?'

'Oh, yes. Thank you so much. I really am sorry for wasting your time.'

She sighed. 'It's okay. You're on the right side, I suppose.'

'You know all about what happened, I take it?'

'The police have been to see me. I told them more or less what I told you — in less detail, of course. After all, they weren't claiming to be doing a research project on twins.'

She let the smallest smile cross her face, and I smiled back.

'Has someone called Tony Bryce been here?' I asked.

'He called. I'm seeing him tomorrow.'

'Don't tell him what you've just told me,' I said urgently.

'No?'

'No. He's the bad guy. Well, a journalist intent on digging the dirt.'

'This is like some kind of horrible dream,' she said sadly. 'It's not every day one of my students gets killed. And then having people turning up like this, lying and looking for information ...'

'Do you believe it was murder?'

'Yes. I suppose so. Laura wouldn't kill herself. I just hope Alex didn't ...'

'What?'

'Nothing. I just hope their rivalry didn't get too out of control.'

'I know. It's a horrible thought.'

'Do you think Alex did it?' she asked me.

'I don't know,' I said. 'But after what you just told me, she's my main suspect.'

What I didn't say was that if it was in fact Laura who was alive, she'd be an even bigger suspect in my mind.

'Why do you think it's Alex?' I said. 'The one who's still alive, I mean.'

'Sorry?'

'Well, the fake suicide note was signed "Laura", but I thought most people believed it was actually Alex who was dead.'

'Really? The police didn't say anything about this. Gosh. That can't be right. I saw Alex in town, with her brother Tim. She was wearing black, of course. And when I went to talk to her I called her Alex and she didn't correct me. No one told me anything about this. So it could have been *Laura*?' She shook her head and frowned. 'This is just too much.'

Dr Ravine looked as if she was about to cry. I decided to change the subject.

'Do any of these words mean anything to you?' I told her the words from the burnt piece of paper: *Lucky, lipp,* and *she looks like the real thing.*

She shook her head. 'No idea,' she said, composing herself a bit.

'Never mind,' I said gently.

She smiled weakly. 'You seem to be doing a thorough job.'

'Thanks. I just wish it would get me somewhere.'

'And you are working for whom?'

'I can't …'

'Would it be Emma Winter?'

'Yes.'

And at that moment we both said together, 'The twins' mother.'

We sat in silence for a moment.

'I suppose she was paying their fees?'

Dr Ravine nodded.

CHAPTER FOURTEEN

Femme Fatale

———————◆———————

On the way home I kicked myself for not seeing it before. Of course Emma was their mother: who else could she be? Once I'd finished being shocked by that, I went back to being shocked by Dr Ravine's implication that Alex could have killed Laura. Could that possibly be true?

If Alex had killed Laura, and made it look like suicide, why on earth would she tell the police that *she* was Laura? I struggled to find a plausible reason, but couldn't. Maybe she was trying to hold up the police inquiry, but by behaving so suspiciously? No. Her behaviour put the spotlight on her, right at a time when she'd want it as far from her as possible.

It was interesting, though, the way that the victim in Dr Ravine's version squared up with Tim's. Laura was dead, and Alex was still alive. And in this scenario, perhaps Alex had killed Kurt as well, because he'd been having an affair with her sister. The more I thought about that detail – that Kurt had been involved with Laura – the more it now made sense. I bet that she'd gone after him. After all, that was what Dr Ravine and Cornelia had said: whatever one twin had, the other wanted.

Unless, of course, it was the other way round, and Laura had killed Alex. But, then, why would she write a suicide note signed 'Laura'? The police believed the death to be suspicious mainly because the note was from the wrong twin. If Laura had killed her sister, and set it up to look like suicide, she would have at least signed the note 'Alex', and would have made sure her sister's fingerprints were all over the note and the knife. All this made me believe that the murder had been committed by someone who really hadn't given it much thought. If Laura had done it, I was sure that she wouldn't have messed it up so badly. Of course, this logic left me with few suspects. If Laura hadn't killed Alex, and Alex hadn't killed Laura, then what had happened?

When I got home I was surprised to find flowers at my door. It was a bunch of red roses, tied up with a big white ribbon. Jack, I thought, trying to win me over again. But when I got them inside and looked at the label I could see they were from Tony Bryce.

'Tell me what really happened that night,' the note said.

And why couldn't he just leave me alone?

I looked at the clock on the kitchen wall. It was two o'clock. In the fridge, all I found for lunch was a lump of Brie, which I combined with some old celery and mayonnaise in some rye bread that I found in the freezer and toasted. It was time to go to the supermarket. And on the way there I thought I would call in on Emma, and start demanding some real facts from her.

When she opened the door to me Emma was fairly drunk. She was holding a glass in her hand and swaying.

'Have you worked it out yet?' she asked.

'I've worked out that you're their mother,' I said. 'Can I come in?'

'Very clever.' She smiled with everything but her eyes. 'Yes, please do.'

Inside, Emma's house smelt strongly of incense. The cottage was by the side of a river and must have been very old.

As we walked into the sitting room I had to bend slightly to avoid hitting my head on a low beam. The large french windows at the far end of the room led right out on to the riverbank, and I could see a small boat moored there. Inside, the room was expensively but minimally furnished. One sofa and two armchairs were clustered around the fire and a coffee table sat between them. The rest of the room was bare, except for a large Indian rug and Emma's desk: a huge pine table with a computer sitting on it. This arrangement faced out on to the river. Underneath the desk were two Labradors, curled up in a large basket.

'Sit down,' said Emma.

'Thanks.'

'Can I get you a drink?'

'I'll have whatever you're having.'

A few moments later I was supplied with a gin and tonic.

'So,' said Emma, 'how did you work it out?'

'Well, it was obvious, really. I should have seen it sooner. But I knew for sure when I went to the school and found out you'd paid for them to go there.'

'Very good. I'm impressed.'

'Why didn't you tell me at the beginning?'

'I didn't trust you. I still don't.'

'Thanks.'

'Look, Lily, I'm a celebrity. My privacy is important.'

'Did the twins know?'

'No. They knew they were adopted, but they didn't know who their mother was.'

'Why not?'

'They chose not to find out.'

'I see. So did you track them down?'

'Yes. A couple of years ago. But I had to wait to be found by them. That's adoption etiquette, you see. So I bought a house here and waited. I'm still waiting.'

'What were you going to tell them?'

'Some bullshit about their father leaving me pregnant at seventeen.'

I frowned. 'What was the real story?'

She laughed. 'Have you ever had your cards read, Lily?'

'My cards?'

'Wait here.'

I sat there looking into the flames of the fire while Emma banged around upstairs. Eventually she returned with a set of what looked like playing cards. They were large, though, with horrible, bright pictures on them. Tarot cards. Great.

'Have you?' she said.

'What?'

'Had your cards read?'

'No.'

'Why not?'

'I'm a Catholic. It's against my religion to conspire with the devil.'

'God, you're uptight.'

'Yeah, well, you've caught me in a particularly unsatanic mood.'

'So you don't want a reading?'

'No, thanks.'

She shuffled the cards around in her hands. I hadn't meant to be so harsh with her, but although cards were one of my great passions, these cards filled me with dread. Ever since I could remember, I had been terrified of anything to do with black magic. Maybe it was all those scare stories the priest had told us at Sunday school, but I wasn't taking any chances.

'I had my cards read for the first time when I was pregnant.'

'With Alex and Laura?'

She nodded. 'Yes. They warned me about what would happen.'

'Sorry?'

'The cards said that history would repeat itself.'

'I don't understand.'

'I'm a twin.'

'I heard it runs in families.'

'My twin is dead.'

'I'm sorry, I didn't—'

'I killed my own sister.'

Emma stood up shakily and the glass fell from her hand and landed with a thud on the rug. She didn't appear to notice. I put my glass down on the table: my hand was shaking, too. She couldn't be serious. Was she telling me she was a murderer?

The gin swilled uncomfortably in my stomach, the taste unnatural in my mouth. Emma had started pacing up and down in the room, walking unsteadily from the french windows to the wall in front of me and then back again. I sat there frozen, not knowing what to say or do next.

'Did you hear me?' she said, her voice raised. 'I killed my own sister.'

I looked down. 'I don't know what to say.'

'Don't you wonder why I'm not in prison? What's your saintly mind thinking now, Lily? Do you think I'm the devil, with my devil cards and my devil sister whom *I* killed? Do you know, I committed the perfect crime? I killed her in the only place where you are immune from judgement. I killed her in my mother's womb.'

She looked at me like she thought I might say something. Her words were coming out all hissed and screechy. She was clearly losing it. Maybe it was the drink, or the guilt, or the grief. She was scaring me, though, and I wished she would stop.

'We were real opposites, my twin and I,' she continued. 'I was born alive and she was born dead. They called her Abigail. Pretty name, don't you think? We were going to do everything together. Our parents had bought us two identical little cribs, two identical little tricycles to ride when we were old enough.

145

That's how I found out, you know. I was going through the attic one day and found all my things up there. All my things in the attic, although I knew they were downstairs. A little dolly just like mine. The little bike, the crib. All the clothes. Just like mine. Can you imagine that? Can you? My dad found me up there. They explained to me then: "You had sister but she died." And then I remembered. I strangled her with the cord, you know. I did it, and now it's happening again.'

Her voice had become louder and louder until she'd seemed to reach a peak and then it had become small, like a whisper, as she sat, hunched, on the sofa.

'Fetch the gin, Lily.'

'I think you've had—'

'Fetch the fucking drink, girl.'

'Okay.'

When I returned with the bottle, she seemed to have composed herself slightly. It was exactly as Star had said: twins sometimes murdered each other in the womb. Of course. But, as was her style, Star had made it sound far too sinister – it was accidental, surely? No one could seriously consider taking the blame for something like that, could they? But, looking into Emma's cold eyes and her distant expression, I understood. It was probably fine if you'd never known, but ... Finding out that way must have been so horrible. And she was so traumatised by it. Poor Emma.

'Emma,' I said gently, 'it wasn't your fault.'

'That's what they all say.'

'What did you mean when you said it was happening again?'

'The curse.'

'I'm sorry?'

'She told me – the woman who read my cards – she told me it was all going to happen again.'

'I still don't understand.'

'Come on, mastermind, who do you think killed the girl?'

I frowned. 'The other girl?'

'Bravo. We're finally getting somewhere.'

'But if you knew that already, what did you need me for?'

'I still need you, Lily. I need to know which one is which. Which one killed, which one died.'

'Well, I'm doing my best.'

'And you will continue?'

'I suppose so, although I don't think it's as simple as you're making out. I can't see evidence that one killed the other. And what about Kurt?'

'It's all connected. If you find out who killed him, you'll be getting somewhere.'

'But how?'

'I really don't know. But you will have to find out.'

'Like I said, I'll try my best.'

'Thank you.'

'Emma?'

'What?'

'Is there anything else you're keeping from me?'

'No. Cards on the table now. You know everything.'

'Okay.' I stood up to leave. 'I'll be in touch.'

'Good.'

I didn't really feel like going to the supermarket after all that. It had been intense, and frightening. In a way, I wished I'd told Emma that I was giving up this whole thing. It was like a nightmare I couldn't get out of: a dark, cold existence in which everything lay in the shadow of its own double. Who were all these strange people? Not just the twins, all of them. Who were they and what was going on? I wished I knew. I drove home fast, with my mind racing.

When I got in I called my mother and cancelled dinner. She was cross, because it seemed that Emma had just cancelled as well. She asked about Jack and I didn't tell her anything. It would have been too embarrassing.

Emma had really done it this time. My heart wouldn't stop pounding and I couldn't relax. I paced the house for an hour or so, pulling sheets off my bed, cleaning things, moving around. Everything seemed all wrong.

In my mind, amidst all the toy tricycles and seaside scenes that now inhabited it, one thing shone through. That little girl, the one with glass eyes, the one called Pippa. She'd said she knew who had gone out that night: she claimed to know which twin was which. I wondered what blind people saw, what insight I had missed out on. As the telephone started to ring I put on my coat and went back outside. I was going to the hotel, to try finally to get some answers.

As I walked out of the door I bumped straight into Jack, who was carrying a soft toy and a box of chocolates.

'If those are for me, don't bother,' I said, pushing past him.

'Please, Lily, just listen to me.'

'I can't, Jack. Time's running out.'

'What? What's wrong with you? You seem all weird.'

'I have to get to Torquay. I haven't got time for this now.'

'Can I come with you?'

'No.'

'I thought we were friends.'

'Friends don't embarrass each other the way you embarrassed me.'

'If I could only make you believe that I couldn't help it.'

'Whatever. Look, Jack, I have to go.'

'Will you be back tonight?'

'Who knows?'

'Can I at least speak to you then? Or tomorrow?'

'Maybe. I don't know. I'll give you a call.'

'Really?'

I looked him straight in the eyes. 'Yes. *I* don't break promises.'

'Be careful,' he said softly, as I climbed into my car.

The roads shone with ice as I drove too fast along the coast. Something was inside me now, telling me I had to escape from this, and that I only had a certain amount of time to get this right: to reach the hotel. Tony was on my trail; Emma was cracking up. It was all too much. I had to solve this and get out. Call me paranoid, but it felt like everything was closing in.

It was hard to get the car up the hill to the hotel. The road seemed more narrow, more slippery and treacherous than it had before. Perhaps it was because I felt nervous that I stalled twice: skidded all the way up.

When I reached the top, something seemed different. For a minute I couldn't work out what it was. The little orange street lamp still glowed at the very end of the road, but I could see less detail here tonight. Then I realised. There were no lights. Neither hotel had any lights on. I got out of the car and walked towards the blackened door of the Tulip Hotel. A small sign said: *Closed until further notice.* The next-door hotel, the one I hadn't really paid much attention to before: it was also unoccupied. I walked to that door, a peculiar chill cutting through me. *Closed,* it said on the door.

My mobile phone started to ring.

CHAPTER FIFTEEN

Crooked

———◆———

'Lily Pascale,' I said, when I answered it.

'It's Ian.'

'Hi, Ian. What's going on?'

'I need you to come and fill out a statement.'

'Sorry?'

'You need to come to the police station. I'll explain when you get here.'

'Fine. I'll be ten minutes.'

Perplexed, I got back into the car and drove down the hill and across town.

The police station was a drab grey building, sixties in design, all flat and gravelled and cold. When I walked in through the glass doors it was quiet; no one else was inside apart from one police officer standing behind the desk. I asked to see DC Ian Nagy and they told me to sit and wait. After ten minutes, there was no sign of Ian and I was getting restless. I went outside and had a cigarette.

What on earth could he possibly want me to make a statement about? I tried running through some possibilities in my head, but the list wasn't very long. Could something have happened to Emma? She'd been in a state when I last saw her. Or could it be somebody else I'd seen recently? I got a sick feeling in my stomach when I considered the possibility that someone else might be dead. That it might be someone I knew. But then I rationalised everything. It was probably just something to do with the night Kurt had been murdered. I remembered I hadn't actually made a statement about that yet.

Eventually, after I'd gone back inside and waited for fifteen more minutes, Ian came through. 'Lily,' he said, and gestured for me to follow him.

I'd been here before, last Easter. The horrible long corridor was still the same; it still felt like I was in some kind of underwater cavern. The light didn't help. It was a fluorescent, unnatural pale yellow with a small, barely there flicker. There was no natural light in here, because there were no windows.

'Here we are,' he said, and led me into a small interview room.

'What's going on, Ian?'

'We've caught him.'

'Sorry?'

'We've caught the murderer.'

'Him?'

'Yep.'

'And his name is?'

'I can't tell you until you've made the statement, I'm afraid.'

'Well, hurry up, then.'

'Okay, I want an account of what happened that night in the hotel. And this time it's official, so don't piss me around.'

'Okay.'

So I ran through the whole thing again. In the end there wasn't much to tell. I left out the details about my conversation with the woman and the girl and stuck to plain facts instead: what time I'd arrived, when I'd heard the door open, and all the other noises and movements I'd heard during the night.

'So the door opened at ten thirty,' said Ian, looking over what he'd transcribed.

'Yes.'

'Okay,' he said, after he'd read the whole thing out to me again. 'That's fine.'

'So?' I said, holding out my hands questioningly. 'What does it tell you?'

'What we knew anyway. Tim Carter killed Kurt, and he also almost definitely killed his sister.'

'Tim?'

'Yep.'

'How? Why?'

'It seems that he went down on to the pier and beat Kurt to death.'

'What with?'

'A piece of his wheelchair.'

'Sorry?'

'You know the metal footrests? They slide out. He beat Kurt to death with one of them. There was even blood left on it. It was quite exciting when we worked it out. Someone in Forensics noticed a tiny little indentation on Kurt's wound, which could only have come from something precisely that shape. We generated the shape on the computer – it was very high tech – and it came out looking like, well, no one knew. But then one of the women there, whose husband's disabled, recognised it and bingo. The only person connected to all this who goes around in a wheelchair is Tim. We brought him straight in.'

'And?'

'He confessed. Well, he says he killed Kurt, although he won't say why. But we're working on him. The problem is, we can't get him to admit that he killed Alex as well.'

'Alex?'

'Well, whoever. That's another loose end I need to tie up. I really believe Laura's telling the truth, and it makes sense that

Tim thought the living twin was Alex if he thought he was murdering Laura. We just need something conclusive, and then we'll be able to charge him properly and get on with the trial.'

'What if you don't get anything?'

'Then we'll have to take Laura's word for it, I suppose.'

'Did Tim definitely kill Alex, or whichever one she was?'

'It seems that way. His fingerprints were on the knife and the note, and although he'd previously claimed that they were there because he discovered the body, it turns out that the suicide note is also in his handwriting. The smudged prints turned out to be just more of his – like he'd gripped the paper really hard or something. It would be helpful if he would confess, though. It's weird. I can't see why he would confess to one thing and not the other.'

'What is he saying?'

'Nothing. He refuses to speak until he's seen Alex.'

'He's still convinced she's Alex?'

'Yeah.'

'She still hasn't put him right?'

'Would you, if you knew that you were his intended victim?'

'I suppose not. But if she actually let him think she was Alex that means she must have suspected him.'

'Maybe.' Ian rubbed his temples. 'I'm just glad it's almost over.'

'Seems that way,' I said, trying to sound genuine. 'Well done, Ian. You got there first.'

'Yeah, well. It's my job.'

'Right. Well …'

'There was just one more thing, Lily.'

'What's that?'

'I need a favour.'

'What kind of favour?'

'It's Laura. She hasn't got anywhere to go.'

'Why not?'

'The hotel's too much for her on her own. She needs people around her.'

'And?'

'Well, she wants to leave the area, but she's going to have to give evidence at the trial. Can she stay with you?'

'With me?'

'It'll only be for a few days. She can't stay at my place, and I thought you would be the ideal choice. She needs some peace and quiet and some sea air.'

'Why can't she stay with you?'

'Think about it. It wouldn't be right.'

'Well, don't you have some witness-protection programme or something?'

'You watch too many American films,' he said. 'We do have a system, but she's not in danger from anyone any more, so she's not really a priority case. I'm just worried because she's lonely and scared, and she's lost all her family. I promised I'd help her find somewhere.'

I sighed. 'Well, when does she want to come?'

'Right now seems as good a time as any.'

Ian led me out into the corridor and then down to another room, where a girl sat, all in white, with a small white suitcase. I recognised her from the night at the hotel and from the club, except that now she wore a pained, nervous expression and her hair was in a high ponytail.

She stood up when we walked in, and she seemed even thinner than she had that night. Her low-slung hipsters and short white jumper didn't quite meet in the middle, and revealed some pale creamy-skinned midriff.

'You look familiar,' she said.

'Never mind that,' said Ian, all smiles. 'Laura, this is Lily Pascale.'

'Interesting name,' she said, raising an eyebrow.

'Hello,' I said. 'Pleased to meet you, Laura.'

'This is who you're going to be staying with,' said Ian.

'Great,' she muttered.

She looked up at Ian and batted her long, thick eyelashes. Then she very slowly and very deliberately looked me up and down.

'Is that all right?' I asked her.

'Yeah. Whatever. Let's go.'

She picked up her suitcase and walked out of the door, not looking at Ian again.

'She's had a rough time,' he murmured to me, 'but she's very sweet once you get to know her. I'm sure she'll be no trouble.'

'Right.' I wasn't so sure, but I was stuck now.

'Let me know if you need anything.'

'Yeah. 'Bye, Ian.'

Laura didn't speak as we walked out to the car. I took her case from her and put it in the boot. We got in and I started the engine.

'Cold, isn't it?' I said, making conversation.

She didn't say anything, just looked at her fingernails, which were painted with some kind of blue-black polish. Driving through Torquay I thought about everything Ian had said about Tim. I didn't understand what could have made him do it. He had no motive, as far as I could see, for either murder. I wondered if they would make it stick in court. I supposed since they had a confession that that would do it. But why wasn't he admitting to murdering his sister as well?

'Can I have the stereo on?' asked Laura, as we hit the coast road after Paignton.

'Sure,' I said. 'Whatever.'

She fiddled with the dial on my car stereo until she found Radio One. They were playing a song that sounded familiar, but which I couldn't place. Something that sounded like some nouveau progressive rock attempt, with a wailing vocal and words like 'rain down, rain down, rain down'.

'Jesus,' muttered Laura, reaching for the dial again.

'Fucking Radiohead. I hate Radiohead. Depressing load of shit. Alex loved them. Stupid cow.'

'Sorry?' I said.

'Nothing,' she replied, starting to look through the tapes in my glove-box.

When we pulled up outside the house I saw Jack looking from his window. He smiled when he saw me, then, noticing I had a passenger in the car, he frowned and made a kind of what's-she-doing-there? expression. I was glad to see him: the atmosphere around Laura was cold and impenetrable – which was understandable – but something about her frightened me, just as it had that first night I'd seen her. I found myself in two minds about whether or not I would actually want to go to sleep with her in the house. But I was probably just paranoid. After all, she was only a teenager.

Jack came over about five minutes after we got into the house. Laura had made straight for the kitchen and poured some Evian from the bottle in the fridge. Then she had glided through to the sitting room and switched on the TV.

'So what's going on?' asked Jack, when I opened the door.

'Sorry?'

'What's with the house-guest?'

'I'm still not sure if I'm speaking to you.'

'Come on, Lily, I've apologised.'

'Mmm.'

'And I've offered to explain.'

'Well ...'

Laura appeared beside me 'Who are you?' she asked Jack, her voice falsely childlike and innocent.

'Who are *you*?' he replied.

'I'm Laura Carter,' she said.

'Why don't you go and watch TV?' I suggested.

'So you can be alone?'

'That was the general idea.'

'Okay,' she said, and, after smiling at Jack, she skipped off.

'What was all that about?' he asked.

'Don't ask. Anyway, you were in the middle of explaining something.'

'We can't do this on the doorstep. Can I come in?'

'It's not going to be very private.'

'Well, come over to my place, then.'

'I can't leave her, can I?'

'Why not?'

'I don't know. She might be suicidal or something.'

'She didn't look suicidal to me.'

'Well ...'

All of a sudden I heard a crash from the sitting room. 'Lily!' came Laura's voice.

'Shit,' I said. 'I'm going to have to go and see what's going on.'

'And where does that leave me?'

'Lily!'

'I'll see you tomorrow.'

When I got to the sitting room I could see shards of glass all over the floor. Laura was trying to pick up the pieces, but in doing so she had cut her hand and she was dripping blood everywhere.

'Come on,' I said, trying not to sound annoyed. 'I'll do that.'

Once it was all cleared up and a plaster had been administered to Laura's hand, I tried to make myself comfortable enough to settle in for the evening. I lit a fire and made coffee. Laura asked for one too: black, no sugar. She channel-surfed for a while, not staying on any one channel for more than two minutes. I hadn't asked her any questions or anything, feeling it would be better to let her start any conversations. I flicked through a magazine instead, paying it about as much attention as Laura was giving the television.

'It's nice here,' she said eventually.

'It's a bit quiet,' I said, 'but okay if you like that kind of thing.'

'Is that your boyfriend living next door?'

'Jack? No. He's just a friend.'

'He's American, isn't he?'

'Mmm-hmm.'

'Does he live here now, or is he just on holiday?'

'It's a long holiday.'

'I'm going to America,' she said.

'After the trial?'

'Yes. After the trial.'

Her black eyes glazed over and I thought I could see tears forming in them. All of a sudden I realised that she must be devastated by all this. I hadn't meant to be stand-offish with her, it was just that Ian had talked me into having her here, and after all the things I'd heard about her, it was hard to believe she was as sweet as she was coming across. But, then, nothing was ever simple.

As I watched her compose herself, I was struck by how similar Laura was to Emma. Emma obviously dyed her hair, but the eyes were the same: they contained the same darkness. Briefly, I wondered if Ian had been right. Was I really sitting here with Laura Carter? She was doing a good job of it: dressed all in white, looking up each time I said Laura. But could this still be Alex? She'd told plenty of people she was Alex: Tim, Pippa, Kurt, Harry Duckling, and Dr Ravine. Had she really just done that to protect herself?

'This must be very upsetting for you,' I said, eventually.

'It's horrible,' she said. 'I've been so afraid.'

'Well, it's all over now,' I said soothingly.

'Is it?' she said, and turned the TV over.

At bedtime, I showed Laura to the spare room. She had been alternately friendly then distant all evening; one minute she was asking me if I permed my hair, and the next she was telling me about her nightmares.

'I kept dreaming about him,' she said, as I took her up the stairs.

'Who?'

'Tim. I kept dreaming that he was holding me down, slashing my wrists.'

I flinched. Her expression didn't change.

'I knew it was me he wanted, and I had to pretend to be Alex for all that time.'

'Why would he want to kill you, Laura?'

'He said I was a bitch.'

'Don't worry. It's all right now.'

'I miss her so much, Lily. She was my very best friend. I mean, we had loads of arguments and stuff, but I loved her.'

'I know. Just try to get some sleep.'

'Thank you. You're being very kind to me.'

When I went downstairs, I found a note had been pushed under the door. Jack, I thought, smiling. I took it into the sitting room and opened it up. 'I'm watching you,' it said. It wasn't signed. I gulped and dropped it on the floor, my heart beating hard and my hands shaking. I should have known this was going to happen: after all, this was what had happened last time I'd investigated a murder. But wasn't this all supposed to be over now? Didn't the police have the bad guy?

I picked up the phone and dialled Jack's number. I could hear it ringing in the cottage next door. Why wasn't he answering? Eventually he did.

'Jack,' I said, relieved to hear his voice at last.

'Who is it?'

I heard my voice peak with fear: 'It's Lily.'

'Sorry, Lily, I was fast asleep. What's the matter?'

'Can you come over?'

'Sure.'

'Now?'

'I'm on my way.'

CHAPTER SIXTEEN

Sweet Dreams

———◆———

We sat at the kitchen table looking at the note.

'Do you think she's asleep?' asked Jack.

'Who knows. Does it matter?'

'I don't trust her.'

'No. Well, the jury's out on whether she's genuine or not.'

'Who do you think sent the note?'

'Tony, possibly. Apart from that I have no idea.'

'It's not his style, though, really.'

'What do you mean?'

'He seems a little more direct, somehow. And he signs his name.'

'I suppose so.'

'What do you make of all this Tim stuff?'

'Well, if he confessed then I suppose that means he did it,' I said uncertainly.

'Yeah.'

I frowned. 'But why, though?'

'Doesn't match up with what we worked out, does it?'

'No. For a start, how would Tim get Kurt to the pier?'

'Maybe he was blackmailing him.'

'Maybe.'

Jack yawned. It was getting late.

'Anyway,' I said, looking up pointedly, 'we shouldn't talk about this now.'

'No.'

'I suppose it's time for bed.'

'Do you want me to stay?'

'Sorry?'

'Well, you must be a bit freaked out just now.'

'I am, actually.'

'Well, let me stay.'

'There's only one bed apart from hers.'

'Well, I'm sure we can restrain ourselves.' He grinned. 'Come on.'

Still wondering exactly why we should have to restrain ourselves, I walked upstairs, with Jack following closely behind. It felt funny, having two new people in my house. The bathroom was between Laura's room and mine, and Jack and I politely took it in turns in there. I went first, cleaning my teeth and washing my face, and then felt him brush past me as he went in straight afterwards, smiling. For some reason this made me feel like we had been married for a very long time. But we'd never even slept together. I felt nervous about sharing a bed with him, although there wasn't any reason to: I wanted something to happen between us and he didn't. Nothing was going to happen, and I was just going to have to get over it. This was platonic, and the only reason Jack was staying was because I was scared.

Nevertheless, I ditched my pyjamas and got into bed wearing a pair of white lace knickers and a white cotton night-shirt: not too full-on, but approachable, just in case he had a change of heart. He undressed by the side of the bed once he'd finished in the bathroom. I noted the tanned, smooth skin and the scar on his back. He was wearing blue and white checked boxer shorts — the only item of clothing he left on as he slipped under the duvet next to me.

'You'll get me excited dressed like that,' I teased.

'Really? Should I put more clothes on?'

'No, I think I can hold back,' I said, giggling at his serious tone.

'Shhh,' he said, muffling his own laughter. 'We'll wake the guest.'

'She isn't asleep,' I said. 'You can count on that.'

'Mmm.'

'Well, goodnight, then,' I said, turning over to face the window.

'Yeah. Sweet dreams.'

Usually I slept right in the middle of my big double bed, but tonight I'd opted for the right-hand side, closest to the window. I drew my knees up to my chest, feeling cold in my nightshirt, and tried to drop off. I could sense Jack lying on his back; staying still. I listened to his breathing in, out, in, and tried not to let my own breathing fall into the same pattern, in case he thought I was copying him. It was hard to sleep with him there. I could smell him; more sensual than any man I'd ever known. Slightly musky, but fresh, with the faint scent of a spicy aftershave.

'Are you asleep?' he asked, after we'd been lying there for about half an hour.

I didn't say anything. I wasn't pretending to be asleep, as such, I just wanted him to feel relaxed – not like I was staying awake spying on him. Call me over-sensitive, but rejection did funny things to me, and I didn't want him to think I was lying there awake, desperate for him to touch me, waiting to have my wicked way with him – tempting though that was. I just couldn't sleep because I was enjoying this too much, but I'd have preferred him not to know that.

'Lily?'

Still I didn't respond. Then, slowly, I felt the heat of his body as he turned over to face my back, and then his soft, strong arm as it slipped around me.

'Sweet dreams,' he murmured into my ear, nestling up close.

Having him this close was so exciting, and so perfect, that I almost stopped breathing altogether. His hand was resting on my stomach, and he stroked my skin with his thumb, so gently that he was barely touching me. Of course, it felt like a million volts passing through my body. I pushed myself closer to him and felt him kiss my neck again. Before long I was so turned on I could barely move. I could feel that he wanted me, too. But he didn't do anything else: he just stroked me softly and every so often he kissed me again.

We stayed like that for several hours. I drifted in and out of sleep, and each time I woke up he was still holding me tight. I remembered how nice it was to sleep with someone; how lonely I got sometimes on my own.

At about four o'clock I was disturbed by Jack getting up. I thought he would be going to the loo, but he went downstairs. I remembered the beach incident and hoped he wasn't going to do that again. But instead I heard the sound of a tap running for a few seconds, then nothing, then his footsteps as he came back up the stairs. The feeling when he took me in his arms again was incredible. I never wanted it to end. Just before I dropped off for the last time I heard his voice in the silence: a whisper, barely audible.

'I love you, Lily,' he said.

CHAPTER SEVENTEEN

Trash

I woke up in Jack's arms. My stirring woke him and he yawned and stretched, before propping himself up on one arm and stroking my face.

'Did you sleep well?' he asked.

'Mmm.'

'And would you like coffee or tea?'

'Is hot chocolate too much to ask for?'

'Your wish is my command.'

'Thanks. And could you bring up my cigarettes? I don't usually smoke in the bedroom, but I don't want to bump into Laura at this time of the morning before I've woken up properly.'

'Makes you wish she wasn't here, doesn't it?'

'Tell me about it.'

'I hope I kept you sufficiently warm last night.'

'Yeah.' I didn't add that after that I had no idea how I was ever going to sleep without him again, I just lay back on the pillows while he went and bustled around downstairs. Had I dreamt it, or had he said he loved me last night? I looked at the clock. It was almost ten. It was a shame Laura was here but at least I didn't have to go in to work, which evened things out a bit. And, of course, there was Jack, who had sent me into orbit.

'Do you want to do something today?' he asked, when he

came back in. He gave me my hot chocolate and my cigarettes and crawled back into bed beside me, sipping his coffee.

'What did you have in mind?'

'I don't know. Go for a drive, get lunch someplace.'

'Yeah. That would be nice. I've got a couple of things to do first, though.'

'Like?'

'Well, I suppose I'm going to have to go and see Emma.'

'Do you want me to baby-sit while you do?'

'Could you?'

'Sure. Oh, one other thing.'

Jack fished down by the side of the bed. He seemed to be getting something out of his jeans pocket. It was a key. He handed it to me.

'What's that?' I asked.

'It's a key to the cottage next door. I want you to have it.'

'Why?'

'Just so that you can get in if you need to. Hey, I might be in trouble one day and you can come rescue me. But mainly it's so you can escape from here if you need to. You know, get some space.'

'Won't you be there, though?'

'If you're lucky.'

I smiled. 'Thanks.'

Emma answered the door in her dressing gown. She was holding a glass of cloudy liquid and she looked incredibly rough.

'Overdid it a bit yesterday,' she said quietly. 'Do come in.'

'Thanks,' I said.

There was a simmering atmosphere in Emma's house today. Someone less perceptive may have thought it was an air of calm; I knew better.

'Have you seen the papers?' she asked.

'No,' I said, 'but I know what's in them. I saw Ian last night. He told me they'd arrested Tim.'

'What do you think about that?'

I shrugged. 'I'm not sure. There's a lot that still doesn't add up.'

'Like?'

'Lots of things. For example, why did Kurt go to the pier in the first place, and how did Tim know he was going to be there? I thought of blackmail, but it just doesn't sound right. What could Tim possibly have wanted to get from Kurt? He had money – he'd just inherited money and property from his parents. I know they were poor but I bet they had life insurance. Also, I don't get why he would want to kill his sister. And, of course, he claims he didn't kill her, which I am inclined to believe.'

'Maybe he killed her for her share of the money.'

'Sorry?'

'Alex's third of the parents' estate.'

'He'd have to share it with Laura, though, surely? It wouldn't really be worth it.'

'So what are you telling me?'

'This isn't over, I don't think.'

'You don't think?'

'Well, the police say that his fingerprints were on the knife that killed Alex, but if he discovered her body then that's plausible enough. The only thing is that the suicide note was in his handwriting and her fingerprints weren't on it. Which I suppose is all fairly conclusive stuff if you want to believe he did it.'

'Do you think someone may have fitted him up?'

'I really don't know.'

'And what are you going to do about it?'

'What do you want me to do?'

'What I'm paying you to do. Do we know which girl is dead, yet?'

'No. People want something more conclusive than just

taking Laura's word for it now, which is what the police wanted to do before the press made such a fuss about it. Incidentally, Laura's staying with me at the moment.'

'Well, that should give you a head start. I still need to know, Lily.'

'Mmm.'

'We don't seem to be moving forwards as fast as the police.'

'Well, it's a very confusing case.'

'Yes.'

'And I am working on my own.'

She sighed. 'I suppose so.'

'By the way,' I said, 'has someone called Tony Bryce been in touch with you?'

'No. Should he have been?'

'He's the reporter that broke the story about the twins.'

'So I shouldn't talk to him?'

'Not unless you want all your secrets in the paper, no.'

'Thanks for the warning.'

'No problem. Well, I suppose I should get going.'

'Yes. I'll expect some results very soon.'

Since Jack was keeping an eye on Laura, I thought now would be a good time to go to the supermarket, particularly as I had another mouth to feed and no food in the house apart from catfood and some stale digestives.

It was raining as I drove into the Safeway car park. I'd intended to rush around the shop as fast as possible and get home, but I soon found myself lingering. I should have been concentrating on what Emma had told me to do: get this whole twin thing wrapped up and over with, but all I could think about was Jack. I wanted him close to me again, like he'd been last night, and I started fantasising, as I walked down the aisles, about what I might cook him soon for a romantic

dinner. If only I could get rid of Laura I was sure there would
be lots of opportunities for candlelit dinners over at my place,
wine and chocolate at his. We could take it slowly — after all,
that seemed to be what he wanted. I wouldn't hurry him, and
perhaps, after a lot of getting to know one another, he'd be
willing to take things further.

Walking around Safeway in this state was not a good idea;
glowing, head in the clouds, fantasising, in love. I barely
noticed as I blankly filled the trolley with things I thought
Laura would like: salads, pizzas and ready meals. I vacantly
selected about ten bottles of wine to refill my depleted collec-
tion, and in each one I saw an evening of unbridled passion.
Me and Jack. Jack and me.

As I walked past the baby aisle I saw a man who looked like
Fenn, his basket full of nappies and Vaseline and baby-wipes.
Now I knew what a real man was, I had no need for pathetic
half-measures like Fenn any more. This was bliss. Before I
started singing and dancing in the aisles I walked to a check-
out and waited in the queue.

Singing and dancing, I thought, as I stood there willing the queue
to get a move on. How ridiculous. Then I suddenly thought. Of
course. Dancing. That was how we could be sure it was Laura.
Suddenly I snapped out of my icky-romance reverie and got real
again. I was making a plan, and I thought it was a good one.

As soon as I'd finished in Safeway I rang Cornelia from my
mobile phone.

'Lily,' she said, 'how nice to hear from you again.'

'You too. Look, Cornelia, I was wondering whether you
would be willing to help me out.'

'Help you out?'

'Yes. You know what you were saying about Laura having
the gift, or whatever?'

'Yes?'

'Well, I was wondering about something. If you saw one of
the twins dance, would you be able to know which one it was?'

'Absolutely. Why? Are you planning to test her out? Laura, I mean.'

'Yes. Would you help me?'

She paused. 'Are you going to tell her she's being tested?'

'I hadn't thought about it, really. The idea just came to me a few moments ago.' I thought for a second. 'I don't see why not. In any case, how would we get her to dance otherwise?'

'With some difficulty, if it's Laura. And she'd probably refuse anyway even if you did ask her outright.'

'Oh.'

'Besides, you have another potential problem.'

'What's that?'

'Well, although Alex could never imitate Laura, Laura does a damn good impression of her sister dancing.'

'I suppose she could if she's that much better.'

'Anyway, I don't think you need to test her. She hasn't been to see me, you know, and that can only mean it's Laura.'

'Mmm. I'd like to be sure. The police don't even know definitely yet.'

'Well, if you think of a way of doing it, I'd be more than happy but ...'

'Yes. I'll try to think of something and let you know.'

All the way home I went over everything in my head. The experiments I'd done with Jack to try to understand Kurt's murder — which made me suspicious about the police's conclusions; everything I'd learnt about Alex and Laura. It *was* Laura in my house, wasn't it? I had to know. And the piece of paper that she'd burnt. I still had no idea what that had been. None of the words meant anything to anyone. And that sentence: *she looks like the real thing.* It kept playing on my mind, as if I should know it, but I couldn't place it. Cornelia was Cornel, but what were the others? Then there were all the other loose ends. I was still intrigued by the implications of the night in the hotel, and particularly the little girl, Pippa. I still wanted to know what she knew, but of course I had no idea where she'd gone now the hotel was shut. And the drink I'd had with Tim. Had he seemed like a murderer? Not one little bit. But, then, he had said all that stuff at his parents' graveside about 'making it up' to Laura. What was all that about?

My thoughts were like spirals of candyfloss. I couldn't separate one thing from another: there was no linearity, no logic to all this. There should have been some obvious thing to do next. There wasn't. I would have to think of something soon. But for the time being I had to get home, relieve Jack of his babysitting, and work out what I was going to do with Laura while I went out with him for the rest of the afternoon.

When I returned she seemed happy. Wearing a white négligé that would only have passed as a dress in some kind of porn film, she could just be seen through the sitting-room window lying on the sofa, giggling coquettishly at something Jack was saying. Neither of them heard the door open, so I struggled in with the shopping-bags on my own, hearing only the fake tinkle of her laugh; the calm vibrations of Jack's voice.

'Am I missing something?' I asked when I'd finished, walking into the room and sitting down.

They both went quiet.

'We were just talking about films,' said Jack.

I raised an eyebrow. 'I see.'

'Yeah. Laura's a fan of *noir* as well, so we were talking about the season they had on at the cinema.'

I didn't respond. I remembered Harry telling me about the way Laura had gone and told him that she was Alex and Laura was dead. It was details like that which kept making me confused about all this. Why on earth would she have done that?

'So,' I said to Jack, 'are you set?'

'For?'

'Going out. I thought we were going to go and get lunch somewhere?'

'What about me?' asked Laura. 'You can't leave me on my own. I'm too afraid.'

'What of? Tim's in prison.'

'I know, but ...' She shivered. 'Please don't go.'

'Actually,' said Jack, 'that suits me. Something's come up anyway.'

I must have looked disappointed. As I walked him to the door he squeezed my hand and told me he'd make it up to me. Mumbling something about having just had a great idea for his new film he walked slowly across to his cottage while I watched from the doorway. Feeling like I could do with some space too I walked down to the beach instead of going back inside.

The tide was coming in. As I sat with my back to the two cottages I started to feel a bit more relaxed. Every few minutes I had to shuffle back a little, trying not to be hit by a wave. The sky was starting to turn pink with the sunset coming.

Before it got dark I decided to go in, my thoughts still unresolved and seeming like they might stay that way for a long time. When I got inside Laura was up in her room, so I read the paper on my own in the sitting room. I wondered if Jack might fancy doing something tonight, since our afternoon plans hadn't worked out. But Laura would probably still be too 'afraid' to be left on her own. But maybe he could come and stay again tonight: at least Laura couldn't disturb us in bed.

She came downstairs eventually, one towel sheathing her thin body, and one up on her head, turban-style. She walked slowly and deliberately into the room and sat down, picking up the remote control as she did so.

'Do you mind if I switch over?' she asked, changing the channel twice.

'Go ahead.'

'Oh, someone rang for you while you were on the beach. Star, or something.'

'Oh. When was this?'

Laura shrugged. 'About an hour ago.'

I unplugged the phone downstairs and took it up to my

bedroom to call Star back, making sure I shut the door firmly before I did so.

'Lily,' she said, when she picked up the phone, 'who on earth was that awful girl who answered the phone before?'

'Laura.'

'Sorry?'

'Or Alex.'

'What, you mean ...?'

'Yep. I've got the twin from hell as a house-guest.'

'You know how she's answering your phone, I suppose?'

'No. How?'

'Like you do. When I called before, she said, "Lily Pascale," and if it hadn't been for her voice I would have thought I was talking to you.'

'Jesus. This is too much.'

'Sounds like a nightmare. Anyway, I just called to say that I'm arriving early tomorrow afternoon, if it's still all right.'

'Sure. Oh, except she's got the only spare room.'

'Oh. Do you have a couch?'

'Yeah. Or there's Jack's place.'

'Is this the American you hate?'

'Hate? You're behind the times. He's fantastic. And last night he said he loved me.'

'Really?'

'Yeah.'

'God. Do you feel the same way?'

'I think so. He is wonderful, Star.'

'Well, I hope you know what you're doing.'

'Why do you say that?'

'Well, last time I spoke to you, you weren't too sure about him. I don't want to see you get hurt again. It was bad enough with that Fenn character.'

'Jack's completely different from Fenn, though. He's alive and interesting and fun. Slightly mysterious, but I think I can live with that.'

'Well, I look forward to meeting him, then. *And* this Laura.'

'Which reminds me,' I said, and told Star my plan.

'So when I turn up you're going to say I'm the casting director for what?' she asked, after listening patiently while I explained everything.

'I don't know. Um ... some big-budget Hollywood romance or something. Say you're looking for the next big box-office actress. Tell Laura that you're looking for a new face and you've just been auditioning hundreds of girls in London, but you haven't found the right one.'

'Okay.'

'And make sure you emphasise the hugeness of the project, so she thinks there's loads of money in it, and that it's a Hollywood thing, because she wants to go to America.'

'Right. So I'm looking for a young girl who can act and dance.'

'Yes. Ballet, though. It has to be ballet.'

'How am I going to know what to ask her to do?'

'Hopefully, you won't have to. I'll get Cornelia to lurk around so she's ready to watch whenever Laura does dance. Hopefully when you tell Laura about all this she'll be more than happy to tell all about being such a great ballet dancer, and she'll provide you with a performance. Just tell her to impress you or something. Don't ask for specific moves.'

Star giggled. 'Why do we always end up doing this?'

'What? Tricking teenagers into performing ballet?'

'No, just ... *this*. I'm sure other friends do normal things.'

I laughed. 'Maybe we'll get to do some normal things as well.'

'You never know.'

'Anyway,' I said, 'I can't wait to see you.'

'Me too.'

'Call me from the train and tell me what time it gets in.'

'Sure.'

CHAPTER EIGHTEEN

Maths

———◆———

Laura was painting her toenails red when I went back downstairs. She still didn't seem very bereaved. Perhaps she didn't care that she'd lost her whole family, or maybe she was repressing it. I'd heard that people did that. Of course, she had a mother she didn't know about who lived ten minutes down the road. I wondered when that particular detail would come out. She seemed to be dressed smartly. She was wearing a white suit and her hair was done up in a clip.

'Are you going somewhere?' I asked.

'Sorry?'

'You seem smartly dressed. Are you going somewhere?'

She replaced the nail-varnish brush in the bottle and looked at me coldly. 'I have someone calling on me shortly. Is that all right?'

'Fine. Who is it?'

'My solicitor.'

Her solicitor. Of course. Silly me.

He arrived about half an hour later in a large white Mercedes. They made it clear I wasn't welcome to listen to their conversation, so I pretended to do things around the rest of the house, catching the odd thing now and then. They seemed to be talking about life insurance: probably Laura's parents'. Laura's voice seemed kittenish and soft, and every so often I heard the same false laugh I'd heard before.

'Oh, Mr Harvey, you're so clever,' I heard her say, as I passed the sitting-room door. 'That's such a very good idea.'

Stopping there, I tried to catch more of what they were discussing.

'It's good that he signed this,' came Mr Harvey's deep voice. 'It would be hard to resolve without it.'

'Yes. That's what I thought.'

'How did you ...?'

'I have my ways.'

'Yes. I know your ways.'

'He's obsessed with me. After all, he killed Kurt because of me. Why wouldn't he give me all the money?'

'Yes. That's fine. And your sister's money will pass straight to you anyway.'

'We'll be able to prove it?'

'It doesn't matter. He killed her and he can't profit from it.'

'But what if he didn't?'

'He did, though, surely?'

'Yes, but ...?'

'Well, to be honest I think this document covers that as well.'

'Great. So when will I get the funds?'

'Not for a while, I'm afraid.'

'There was a small property deal I wanted to arrange.'

'Buying or selling?'

'Both.'

'Give me the details and I'll act for you.'

'Thanks. I need something to keep me busy. All this has been so dreadful.'

'I know, dear. I know.'

'Hang on, I just need to get something.'

I could hear her getting up so I moved off towards the kitchen, wondering why I was being forced to creep around in my own house, and also what the hell this document was that Laura had made Tim sign.

The phone rings. She picks up and speaks slowly. She has such a common voice.

'Hello?'

'It's Alex.'

'Alex?'

'Yes. I wanted to make you an offer.'

'What kind of offer?'

'The hotel. I'll give you fifty grand for it.'

'Fifty? You know it's worth more.'

'Yes, but you're in trouble, aren't you? There are all those legal costs, and now a funeral to arrange. I just wanted to make it easy for you. Take it off your hands.'

'You little slut.'

'Ouch. Forty grand.'

'A minute ago it was fifty.'

'And it'll go down every hour until you give me an answer.'

Can you see her face as it drains of blood? This can't be how it's ending. She writes the address down on a piece of paper. She has to get there within an hour. Of course she doesn't have to sell, but what else can she do? She's not good with the accounts, and she doesn't want to stay here anyway. She slips on her jacket and calls a cab.

I wandered around the house doing some tidying up, vaguely wondering if Jack would ring or call round. Laura had started to watch some Australian soap so I decided to go and sit with her for a while, wondering what was going on in her head.

As I walked through the door into the sitting room I could see that her eyes looked vacant, as if nothing was going on. She wasn't really watching the programme. Every so often she flicked through a magazine she'd found, or else she just stared into space.

'Are you okay?' I asked, sitting down opposite her in the armchair.

'Yeah. Of course.'

'Was that your solicitor who was here before?'

'Yes. There's a lot to sort out.'

'I can imagine. It must be very upsetting.'

'It is. When's Jack coming back?'

'I don't know. Why?'

'No reason. He's sexy, isn't he?'

'I suppose so.'

'And very strong.'

'Hmm.'

Lighting a cigarette, I reached for the remote control. I switched over for the news.

'I was watching that,' said Laura, scowling.

'Sorry,' I said, switching it back.

'He's very well ... *endowed*, isn't he?' she said, almost to herself, with the smallest little red-lipsticked smile emerging on her pale face.

'I'm sorry?' I said, stunned.

'Jack. He's got a really big one.'

'Look, Laura, if you're trying to really wind me up you're succeeding.'

'I was just making conversation.'

'No, you weren't. You were trying to piss me off. So I'm pissed off. Are you happy now?'

'Don't you want to know what went on with me and Jack?'

'Not really.'

'He said he loved my hair, because it's straight and shiny. And he says that he really likes incredibly slim girls like me. In fact, he said I was his ideal woman. I was very flattered.'

Of course she said all this very nicely. But she was succeeding in making me insecure. And that made me angry.

'Stop fucking me around, Laura,' I said coldly. 'I'm trying to be kind to you. You can always go back to the hotel if you don't like it here.'

'I thought you said he wasn't your boyfriend.'

'He isn't.'

'Then what's your problem? I fancy him and he fancies me.'

'Did he actually say that?'

'Yes. And he says I can stay with him in America.'

'Really?'

'Yes,' she said, slightly huffily, as if I'd offended her in some way. 'Anyway, I'm going to go and have a lie-down, since I'm not welcome down here.'

'What a good idea.'

Although I was fairly sure that she had just been trying to wind me up (how did she know my weak spots so well?) what she had said started me thinking. Could something have gone on between her and Jack while I was out? They'd seemed very friendly when I had returned, and Jack hadn't seemed very keen on spending any time with me after that. Could she have been telling the truth? Although my heart was screaming, *No*, some insecure part of me was whispering, *maybe*. What the hell was going on here?

Needing to be on my own, I picked up my car keys, intent on heading out for a drive, to pick up some cigarettes and keep out of Laura's way for half an hour while I got my head together. Just as I was ready to go the phone rang. It was Jack.

'Hey,' he said.

I mumbled some sort of response.

'Lily, what's wrong?'

'Nothing. It's a bit claustrophobic here. I was just heading out.'

'I thought we might do something tonight.'

'Sorry. I'm in a bit of a bad mood. I wouldn't be very good company.'

'Maybe some other time.'

'Yeah.'

He didn't seem to be trying very hard to convince me otherwise. Oh, well, maybe he would prefer to spend time with skinny little Laura. Maybe something really had gone on between them. After all, we didn't have an official claim on one another. He could do what he liked.

'I enjoyed last night,' he said.

'What, more than this afternoon?'

'Sorry?'

'You heard.'

'What *is* your problem?'

'*I* haven't got one.'

'Whatever.'

'Anyway, look, my friend Star is coming to stay tomorrow.'

'Uh-huh.'

'And I was wondering if you could do me a favour.'

Suddenly not trusting him completely, I didn't tell him exactly what I'd planned. I just said that she was a friend and she was coming to stay. He seemed quite happy to let her stay in his spare room, and even jokingly suggested that we could send Laura over there as well and that he could come stay with me. But my mood wasn't lifting and, without meaning to, I came across as cold and humourless. I didn't like the idea of Laura getting her claws any further into him or his house or anything to do with him. I just wished she'd go away.

As I drove to the village shop, I calmed down a bit, realising I was being irrational and not acting my age. But Laura was. I remembered when I was eighteen I'd desperately wanted attention as well. Was that all she was doing, demanding attention? Almost everybody I'd spoken to had confirmed that Laura wasn't particularly nice, that she wanted the spotlight to remain totally on her. Perhaps with Alex gone she was looking for other rivals to fill her place. Perhaps for the time being that was what I was: her rival; her replacement twin. And I should have expected this. It wasn't as if I hadn't known about her.

Driving home I felt a little more relaxed. And I had resolved not to lose my rag with her any more. She could try and bait me, but I wouldn't rise to it.

And poor Jack. I'd have to apologise to him as well.

As I pulled up in the driveway I could see the image of someone walking quickly around inside my cottage. In fact there were two people, facing one another, pacing and moving back and forth, gesturing with their hands. Getting out of my car I was startled to hear shouting as well: two high-pitched female voices. I walked inside and waited in the doorway of the sitting room where Laura stood, defiantly gesticulating at a middle-aged blonde woman who seemed to be in quite a state.

' ... would have killed myself too if I'd been married to you,' was what I heard Laura say, as soon as I was within earshot.

Neither of them noticed me at first, so I was able to take in the whole scene. The woman was dressed all in red. Her grubby sweatshirt seemed a size too big, her faded leggings two sizes too small. Her hair was bleached almost white-blonde and her roots more than showed: they made up about a quarter of her hair's length. It needed washing as well, and sat lankly on her head, as if someone had stuck it down with a block of lard. Her face was pasty and white; the colour and texture of birdshit. Laura glowed in comparison, her porcelain face slightly red with anger.

Her words had caused the scene to freeze. Clearly this was a climax they had been building up to for some time. The look the woman was giving Laura was intense and long. It was hate, undiluted, and it spilled out of her like a laser beam. After a few moments the scene became animated again, and the woman slapped Laura jerkily around the face.

Laura's reaction was interesting, in that she did not react at all. She just stood there defiantly, as though nothing had happened. Then, after about thirty seconds, she simply raised an eyebrow and smirked.

'Is that the best you can do?' she asked.

'I'll do a lot worse in a minute. Your sister was trash and you're fucking worse, Alexandra Carter. You're a pathetic slag and so was she. There's no difference between you, none at all. I thought you were nice, once, but now I can see that you're as big a tramp as she was. Laura was fifteen years old, for Christ's sake. What did she want with a married man like my Stan?'

'It's easy to see what he wanted with *her*,' said Laura, looking the woman up and down. 'You seem to have let yourself go, Mrs Green.'

I decided that it was time to make my presence known.

'What's going on here?' I demanded, walking into the room.

Laura's face instantly lost its hardness once she realised I was there and crumpled into the victim expression I recognised so well.

'Lily! This horrible woman has been threatening me. Please call the police.'

'Who are you?' I asked the woman.

'Fuck you, whoever you are,' she spat. 'I'm on my way out.'

'I'm so afraid,' said Laura, clinging to me like a boa-constrictor.

'There, there,' I said, or something like that, as Laura buried her face in my jumper.

The door slammed. The woman had gone.

'What the hell was that all about?' I asked, pushing Laura off me. Then, because I thought I should at least feign concern for her, I added, 'Are you okay?'

'Yes,' she said, beginning to snivel delicately. 'Please would you get me a glass of water?'

'Sure. You just sit here.'

Having sat her down on the sofa I went through into the

kitchen and poured a glass of water for her and a Scotch for myself. This was turning into one hell of a day, and I was going to kill Ian when I next saw him. He must have known what he was setting up for me here. Or maybe he hadn't known. Maybe he was that naïve.

'So, do you want to tell me what was going on there?'

'She came here to threaten me she—'

'In your ordinary voice will be fine, Laura. You're not fooling me with that wounded-little girl routine.'

She smiled. 'Sorry.'

'That's okay. Now just tell me what was going on.'

'She came here looking for me because she claims I was having an affair with her slimy overweight husband, who, incidentally, killed my parents.'

'Is that why you were pretending to be Alex?'

She nodded. 'Yeah. That trick still seems to work, at least.'

'Did you do that a lot when Alex was alive?'

'Yeah. Of course.'

'What about pretending to be Laura?' I said.

'Sorry?'

'Well, are you pretending now?'

'No, I'm not.'

'So did you have an affair with the woman's husband?'

'Euugghh! No way. He was gross.'

'Why did she think you had?'

She shrugged. 'God knows.'

'Did Alex have an affair with him?'

'Possibly. I wouldn't know.'

'Laura, did Tim kill Alex?'

'Yes.'

'Did he kill Kurt?'

'You know he did. What is this, *Twenty Questions*?'

'I need to get this all straight, Laura. Tonight wasn't the first time you've pretended to be Alex, was it? I saw you at Juno's on the night Kurt was killed. Then I stayed in the hotel

— you know that, you remembered my name. Is that why you've been giving me such a hard time?'

'Maybe.' She frowned. 'I still don't know why you were watching me.'

'Never mind that. I was doing a favour for a friend.'

'What kind of favour?'

'Someone wanted to know who the murderer is.'

'And which one of us was dead?'

'Yeah.'

'Was it Tony Bryce?'

'It doesn't matter who it was. Anyway, I think it's about time I heard your version of events. And no pissing me around, Laura, because this is serious.'

'Why is it serious?'

'Because I still want to know who killed Alex.'

'Tim did. Are you stupid or something? Tim did it.'

'He says he didn't.'

'Well, he would, wouldn't he?'

'He admits to killing Kurt. Why not Alex?'

'Because he thought he was killing me.'

'Why would he want to kill you, though?'

'Because he wanted my money. And he hated me.'

'Why?'

'Because he was obsessed with Alex, and *she* hated me.'

'I see. What do you mean he was obsessed with Alex?'

'He was in love with her. Disgusting, don't you think?'

'Is that why Tim killed Kurt? Because he thought he'd raped Alex?'

'Yes.' She paused. 'How did you know about that?'

'Never mind. But it wasn't Alex, was it? It was you.'

'Yes, well, I had to pretend to be Alex, since whoever had killed Alex had actually wanted me dead. I suspected Tim, but I also suspected a couple of other people, so I thought it would be best to just lie low and play detective, cunningly disguised as my sister.'

184

'Why did you suspect Tim?'

'He'd been threatening me for ages. When our parents died we all went a bit crazy. He kept saying he wanted my share of the money we all inherited. I don't know what he was going to do with it, but he had some plan that supposedly we were all going to benefit from. He used to beat me when I refused to do things for him, and we used to get into arguments and he used to hit me all the time. You might think that would be difficult in a wheelchair, but it made it worse. He could trap you in corners and pin you against the wall with it, put his brakes on and you wouldn't be able to get away. He ran his wheel across my toe once and broke it. I was just lucky that the day he tried to kill me Alex was pretending to be me.'

'Why was she pretending to be you?'

'To test Kurt. We'd been having a bit of a thing together. Alex suspected that something was going on so she pretended to be me, to see what reaction she would get from him.'

'And do you know what happened?'

'No. The next time I saw her she was dead.'

'So then you pretended to be Alex.'

'What else could I do? I wanted the police to know I was really me, but I couldn't let Tim know. He frightens me so much, Lily. And even if it wasn't him, anyone else could have come back to get the job done properly. It just wasn't worth the risk. Someone wanted Laura dead, so I let them believe she was dead.'

'On the night that Kurt died, you were down at the club pretending to be Alex. Did you suspect him?'

'Well, for a while I thought he might have killed her. He was scared that I was going to tell Alex that we'd slept together, so I could understand why he would have wanted me out of the way. It made sense to me that he would have killed her by mistake while she was pretending to be me. He would have thought he was doing a nice job of getting rid of me, Laura, the only person who had something on him.'

I rubbed my temples. 'Didn't you both ever get confused with all this swapping around?'

She smiled. 'All the time. But it was fun. I never really hated her, you know.'

'Why would I think you did?'

'Everyone else thinks it.'

'Why did you tell Pippa that you were Alex — and Harry Ducking and Dr Ravine?'

She shrugged. 'I just did. Pippa had to think I was Alex because she was in the hotel, I was with Tim when I saw Dr Ravine and I didn't want to blow my cover. As for Harry, well, he was a dirty old man and I didn't want to work for him any more.'

'Hmm.' I downed the last of my Scotch. 'So *did* Kurt rape you?'

'No.'

'Did you tell him you were really Laura?'

She shook her head. 'No.'

'But that's what you told the police.'

'Yeah. It seemed simpler.'

'Simpler than what?'

'Telling them what really happened.'

'Which was?'

'Nothing. We had sex after Stoosh's set — he thought I was Alex, of course. But then Kurt told me that he was going to America the next day at the last minute to do some gig. I thought he was running away after killing Alex, and I needed to keep him here so I could try to find some evidence on him. I made up the story so that the police wouldn't let him leave the country.'

'When did you find out he was dead?'

'The next day, same as everyone else.'

'But you reported the rape before you found out?'

'Oh, yes. His body wasn't discovered until much later. There was no way I could have known. Obviously if I had

known, I wouldn't have bothered reporting it, since I'd made
it up to keep him here in the first place.'

'When did you find out that Tim murdered him?'

'Not for a few days. I can see how it all makes sense now,
of course. I went back to the hotel all dishevelled and Tim
wanted to know what had happened to me. I had to tell him
what I was planning on telling the police, to make sure my
story was consistent. But evidently after he'd seen the state of
me, and because he thought I was Alex and he was in love with
her, he went and bashed Kurt's brains in. I had no idea he'd
done something so stupid until later. I can't believe I didn't
see it.'

'Who was your other suspect for the murder?'

'That bitch Sylvia, who was just here. I thought she'd want
to murder me for sure.'

'Because you slept with her husband?'

'I told you, I didn't.'

'But she thought you did?'

'Yes. What a horrible idea. I don't know where she got it
from.'

'And this guy Stan, he murdered your parents?'

'Yes. He owned the hotel next door. He'd always wanted
my parents out of the way, so he could buy out their land or
something. I never really understood what that was all about.
But he tampered with their brakes, and that was what caused
the car crash – he drained off the brake fluid or something. He
admitted it and everything. She kept saying he didn't do it,
but she's mad.'

'I see.'

'Now do you understand how awful it's all been? I've had
to lead a double life, always knowing that there was someone
out there wanting to kill me. It's been so bad. I'm just glad it's
all over now.'

'Is it, though?'

'Yes, obviously.'

'But maybe Tim didn't kill Alex. What if one of the others did it?'

'I thought the police had evidence that it was him?'

'Oh, yes.' I remembered what Ian had told me about the fingerprints and the handwriting. 'I suppose they have.'

Later, as I went up to bed, I tried to work out what it was Laura had said that hadn't seemed right. Hard though I tried to see it, there just wasn't anything. Her story was entirely plausible.

My bed was cold and empty tonight. Even with a T-shirt on under my pyjamas I didn't seem able to get warm, and I could hear the TV blasting downstairs and Laura walking up and down every so often. I was tired and headachy and I wished I hadn't fought with Jack. I fell asleep in the end with Maude providing the smallest amount of warmth around my feet.

CHAPTER NINETEEN

Pas de Deux

———————•———————

The next morning I was awoken by the sound of somebody furiously banging on the door. Hoping it wasn't another one of Laura's arch enemies, I slipped on a dressing gown and walked down to open it. It was Jack.

'We have to talk,' he said.

I yawned. 'It's eight o'clock in the morning, Jack.'

'We still have to talk.'

'Do we?'

'Yes.'

He looked like he had been awake for ages. I wondered if he was still jetlagged. He was wearing black jeans today, and a thick black roll-neck jumper. He looked good in black. His hair was slightly ruffled, but he was clean-shaven and bright-eyed. Remembering the way he'd made me feel the night I'd slept in his arms I suddenly ached for him again. I wondered what he wanted to talk about.

'Hang on, and I'll get dressed,' I said. 'Could you put the kettle on?'

He shook his head. 'Uh-uh. We're not staying here.'

'Fine. Give me five minutes.'

'Okay.'

I dressed quickly in jeans and a jumper and my Converse trainers. I put my hair up in a high ponytail and applied a bit of red lipstick. On my way downstairs I stopped for a second outside Laura's door and listened. It sounded as if she was asleep; there were no noises coming from behind the door. But she could have been pretending. I didn't particularly care either way, though. Jack was right. If we were going to talk, we couldn't stay here.

He took me up the coast to a small café right on the edge of the water. We didn't talk much on the way over there: he seemed focused on something he wasn't sharing, and almost angry. We were seated by a freckled teenage girl, who looked too young to be working. The tables were all square and covered with the same red and white checked plastic table-cloths. On each table was a napkin dispenser, a sugar bowl and tomato ketchup in a squeezy red tomato. There was an old man sitting over in non-smoking. Apart from that we were the only ones there.

Jack still wasn't saying anything. I lit a cigarette and looked at him anxiously.

'Have I done something wrong?' I asked, responding to the atmosphere creeping around the table.

'Have you? You tell me.'

'Jack, you've completely lost me. Have you come here to break up with me or something? Because if you have you don't have to bother. It's not like we were ever really together in the first place.'

'Right. That's convenient.'

'Yeah, convenient for you,' I said, remembering what Laura had said.

'What?'

'Nothing. Anyway, what do you mean?'

'Why didn't you tell me you were involved with someone else?'

'Maybe because I'm not.'

'Yeah. Whatever.'

He looked away from me and out to sea. I could feel tears

beginning to well up in my eyes. His tone was horrible: accus-
ing. What could I possibly have done to upset him this much?

'Jack?'

'I was really beginning to feel something for you, Lily.'

'So what's changed?'

'This.'

He reached into his pocket and pulled out a single piece of
paper. Pushing it across the table towards me, he looked away
again. I picked it up and smoothed it out. Then I started to read.

Dear Fenn, I can't wait to see you again. When you said
you'd leave her for me I was so thrilled. Oh my darling, I can't
wait to be back in your arms again. No one compares to you.
Call me soon. Lily.

'Where did you get this?' I asked.

'It doesn't matter where I got it. When were you going to
tell me that you were running off with him? How far were you
going to string me along?'

'Where did you get it?' I asked again, calmly.

'It's a long story,' he said evasively, toying with a napkin.

'Well, I think you'd better tell it,' I said. 'Because I didn't
write this.'

It turned out that what had happened was this: Laura had
gone over to Jack's in tears last night while I was at the shop,
saying I'd given her this letter to post but that she had spilled
water all over it and the address had run too badly to see and
she didn't know what to do. Jack had helped her ease the letter
out of its envelope, saying he'd help her address another one
and I would never know.

'So how did you get from that to reading and keeping the
letter?' I asked.

'I wasn't going to. But while I was looking for an envelope,

Laura read it and then when I came back downstairs she looked all weird and said she thought I should read it.'

'So you did?'

'Yeah. I didn't know it was going to be to another boyfriend. I just thought if she said I should read it that there might be something important in there. I guess I didn't think about what that might be.'

'And you just believed it, did you?'

'Sure. Why wouldn't I?'

'Couldn't you trust me?'

'What? Like you trusted me? What was all that stuff about yesterday, asking me whether I enjoyed the afternoon or whatever? You were jealous as hell. There was no way you trusted me.'

'Right. And do you think I would be that jealous if I was planning to run off with Fenn?'

'Uh ... I guess not.'

'And do you want to know why I was jealous?'

'Because I'm a swell guy?'

The tension snapped and I started to laugh. It was a combination of Jack's sorry expression and the sudden realisation that everything was okay with us; the only problem had been Laura, being a conniving little cow, all along.

'Yeah,' I said. 'Because you're a swell guy.'

'I feel a bit stupid.'

'So you should. I would never write something that bad.'

'Oh, my darling, I can't wait to be back in your arms,' said Jack, fake-swooning.

'You know, yesterday she told me you were well endowed,' I said, giggling.

'I am,' he said.

'I know. You almost ruptured my back with it the other night. Anyway, she said that as well as getting to know you well enough to be able to comment on the size of your ...'

'Ding-a-ling?'

I laughed. 'Whatever. She said that you'd got very friendly while I was out, and that you were even going to take her to America.'

'And you believed that?'

'Not as much as you believed that whole fake letter crap.'

'*Touché.* Jesus. She really said all that stuff?'

'Yeah.' I looked down. 'She also said that you thought she was prettier than me.'

'Little bitch. Lily, you are the most beautiful woman I have ever seen in my life.'

I smiled. 'Really?'

'Sure. Really.'

'God, she's a slippery character. Where do you think she got Fenn's name and everything?'

'I don't know. Do you keep a diary or anything like that?'

'Not really. I used to, but I don't have time any more.'

'Did you have his name written anywhere?'

'No.'

'Oh, my God ...' he said.

'What?'

'She's read my journal. She must have done.'

'You wrote about Fenn in your journal?'

'I wrote something about that night, when I had to kick him out of your house. And if she read about all that, she would have known how I felt about him and realised he was exactly the person to choose for her fake letter.'

'Well, at least that mystery is solved.'

'Yeah.' He looked distracted.

'I think it's really sweet that you keep a journal.'

'You do?'

'Yeah. It's a great thing to do.'

'Hmm.'

'What's wrong?' I asked him.

'We have a problem.'

'Which is?'

'If Laura has read my journal then she knows too much about me.'

'Sorry?'

'There is some stuff ... Stuff I've been meaning to tell you.' The more he thought about this, the more wound up he seemed to get. 'Shit! She fucking knows everything. I'll kill her. I'll fucking—'

'Jack, calm down. If it's stuff you've been meaning to tell me then just tell me.'

'I don't know if this is the right place or the right time. I'm afraid it's going to have to be dark, and I'm going to have to be drunk.'

'Is it that bad?'

'Yeah.'

'Fair enough. Tonight, then.'

'Yeah. Tonight. I just hope she doesn't fuck everything up before then.'

'Look, Jack, Laura's tried to come between us and she's failed. I don't know why she did it ... It's probably just a pathological thing with her, wanting to tell lies and cause trouble. Anyway, she hasn't succeeded, and since neither of us will ever believe her again there shouldn't be a problem.'

'Maybe.'

'Definitely.'

'She knows how I feel about you, if she's read my journal.'

'And how's that?'

'Come on, you heard what I said to you last night. You weren't asleep.'

'Did you mean it?'

'Uh-huh.'

Suddenly I went all gooey, and Jack took my hand in his. I expected to move on to the romance part now, but he still looked concerned.

'What is it?' I asked.

'She will have read all that stuff about Kurt and everything.

All the role-play, and what we both thought about the murders. I hope this hasn't screwed everything up for you.'

'I doubt it. We have a plan, anyway.'

'Do we?'

'Oh, yes.' I filled him in on the ballet idea.

'With your brains and my looks we'll go far,' he said.

'Let's hope so.'

We walked to the car hand in hand, and kissed before we got in.

'I love you, Lily,' said Jack.

'And I love you, too,' I said.

CHAPTER TWENTY

Sticky

Star called at about twelve to say that her train was passing Exeter. This was my cue to hop in the car and get over to Totnes to collect her, since the last part of her journey took exactly the same amount of time as it took me to get there. After Jack and I had arrived home, we'd gone our separate ways. I didn't know what he was doing in his cottage, but in mine I was simultaneously floating around feeling in love again, and trying to stop myself killing Laura.

She was still in bed when I left the house, which was good. I hadn't told her I had a friend coming, although she probably knew. I just hoped she hadn't got wind of what we were all planning. I got to Totnes station in plenty of time and sat waiting for Star's train to pull in. When it did I felt excited about seeing her again. She stepped off the carriage, looking immaculate as always.

'Smell that air,' she exclaimed, after we had kissed hello. 'It's so good to be out of London.'

'Mmm. Maybe you should move down here,' I said hopefully.

'When I'm old, probably. I'm too attached to my work to leave.'

'Yes, I can see how it would be hard to leave a load of psychos behind.'

'You know what I mean,' she said, laughing. 'It's freezing in London, though.'

'It's cold here, too,' I said. 'Wait till you get near the sea.'

We chatted all the way home, Star commenting on all the scenery, the hills in the distance and the hedgerows. She loved the area in the way that all visitors did; but I couldn't see her living here all the time, even when she did retire. She and Henri regularly went to the theatre and the cinema and out to art galleries. There wasn't too much of that kind of thing here, just wilderness as far as the eye could see, which I found exhilarating.

'So, am I going to have to pretend to be some kind of casting director all weekend?' asked Star suspiciously, when we were about five minutes from home.

'No, I shouldn't think so. I'm going to try to get rid of the terrible twin shortly anyway. I can't handle her messing around in my private life and well, just ... *being* there. I never realised how much I valued my own space.'

'Nothing like a teenager to make you wake up to that. Where are you going to send her to?'

'I don't know. And, at this precise moment, I don't really care.'

'Oh dear. I can see I'm entering a can of worms.'

'Don't worry,' I said. 'It'll be fine.'

'So tell me about Jack.'

'I'm in love,' I said, grinning madly.

'Well, I can't wait to see him.'

'He's gorgeous. All tanned and strong and lovely.'

'And clever?'

'Oh, yes. Didn't I tell you he's a screenwriter?'

'No. What films has he written?'

'*Broken* was his first. Did you see it?'

'No. But I read some of the reviews. That's amazing.'

'Yeah.'

'He actually sounds like he might be suitable.'

'Laura almost messed everything up between us, of course,' I said.

'Really?'

'Yeah. I don't think she can help herself. It's just the lengths she goes to to deceive people that bothers me.'

I told Star about the letter business and all the other stuff.

'How bizarre,' she said. 'Well, I can't wait to see this creature for myself.'

'Hmm.'

'And if we can turn the tables and play some tricks on her, so much the better.'

Tony's got his dick in his hand. Watch it get hard as he spreads the pictures out in front of him. There she is, looking at him with her black eyes. In the pictures her gaze is vacant, but in real life it is hard. Harder than his cock is getting.

'Come on, Tony, I haven't got all day,' she says.

'All right. I'm trying.'

His face is red. This seems difficult. You'd think she'd help him, but she just stands there with a pen in her hand, watching. The pictures don't help either.

He strokes the shaft of his dick and she watches, biting her lip.

'Like this?' he asks.

'However you want. Just make yourself come.'

'It would be easier if you helped me, darling.'

'I'm sure it would.'

Tony is in a sticky situation, and he knows it. Why is his life so shit? How is it that even when he has a beautiful eighteen-year-old in front of him he still ends up masturbating into a beaker? Actually, he usually doesn't use a beaker. But this is all part of the agreement.

It dribbles out eventually, catching the rim and sticking to the side. It takes at least a minute to settle on the bottom of the beaker.

'Now drink it,' she says.

'And then you'll sign?'

'If your price is still right.'
'As we agreed.'
'Good,' she says, tapping her cheek with the pen. *'Now drink it.'*

Jack came out of his cottage when we pulled up in the driveway and introduced himself to Star. He kissed me hello and I grinned at him. We all walked into my cottage and found Laura cleaning the kitchen.

'Hello, Lily,' she said, then, slightly more seductively, 'Hi, Jack.'

We all watched as she got up and smoothed her hands on the apron she was wearing. As well as the apron she had on some kind of scarf over her hair and her face had streaks of dirt and grease on it. Of course she still looked breathtaking, and I thought that this whole effect had been very well created. Her lipstick was pale pink and glossy, and her make-up subtle. I wondered what Jack and Star were thinking.

'Who wants coffee?' said Laura, brightly.

'We all do I think,' said Jack, speaking first. He looked at me for confirmation.

'Yeah,' I said icily. 'Thanks.'

We walked through into the sitting room and sat down, Star and I exchanging glances and Jack seeming unmoved by the whole Laura experience.

'So,' Jack said to Star, 'you're Lily's stepmother?'

'No,' she laughed, 'not quite.'

I wrinkled my nose. 'I don't think I could ever see you as that.'

'No, it's quite a disturbing thought,' said Star, still laughing.

'And I hear you work in the movies,' said Jack, with a twinkle in his eye.

'Oh, yes,' said Star. 'But let's not talk about that yet.'

'No,' said Jack, winking at her.

I shifted uncomfortably in my chair as Laura swanned in carrying a tray with coffee and biscuits. I looked at Jack. He looked at Star. I hoped Laura wasn't going to try and make conversation with Star before I got Cornelia here. But Star and Jack would have to handle that, because I had to go and ring Cornelia. The moment of truth, if it happened, would have to be soon.

Was this going to work? As I walked up the stairs my head felt light with deception. My insides turned around on themselves and I realised I would probably never make a great con-artist. Unless, of course, I could be based in a casino, because card crime didn't really bother me as much. The phone was still upstairs after I'd moved it there yesterday. I dialled, feeling nervous.

'Cornelia,' I said, when she answered the phone, 'I think we're all set.'

I had called her briefly yesterday to tell her that this was probably going to happen around now, and just as we'd arranged she was ready to come over immediately.

'I'll be about half an hour,' she said.

'Great.'

'Where am I going to hide when I get there?'

'I'm not sure.' I thought quickly. 'Look, when you get here, knock on the door and then go round to the back of the house. I'll answer the door and then say maybe I imagined it or whatever. That'll be our cue to get things moving. You'll see a log shed around the back. From there you should be able to see in through the back window of the sitting room. If she decides to do her demonstration somewhere else we'll have to play it by ear.'

'And what if she still refuses?'

'Well, I'm kind of hoping that we won't even really need to ask her. If everything goes according to plan, she'll offer.'

'Very clever.'

'I just hope it works. It'll be nice to have the upper hand

for a change. Let her know that she doesn't have a monopoly on sneaking around, pretending to be something she's not.'

Cornelia laughed. 'Hear hear.'

'Well, fingers crossed.'

'Oh,' said Cornelia. 'I just thought. She won't have *pointe* shoes there.'

'Sorry?'

'*Pointe* shoes. She'd need them to do anything impressive.'

'Oh dear. What can we do about that?'

'I could bring some over.'

'But how will we get them to her?'

'She's a size five. If I slip some to you, maybe you could say you're the same size and you used to dance. You could lend them to her.'

'Okay,' I said, feeling that this was almost becoming too complex.

When I went back downstairs there was an uncomfortable silence in the sitting room. Laura looked as though she had just finished speaking and Jack was looking slightly pissed off.

'I was just commenting on how well Jack looks, considering what he's been through,' said Laura. Star looked at me and raised an eyebrow like she didn't know what was going on here. Well, she could join the club. I didn't want to let on to Laura that she knew something I didn't, so I just smiled nicely.

'Yes, doesn't he?' I said brightly. 'So, Laura, what have you been up to this morning?'

'Just cleaning up a bit.' She looked at Star. 'I take it you're a friend of the family.'

'Yes,' said Star.

'And where are you from?'

'London.'

'Really?'

'Uh-huh.' Star was being guarded not giving anything away. I could tell Laura was intrigued by her. As well as being beautiful, sophisticated and well-dressed, she had a very slight

French accent, dark skin and long black hair. I could see Laura
going mad trying to work out what kind of person she was:
trying to get her number so she could spin her some lines too.
But Star wasn't that easy to figure out. She worked with psychopaths who were much more cunning than Laura, and it was
easy to see who was going to win this particular battle of wits.

'Lily's been so good having me here, you know. Did she tell
you what happened to me?'

'No,' said Star. 'Why don't you tell me all about it?'

The next twenty minutes or so was taken up by Laura
telling her sob-story to Star. She did it very well, and all three
of us were biting our lips trying not to laugh by the end. It
wasn't that the story was at all funny – far from it – but it was
kind of entertaining watching Laura as she tried to wring
every ounce of sympathy from us, clearly struggling to
remember what she'd already told Jack and me, still not really
sure who the new member of her audience was.

The knock at the door came slightly sooner than I'd anticipated.

'I'll go,' I said.

'I'll just take these cups through,' said Jack.

I opened the door just to check it had really been Cornelia.
There was a small carrier-bag on the step and when I picked it
up there was a pair of pink, slightly battered ballet shoes
inside.

'What's going on?' asked Jack, grabbing me around the
waist and kissing my ear.

'That was Cornelia,' I hissed.

'So we're all set?'

'Yep.'

CHAPTER TWENTY-ONE

The Black Swan

———◆———

Star was clearly enjoying herself when we returned to the sitting room.

'How tragic for you,' she was saying when we walked in. 'I don't think I've ever heard a more sad story.'

'Anyway,' I said, sitting on the arm of her chair, 'I bet everyone would like to hear about what you do.'

'Yes,' chimed Laura. 'What do you do?'

'I work in the movies,' said Star. 'I'm a casting director.'

'Hey, I thought I'd seen you somewhere before!' exclaimed Jack. He looked at Laura and me. 'Hollywood's such a small world, you see. Star, tell me you didn't work on the *Terminator* movies.'

I turned round and lit a cigarette, biting my lip. Jack was camping it up almost too much. I wondered if Star had even heard of the *Terminator* films. She held her hands up, clearly improvising.

'Guilty as charged.'

'How's James?'

'He's fine.'

'Are you talking about James Cameron?' asked Laura, her little pink mouth open wide.

'Sure,' said Jack.

'And did you meet Arnold Schwarzenegger?' she asked Star.

Star looked blank; luckily Jack was on the ball.

'She cast him, dummy. He had to read lines for her.'

'Seriously?'

'Oh, yes,' said Star.

'So what have you been doing in London?' I asked Star.

'Casting a new movie,' she said. 'I've had people audition-ing for the female lead. The girl we're looking for has to be British, and has to be a new face – which is a great challenge for me, and a great opportunity for the girl. But, really, I haven't found anyone I like yet.'

'What's the movie about?' asked Jack.

'It's about a young ballerina who falls in love.'

'Is it a very big-budget thing?' I asked.

'Oh, yes. I can't reveal who the male lead is, but he is prob-ably the most famous young actor of the moment. We're paying big for him, and we'll do the same for the right girl if we can find her.'

'So what are you looking for, ideally?' asked Jack.

'Someone dark – blondes are so out just now. Pretty. She has to be able to act and dance.'

'And you say this is ballet?'

'Oh, yes. It has to be ballet. I need someone who has been trained.'

As we spoke Laura's face started almost to vibrate with anticipation. This was working so well I almost believed what Star was saying myself. Jack and I amused ourselves for the next few minutes pointedly ignoring Laura and running through a list of people we knew who could try out for the part.

'There's my cousin Anne,' said Jack. 'But she's already starred in a film.'

'She'd be American too, wouldn't she?' said Star.

'Oh, yeah.'

'I know this girl, Beth,' I said. 'She goes out with my brother. I don't think she dances, but she's got the most wonderful long dark hair and she's stunning to look at. She—'

'Excuse me Star,' said Laura in her smallest voice.

'Yes?'

'I dance.'

'Do you? What kind?'

'Ballet. I've been doing it since I was five.'

'Really? Can you act?'

'Yes. Definitely.'

There was a moment of silence as we all held our breath, trying not to laugh. We all knew how well Laura could act: it was her biggest asset.

'Right,' said Star. 'Let's see you dance, then.'

'What? Now?'

'Yes. If you can, that is.'

'I can. But I haven't got the right shoes or anything.'

'Oh dear,' said Star.

'What size are you?' I asked.

'Five.'

'You're in luck, then. I've got an old pair from when I used to dance.'

'You used to dance?' said Laura.

'Yes. Do you want them or not?'

'If you don't mind.'

I went upstairs and pretended to hunt around for them. After a couple of minutes had elapsed I went back down, picked up the bag from the kitchen and took the shoes out. Back in the sitting room I handed them to her and she looked at them carefully before putting them on and tying the long pink ribbons around her ankles.

'Well, what do you want me to do?' she asked Star.

'Impress me.'

'Well, where can I do it?'

'Here?'

'There's not enough space.'

'Down on the beach?'

'It'll be too soft on the sand.' She bit her lip as if she was about to cry.

'You're going to have to do it somewhere,' said Star.

Laura looked at me. 'Are there any hard, flat surfaces around here?'

'There's the flat rock down at the end of the beach. Would that be too hard?'

'Probably. But it'll have to do.'

'Right,' said Star authoritatively. 'Let's go.'

Laura walked out of the room looking happy and curiously *hungry*: as if she wanted this very badly. Star winked at me as she followed Laura out of the house and I heard the door slam. I almost felt sorry for her then: because, of course, there was no part. Then I remembered what she had done to Jack and me. She deserved this.

'Shall we go as well?' asked Jack, squeezing my hand.

'Yeah. I don't want to miss this.'

'Just don't look at me or I'll laugh.'

'Ditto.'

There was no sign of Cornelia as we walked out of the door and down on to the beach. The sky was a strange kind of purple and the sand looked dusky and dark under the cold weak light. The sea was calm today, lapping gently at the sand, and over on the flat rocks a pair of birds sat, shielding themselves from the wind, which blew icy gusts at us.

We all walked down towards the rocks and, as I looked behind me, I could see Cornelia moving out from her hiding place, trying not to be seen. Laura climbed on to the rock and the two birds flew away. She had been wearing white leggings and a white jumper: she took off the jumper and dropped it on the sand, revealing a tight white T-shirt underneath.

'Are you sure she's really horrible?' asked Star as we stood watching her.

'Yeah,' I said. 'Why?'

'Well, I just feel a bit guilty.'

'Yeah, I know. But don't. She's brought this on herself with all this swapped-identity stuff.'

'So this is going to be the moment of truth, then?' she said.

'Yep. Soon we'll know one way or the other.'

'Are you ready?' called Laura.

'Whenever you are,' Star called back.

Jack pulled me close to him as we watched her begin. It was freezing, but his arms kept me warm. Star focused on Laura as she moved into what I recognised as the fourth position, raised her chin defiantly and raised her thin arms delicately over her head. Slowly, she raised herself up on *pointe*, held the position and then came down again, bending her knees in a *plié*. I couldn't name the next few moves. She did a couple of small jumps and what looked like an *arabesque*.

Then she stopped still for a moment and arranged her arms in an arc in front of her. She moved into an upright position and straightened her knees. Then she took her right foot off the ground, and, raising herself up on her left foot, on *pointe*, swung her leg out backwards, bringing her foot in almost to touch her knee. This movement caused her body to turn almost effortlessly, her head straight, focused, her dark hair blowing in the wind. When she had completed a full turn she came off *pointe* for a second, but her right leg didn't touch the ground and she swung into another, identical turn, pushing herself back up on *pointe* her leg turning with mathematical precision.

She performed this turn more than twenty times, bobbing gracefully, her strong gaze never seeming to move from some point behind us, her head remaining perfectly straight. I didn't know anything about ballet apart from the basic positions and movements, but I could tell this was good.

Like a speck of fluff caught in a gust of wind she just kept twisting, her small body cutting through the air like the trail of a firework. She ended the sequence by flinging herself on the rock dramatically. We all stood there impressed beyond words: the display had been fantastic.

'Bravo,' said a voice coming from behind us. It was Cornelia, moving slowly but gracefully with the help of her walking stick.

Laura had started walking towards us, carrying her jumper limply in her hand. She was slightly pink, and breathless, to all appearances the fit young ballet dancer she was trying to convince us she was.

'What's she doing here?' she demanded, pointing at Cornelia.

'Hello, Laura,' said Cornelia. 'The dance of the Black Swan. Very appropriate.'

'What's going on?' demanded Laura, looking first at me, then Jack, then Star. 'Why is she here?'

'You need to work on your line, of course, but that wasn't bad, considering you haven't been in training for so long.'

'I don't need you any more,' she hissed. 'I'm going to Hollywood.'

'She hasn't figured it out yet, huh?' said Jack quietly.

'Figured what out?' she said crossly. 'What's going on?'

'This is definitely Laura,' said Cornelia to me. 'She just performed the dance of the Black Swan from *Swan Lake*. You wouldn't know, but it's one of the hardest and most demanding routines to perform. And of course she did exactly thirty-two *fouettés*. Alex only ever managed ten without ruining them.'

'You did this to work out who I was?' Laura said indignantly to me. 'You fucking bitch. So there was no Hollywood film or anything. You tricked me!'

'The penny drops,' said Jack.

'And you,' she pointed at Star, 'you're no casting director. I bet you're just a fucking secretary or something.'

'I'm a psychologist,' Star said. 'And you're barking mad.'

'Fuck you,' said Laura, and stormed off into the house.

210

'What was that about the dance of the Black Swan?' I asked Cornelia.

'Do you know the story of *Swan Lake*?'

'No. Well, I probably did once, but I've forgotten.'

'An evil sorcerer turns a princess, Odette, into a swan. She becomes the queen of the swans: the White Swan. Each night she becomes human for one hour only. During one of these times, she meets and falls in love with a prince. He declares that he is going to ask her to marry him, but on the night that he does this, Odile, the Black Swan — the evil sorcerer's daughter — takes her place and tricks him into proposing to her instead.'

'So it's all about mistaken identity?'

'Absolutely. Pretending to be someone you're not to get what you want.'

'Post-modern,' commented Jack.

'You said before that Laura took the lead in *Swan Lake*,' I began. 'Which did she play, the White Swan or the Black Swan?'

'Oh, both,' said Cornelia. 'Traditionally they are danced by the same person.'

'Interesting,' I said.

Cornelia looked at her watch. 'Well, I'm going to have to get back.'

'Thanks,' I said to her. 'You've been incredibly helpful.'

She smiled, and walked off across the sand.

'Well, that was a success,' said Star.

'Mmm. I suppose so,' I said.

'Did you think she was Laura anyway?'

'Yeah, pretty much. But what bothers me is that was exactly what she wanted me to believe. What if she has told the truth all along?'

'Do you think she has?' asked Star.

'No. But I'm struggling to find the inconsistencies.'

'How about we all try and find them over dinner tonight at my place?' suggested Jack.

'That sounds good,' said Star. 'Lily?'

'Yeah. Let me just get rid of Laura and I'll come over. What are you cooking?'

'You'll see. How are you getting rid of her?'

'I'm going to call Ian and tell him to come and get her. I don't want her interfering any more. And then I'm going to get to the bottom of all this.'

CHAPTER TWENTY-TWO

Desire

———————•———————

Star and I went over to Jack's at about eight, each carrying a bottle of wine. I'd dressed in a short black dress with black stockings and high heels. Star was wearing a yellow twinset and a knee-length yellow skirt with little blue flowers on it. She looked stunning; I hoped I looked okay.

Ian had come to collect Laura about an hour before. She hadn't spoken to us since the beach incident, so I'd had no idea about what she was thinking. Ian was pissed off. You could tell: he hardly spoke to us either, seeming more concerned about Laura.

'Where are you going to take her?' I asked him as they were leaving.

'Back to my place. After all, she's got nowhere else to go.'

'I'm sorry it didn't work out here,' I said.

'Yeah, me too.' He looked down at the ground, avoiding direct eye-contact.

'Look, Ian, she really has been a pain. I'm not just offloading her for my own convenience.'

'Whatever. She's always been very sweet to me.'

'Fair enough. Maybe we just didn't hit it off.'

He sighed.

'She's definitely Laura, by the way,' I said, and briefly told him what we'd done. He looked impressed, but still pissed off, so I just let it go. The main thing was that I knew for sure who she was.

Once Laura had left, my house took on its normal atmosphere of peace and tranquillity, and even Maude decided she would hang around purring and sleeping for the rest of the afternoon while Star and I got ready for the night ahead and gossiped like crazy.

There are two people in the car. Watch them as they sit there in silence. He wants to say something, to tell her it will be all right, but he can't think of the words. He's pissed off that his friend has let him down.

His work isn't going very well. Look at the bags under his eyes; the lines on his face. Poor bastard.

He glances at her a few times, but she just looks lonely.

He's lonely too.

Two lonely people driving into the night alone.

She puts her hand on his leg

'Don't worry,' she says.

Jack was playing a jazz CD and stirring a pan of something in his small kitchen. His cottage was laid out pretty much the same as mine. Kitchen at one end of the downstairs hallway; sitting room at the other. The music was loud and filled the house. Whatever he was cooking was heady and sweet.

'Smells good,' said Star, as we walked into the kitchen.

'What is it?' I asked, hovering.

'Risotto. Now go away.'

'Shall I open some wine?' asked Star.

'Yeah, good idea,' said Jack.

Half an hour later Jack seemed ready to serve dinner. We all sat around his small dining table, which was in the sitting room. His fire was lit and the room was warm. Two candles flickered in silver candlesticks on the old pine table and jazz still spilled out of the small stereo system in the corner. Everything was perfect.

His risotto was fantastic; so was the wine. We'd polished off one bottle before dinner and we were well into the second before we'd even finished eating. Conversation moved from Jack's film career to Star's research project.

'Psychological profiling,' repeated Jack, after she'd filled him in. 'Very exciting.'

'I think so,' she said. 'If it works it should lead to a radical new methodology.'

'You really want to understand these people, don't you?'

'I think we all do,' she said. 'Look at the three of us. There's Lily with her crime fiction, on the verge of being a private investigator. There's you with all your *noir* stuff, obviously fascinated with murder and so on, and me with my psychopaths, trying to work out what really makes them tick. We all want to know more about what motivates people to kill or deceive, particularly since we think we wouldn't do those things ourselves.'

'Why is that?' I asked.

'What, why are we so fascinated?'

'Yeah.'

'It's all about desiring the other,' she said in a mysterious tone.

'Desiring?'

'Yes, in a loose sense. We are attracted to that which we abhor. It's a basic psychoanalytical fact. Read Lacan.'

'What's it like being with people who kill?' asked Jack.

'Normal.' She shrugged. 'They're fairly normal people.'

'Really?'

'Yes, of course. If they all ran around with bloodstained axes all the time they wouldn't be so hard to understand and identify, would they?'

Jack laughed. 'I guess not. So does our friend Laura fit into this category, do you think?'

215

'You mean is she a psychopath?'

'Yeah.'

'Who knows? She has a problem relating to people, I think. From everything Lily's told me I'd say she doesn't think too much of the human race. You very occasionally find this with twins. Usually, of course, members of sets of twins are completely well adjusted, pleasant individuals who have the benefit of having a ready-made best friend. But with Laura it would appear that she has been alienated by having a twin. For her it has been a huge identity crisis. It probably didn't help that they were so identical. She seems, from what you have told me, to have felt *split* all her life – like there was a part of her she couldn't control and she didn't know whether to consume it, kill it or what. Whether all that would translate into a total disregard for human life – which is what really pushes you into the category of psychopath – is another issue altogether.'

'So this other part of her would have been Alex, then?' asked Jack.

'Uh-huh.'

'Kind of a coincidence that she's dead, then.'

'Maybe, maybe not,' said Star. 'That's what Lily is going to find out.'

'That reminds me,' I said. 'You know that note that was pushed under my door?'

'What the "I'm watching you" one?' said Jack.

'Yeah. Well I checked the handwriting against that bogus letter Laura gave you, and the handwriting is exactly the same. She must have written it and slipped it under my door herself.'

'Not exactly out of character, is it?' commented Jack.

'No. Although I was pleased it wasn't from someone more sinister.'

'She seemed fairly sinister to me,' said Star.

'Yeah, but she's just a kid, really.'

'Don't let that fool you. Don't ever underestimate these people.'

'No. I suppose not. Anyway, she's gone now, thank goodness.'

'But you're still on the case, right?' asked Jack.

I nodded.

'Where do you go next?' asked Star.

'To see Sylvia,' I said. 'Laura's ex-neighbour.'

At about midnight Star excused herself, saying she was tired.
Since Laura had gone she was able to stay in my cottage after
all. Once I'd seen her inside, and showed her the bathroom
and so on, I slipped back over to Jack's.

He was still sitting at the table, smoking a Marlboro Light.

'Thanks for dinner,' I said.

'No problem.'

'So,' I said slowly. 'Weren't you going to tell me something?'

'Yeah.'

We sat in silence for four or five minutes. Jack's expression seemed to become more troubled as he sat there, probably thinking through what he wanted to say and stalling before
the first word came out.

'Do you want to go upstairs?' he asked eventually.

'No,' I said. 'I want you to tell me what's going on.'

'Yeah. I know you do. Coffee?'

We sat on the sofa with our coffee, which Jack spent ages
making in a small espresso machine that he said he'd picked
up in a little shop in London.

'So you went to London before you came here?' I asked.

'Yeah. Only for about a day and a half. I had a meeting.'

He moved closer to me and started stroking my face.

'What kind of meeting?' I asked.

'Just a meeting,' he said, moving even closer.

'You're very mysterious.'

'Am I?'

'You know you are.'

He took my coffee cup out of my hand and placed it gently on the floor, then, in one smooth movement he scooped me up in his arms and stood up. He carried me through the door and up the stairs to his bedroom, where he put me down gently on his bed.

'Shut your eyes,' he said.

So I did. Almost all of me felt relaxed, incredibly turned on by him. But somewhere in my head a voice kept telling me that this could be some kind of diversion. After all, he was going to tell me something, and so far I had no idea what that thing might be.

Gradually this voice became silent as Jack stroked my face and my hair and then leant down and kissed me gently on the lips. His face was slightly rough with a day's stubble, but his lips were soft. I opened my mouth slightly and felt his tongue move inside, tickling and teasing mine. This was different from the passionate kisses we'd shared after my experience on the pier: this was more tender and thoughtful – and it was driving me crazy.

Pushing my dress up he started caressing my legs. My shoes seemed to slip off of their own accord, and he massaged and stroked my feet before moving upwards again, pressing down on me, kissing me more intensely. His breathing was heavy and urgent. I could tell that he was serious about this. All of a sudden I realised that it was finally going to happen. What I'd wanted so desperately. It was going to happen.

'Take your dress off,' he said huskily, sitting up and removing his shirt.

'Okay,' I said quietly, and slipped it over my head.

This time there was no messing around. He immediately took both my breasts in his hands and pushed me back down on to the bed, kissing my neck, holding me close.

'I want you so much,' he murmured, pulling at his belt.

'Oh, Jack,' I whispered.

I could hear his zip unfastening, then I felt him pull off my knickers. He left my stockings on, which was what I had expected. Suddenly he was inside me, as if he couldn't wait any longer. As he'd promised (and I'd felt in my back the other night) he was very big. Pushing in deeper and deeper he pressed his chest to mine and kissed me hard.

'Lily,' he murmured. 'Oh, God, Lily.'

It was over in a few minutes; passionate, desperate, urgent. Jack didn't even take his trousers off until afterwards. Then we lay naked next to one another, smoking cigarettes. The second time we took it more slowly. He licked and stroked me all over until I came, and then he let me do the same to him. This time when he entered me it lasted for what seemed like hours.

As we fell asleep in each other's arms, I didn't think to ask him what it was he'd wanted to tell me. It didn't seem to matter much any more. Maybe he'd talk to me tomorrow, I thought as I fell asleep.

The next morning I woke up with a peculiar feeling, like something was going on that I didn't know about. It was. The first thing I saw when I sat up in bed was Jack, possessed with an air of being incredibly busy, opening cupboards and drawers and pulling things out of them. On the floor by the bed was a suitcase, which he seemed to be filling haphazardly with the stuff he was pulling out from everywhere.

'What's going on?' I asked groggily.

'Oh, you're awake.'

'Well, I can't sleep with all this slamming going on.'

'Sorry.'

'Are you going somewhere?'

'Hmm?'

'I said, are you going somewhere?'

He came and sat on the edge of the bed and gave me a small kiss on my cheek. 'I have to go away for a few days.'

'Where?'

'Just somewhere.'

'Was I that bad?'

'Were you ...? No! Jesus, Lily. You were fantastic. I want to spend the rest of my life in bed with you.'

'Yeah, it really seems like it,' I said, looking at the suitcase.

'Oh, God, don't take offence. This was planned long before ... you know.'

'When are you coming back?'

'I'll call you and let you know.'

'Are we talking weeks? Months?'

'No. I'll be back in a few days. You won't even know I'm gone.'

'Fine.'

Jack didn't seem to notice as my mood took a nose-dive. Surely the morning after was supposed to be spent walking along the beach hand in hand, having breakfast, reading the papers? This wasn't what I'd expected. But I wasn't going to humiliate myself by causing a fuss. After dressing quickly I kissed Jack goodbye, wished him a happy trip and left.

Star was sitting at the kitchen table drinking tea and tapping away on her laptop computer when I let myself back into my cottage.

'I see somebody didn't make it home last night,' she commented, smiling.

'Mmm.'

'What's wrong?'

'Well, we had a fantastic night and everything ...'

'Yes?'

'But I don't know if I've done something wrong or what, but he says he's going away for a few days.'

'That's odd. Is this the first you'd heard about it?'

'Yeah.'

'Hmm.'

'What does that mean?'

'It means I agree with you. It's odd.'

'Thanks.'

'Well, I'm not going to lie to you.' She gestured at the pot. 'Do you want some of this tea?'

'No, thanks. I'll make a coffee.'

'What are you up to today?'

'I'm going to go and see this Sylvia woman. See if I can find out what all the fuss was about.'

'What did she say to Laura exactly?'

'Just a load of stuff about her being a little tart and so on, and sleeping with her husband. But one thing was really weird. As I walked in I heard Laura say something about somebody committing suicide.'

'Alex?'

'No. She was saying something like, "If I was married to you I'd kill myself too." It must have been Sylvia's husband she was talking about. He's the one who was arrested for the murder of Laura, Alex and Tim's parents.'

'The plot thickens.'

'Mmm. It should be thinning out by now.'

'It will. You'll work it all out.'

'Yeah, maybe. What are you doing today?'

'I've got some files to look through, so don't worry about entertaining me.'

'Are you sure?'

'Of course. Go and find out whodunnit.'

I laughed. 'Yeah, right.'

It wasn't until after I'd finished in the shower that I realised that the silver crucifix I always wore around my neck was missing. I remembered having it on last night, and, as I cast my mind back, I also remembered taking it off, somewhere between fuck one and fuck two. Shit. Then I remembered I still had the key to Jack's cottage. I'd seen the BMW leaving while I was sitting downstairs with Star, so I knew Jack had gone. He'd said I could go over there anytime. Surely he wouldn't mind if I just popped in and got my cross back?

The trouble with me, though, was that I was a natural snoop. That was how I always ended up solving crimes I'd rather have had nothing to do with. So it came to be that I was still in Jack's cottage half an hour after I'd found my chain, looking at his clothes, his books and the brand of shampoo he kept in his bathroom. I was sure anyone would do the same, after all, I was in love with him.

But after this morning's episode, and all the other stuff – like finding him on the beach in the middle of the night, and his mysterious outing in Torquay – I was certain there was a mystery about him. So I was looking for clues.

His clothes were simple and stylish, and I'd already seen most of them before. His plain shirts and T-shirts; that cashmere jumper that Maude liked so much; a few pairs of jeans and a couple of sweatshirts. His socks were all autumn colours; some striped but mostly plain, in browns, greens and blues. His underwear was mostly white: jockey shorts, mainly, and a couple of pairs of striped or checked boxers.

His books were all crime classics; most of which I recognised from my own bookshelves: a couple of Raymond Chandler novels; Dashiell Hammett and a *Pulp Fiction* anthology. There were a few notebooks around here and there, but I didn't want to pry. But I was lying to myself. If I hadn't wanted to pry, how was it that I ended up downstairs with a cigarette and the largest notebook from the pile, which had said on the front *My Journal: Winter* 1997?

There was no way I could justify it. I'd never read anyone's diary before – not unless they were dead, of course. But I just had to know. What did he really feel about me? What was all the mystery about? I opened the book and started flicking

through. I found the entry Jack had made after we'd been out
to Torquay for the first time, role-playing in the rain.

She doesn't know how much I already love her. The rain
drips off her face as we walk through town. She is beautiful. I wish I could hold her hand, but she is playing murderer and I am her quarry. It's not very romantic, but I'm
hooked. I'm hooked on her.

Of course I'm not supposed to use that language any
more. The language of addiction is forbidden. But it's
getting to be too much. I hate myself for what I have done.
I left her in a café on her own and went out to score.
Walking in the rain towards oblivion; my own death for a
few dollars. The guy charged me fifty pounds for a wrap of
coke. About seventy dollars. I don't know if that's cheap or
expensive any more. I saw her face in the powder. I saw our
children: the ones we will never have. I'm a dumb fuck. But
to my credit I just stood there with the white powder in its
virginal little white wrap and tipped it in the sea.

I was supposed to be alone here. So how did I end up
next door to the most beautiful, clever woman in the world?
How can I tell her that I'm an addict, that while I'm trying
to kick the habit I'm not supposed to have girlfriends, have
sex or anything. How do you tell someone that? How do
you tell someone you are in love with that you just can't
love them? I think I'd better keep my distance for a while.
It's only a matter of time before this gets too complicated.

The shakes still come at night. The sea air helps.

'Lily?'

The voice came from behind me. I jumped so high in my
chair that I dropped the book and it fell on the carpet. It was
Jack.

'Hi. I, uh …'

'Save it, Lily. I thought I could trust you.'

'You can, I just ...'

He walked over to where I was sitting and picked up the book from where it had dropped. He looked at me accusingly. 'Just what? Jesus Christ. Maybe I should publish this thing so everyone can see inside me. You've seen inside me now. Like what you see? I didn't think so. Why do you think I couldn't bring myself to tell you all that stuff? It sure ain't pretty.'

'Jack ...'

'Save it. I just came to pick this up.'

He started walking out, carrying his book.

'I still love you, Jack.'

'You think you do.'

'Please don't go.'

'We'll discuss this when I get back. You've fucked me up enough as it is.'

'What the hell's that supposed to mean?'

'You've read the goddamn book. You work it out.'

And he left, slamming the door behind him.

CHAPTER TWENTY-THREE

Death Lily

So I cried.

This was not usual for me. Men didn't often screw me up, I made sure of that. What made me so upset about this was the guilt. I shouldn't have read his journal – of *course* I should-n't. But it's easy to say that afterwards. And in my defence he'd made it clear that there was stuff in the book that I needed to know, that he'd wanted to tell me. But his face when he'd discovered me. And his secrets. They were *his* secrets, and I'd stolen them.

At least it all made sense now. I'd got the rest of the story from other sections in the journal. He'd come to Devon to overcome a drug addiction, something which had got a hold of him in Hollywood and which he'd been seeing a therapist about. No friend had recommended this place. Perhaps there wasn't even a new screenplay. He was just trying to be on his own.

This was the deal with his therapist: no girls, no sex; no going out to clubs. These were all things he associated with coke, and therefore things he was supposed to avoid if he wanted to kick it. He'd gone to Harry's cinema that night to try to take his mind off everything: the shakes, the headaches, the paranoia. The journal had said that he'd only gone into the jazz club because I had; he'd seen me and remembered me from the beach and he'd been so lonely … But it had been inside Juno's that he had met – within three minutes of being inside – a local coke-dealer, who'd taken one look in Jack's eyes and given him his mobile number.

The journal had described how he had felt when I hadn't come back that night: how he had gotten more and more drunk and thought he was boring and a failure and I hated him. Later it detailed how he had reacted when I'd tried to get him to have sex with me that time, when I'd pulled off my dress and he'd refused to go upstairs with me. He'd gone home, cried and thought about going out to score coke. And I thought *I'd* felt bad.

As well as hating myself for being so intrusive, I felt my heart leap out towards Jack. How could he think I wouldn't want him any more? It made things more complicated, sure, but he'd get over it, wouldn't he? I just wished he was here still so I could apologise, and make it up to him in person, but I doubted that he'd want anything more to do with me now. That was what the tears were about. He was the best thing that had ever happened to me, and I'd driven him away.

'Sounds like he was more embarrassed than anything else,' said Star, when I told her everything that had happened, everything that had been said. She was down on the beach reading through a stack of papers so we both sat there together, smoking in the calm, cold air.

'Really?'

'Yes, absolutely.'

'He obviously didn't want to have anything more to do with me.'

'Don't be ridiculous. He wrote all those pages about how in love with you he is. That doesn't just go away.'

'No?'

'No.'

'Don't you think I'm a despicable person, though, for reading his journal?'

She laughed. 'No. I would have done the same.'

'Really?'

'Of course. You slept with him, I assume?'

'Yeah.'

'Well, then, given what had already happened, you had a right to know what was going on. Of course, in other circumstances it would be quite different, but since Laura had already read the journal and he'd told you that she knew his dreadful secret, it put a different spin on things. I mean, that would be enough of a teaser for most people to go over there and rummage through his drawers immediately. Then promising to tell you last night and then not going through with it was just unforgivable, really. *Then* to be in the middle of packing to go away when you woke up the next morning. Really, Lily, you are not the one in the wrong.'

'Really?'

'Yes. He wanted you to read it, anyway.'

'How do you work that out?'

'He gave you a key to his cottage. I'm a psychologist. People do not give away the key to their secrets unless they want someone to find them. He knew you had access to the house. He'd told you about the journal. It was an open invitation.'

'Hmm.'

'Just wait until he comes back. It'll all work out.'

'Maybe.'

'Anyway, while you were over there playing Miss Marple, someone called Emma Winter rang.'

'When?'

'About half an hour ago. She sounded pissed off.'

'She always does.'

'Is she your client?'

'Yep. And she never lets me forget it.'

'Well, you'd better get out there and make her happy, then.'
I smiled. 'Yeah. Thanks, Star.'
'Any time.'

Sylvia was staying at her sister-in-law's council house on an estate in Torquay. It had taken me a while to extract this information from Ian. He was not in a good mood today. I didn't bring up the subject of Laura, but I wondered how much fun she was having with him, wrapping him around her little finger and then unwrapping him *ad nauseam; ad libitum.*

The sky was bright white as I drove into town. It looked like it might snow. I tried not to think about Jack as I drove past what were already landmarks of us: the piers, the walkway and the theatre all looming inconsequentially over the bleached-out sea.

I reminded myself that these were actually landmarks of murder as well, and that I had to get some answers. Tim hadn't murdered Alex, I was pretty sure of that. But who had?

The house I was looking for was on a large estate in which small corner shops and bookies punctuated the acres of grey prefab buildings. Outside the house sat two blue taxis in differing stages of disrepair. On the side of each were the words Happy Cabs. I banged on the door of the house and waited. Eventually it was answered by a woman who looked a little bit like Sylvia. She was twice the size, twice as blonde and twice as greasy. She wore a grey sweatshirt with Happy Cabs written on it; black leggings and green stilettos.

When I explained that I was here to see Sylvia she looked me up and down, sneered before calling, 'Sylv!' then turned and walked inside. When Sylvia came to the door she seemed not to recognise me. I introduced myself as the woman Laura had been staying with and her expression changed. Specifically as I said the word Laura she seemed physically to sag. Her face literally wilted.

'I don't want nothing to do with her,' she said firmly.

'Believe me, I understand why.'

'What was she doing in your house, then?'

'Causing trouble. I'm not her number-one fan.'

'So what are you doing here, then?'

'I wanted to get your side of the story.'

'Why? You're not a copper, are you?'

'No, but if I could just come inside I ...'

'I ain't talking to the press.'

'Sylvia, I'm trying to find out who killed Alex Carter. Please let me in, it's freezing out here.'

Reluctantly she stepped aside and held open the door for me. Inside, the house smelt of chip pans and lard; the smell clung to you the instant you walked into it, and I made plans to wash my clothes as soon as I got home. I followed Sylvia into a small sitting room at the front of the house, in which mismatched brown armchairs huddled in front of an old portable TV. On the floor, in a box, sat a small, red-haired girl of about four. She was picking her nose.

'Do you want a fag?' Sylvia asked me, holding out a packet of Superkings.

'Yeah, cheers,' I said, and took one, wanting her to trust me, wanting her to talk.

'Who are you?' asked the small girl, still standing in the box. She had a nice smile and I worried about smoking in the room with such a small child there. Sylvia didn't seem to care, though, and neither did her sister-in-law, from the look of all the ashtrays clustered around the room on the floor and on the arms of chairs.

'I'm Lily,' I said, smiling back at her.

'Piss off, Louise,' said Sylvia.

The girl climbed out of the box and came over to sit next to me on the sofa. I instantly wanted to take her out of here, she was so sweet and so small. She pushed her small thin body close to me and grinned. Taking a lock of my hair in her freckly hand she started playing with it. I didn't mind, but

Sylvia went for her like a pit-bull, and pulled her away by the arm.

'Pack it in, Louise,' she hissed.

'Ow!' said Louise, and I could see her bottom lip start to tremble.

'I really don't mind ...' I started to say. But it was too late, Louise had started to cry, quietly at first, then more loudly. Sylvia's harsh face betrayed no reaction at all, apart from mild frustration at the noise. After a couple of minutes of this, the other woman stormed in.

'For Christ's sake, pack it in,' she yelled, pulling Louise towards her and giving her a hard-looking smack on her legs. 'Get outside. Now!'

Feeling sick, I watched the girl wander towards the back of the house. Poor little thing. Suddenly I began to feel that whatever Laura had done to this woman couldn't be as bad as this. But I needed information from her, so I smiled through my disgust and put out my cigarette.

'So tell me about Laura,' I said.

'Was that Laura over at your house the other night?'

I nodded.

'Little slut. She said she was Alex. Is Alex dead, then?'

'Yeah.'

'Fucking bitch.'

'What, Alex?'

'No. Laura. She killed my husband, you know.'

'She killed your husband?'

'That's right. My Stan.'

'So why isn't she ... I mean, if she killed him, why hasn't she been arrested?'

The woman shrugged. 'He killed himself. But she was the last person who saw him before he did.'

'You think she drove him to it?'

'I know she did. It was because of her that he done it.'

'Why?'

'They were having an affair. Since she was fifteen, dirty little slag.'

'And that's why he killed himself?'

'Dunno. It wasn't exactly news to me.'

'You already knew?'

'Yeah. I knew.'

'God. I'm sorry.'

'Yeah. Of course you are.'

'So you ran the hotel next door to the Tulip?'

'Yep. For twenty-five years. We didn't get on with our neighbours. That's why the police reckon Stan did the Carters' brakes.'

'The brakes on their car?'

'Yeah. They found evidence and all that, but I know my Stan didn't do it. He wasn't a bad man, just ambitious.'

'Sorry?'

'That was why they reckoned he did it. He always wanted to buy them out, next door. It was a bleeding nightmare up there. Two hotels, both making a loss. He wanted to knock them down and build something better. Start afresh. They wouldn't let him buy them out. *They* kept making *us* offers but we refused. It was a ... what do you call it? Like a stalemate.'

'How long did this go on for?'

'The last five years or so. But it's over now.'

'Sorry?'

'I've sold — to her.'

'Laura?'

'Yeah.'

'Why would she want to buy the hotel?'

'I don't know. I doubt she wants to build on that land.'

'But that was supposedly Stan's motive?'

She nodded. 'They said he'd done it so he could buy out the Carter kids for a small price, you know, so they could divide the estate. But he wouldn't have done it for money.'

'So who did do it?'

'I don't know. I don't care. None of it'll bring him back.'

'No.' I paused for a few moments, then said, 'Sylvia, do you know what any of these words might mean?'

I said each part of the note slowly and carefully like I was talking to someone who didn't understand English. *Lucky*; *she looks like the real thing*; *lipp*; did they mean anything to her?

She shook her head. 'No,' she said firmly.

Sylvia went quiet after that. She offered me a cup of tea, but I refused, saying I had to be somewhere. She walked me to the door and we stood there for a moment, saying goodbye. Outside the door were some huge oversized lilies. I always recognised lilies because the flower was my namesake, but I didn't really know anything about gardening. These particular flowers seemed out of place here: the rest of the small front garden was overgrown and full of weeds and rubbish. A crisp packet fluttered in the cold wind, pushed up to the fence. But the lilies were intriguing: I'd never seen them that big before. Sylvia saw me looking at them and smiled a sinister smile.

'Death lilies,' she said.

'Sorry?'

'Death lilies. The kind you have at funerals.'

'Oh,' I said.

Back in my car I lit a cigarette and thought about where I should go next. Had Laura been lying to me about not sleeping with Stan? Sylvia had been very sure that she had. Why would she have visited him in prison? And why would that make him want to kill himself? More and more, all these murders seemed inextricably linked to one another: the Carters; Alex; Kurt. But how? Laura had certainly gained from all of them, apart from Kurt's. She'd sounded smug talking to her solicitor and now I realised what it had been about. She'd got Tim's money, Alex's and her parents', and she'd bought Sylvia out. Although I had no idea why she would want to do this, it seemed very convenient that Tim was in prison and Stan, Alex and Mr and Mrs Carter were dead.

Taking my mobile phone out of my bag, I then fished around in my pockets until I found the number Tony Bryce had given me. There were two. I selected the one that looked like a mobile number and dialled.

'Hello?' came his harsh, crackled voice.

'Tony. It's Lily Pascale.'

'Yeah? What do you want?'

'I think we should meet,' I said.

CHAPTER TWENTY-FOUR

Tabloid

We agreed to meet at a bar overlooking the sea in Torquay. The place was large and almost empty when I arrived. There was no sign of Tony, so I ordered a bottle of Budweiser at the bar and sat down to wait. Through the windows I could see the long empty beach: waves crashing furiously against it. The sky was still blank. No clouds; no colour. Maybe it would snow soon, I thought again.

Tony turned up about ten minutes after I'd ordered my second drink. He looked exactly as he had when I had seen him on the pier. The windswept look was obviously a permanent feature; the stubble as well.

'Miss Pascale, hi,' he said, almost drawling his words.

'Lily, please.'

'You've left it a bit late, haven't you?'

'A bit late for what?'

'To be blunt, I'm not really interested in your story any more. They've got Tim Carter for Kurt Venga's murder, and as of this morning, he's confessed to murdering his sister as well. So it's all over, really.'

'Tim's confessed?'

'That's right.'

'My God.'

'That bother you, does it?'

'Not as much as it should bother you. You've got the exclusive rights to tell Laura's story after the trial. Am I right?'

He shrugged. 'Maybe. How do you know that?'

'It's just a guess, really. But since what you published in your paper the other day matches up exactly with what Laura told me I thought she was probably your source.'

'Yeah, well, she only did it to cover her back, poor little cow. She's going to tell us the whole thing after the trial. The actual true story, including why she felt she had to lie in the first place.'

'Yeah, right.'

'So why did you want to meet me?'

'Because she's sucked you in, and I just wanted to warn you that she's not what she says she is.'

'Who?'

'Laura.'

He looked at me coldly. 'Jealous, are you?'

'Of what? She's clever, but that's it. She's lied to us all. She's still lying to you.'

'Keep talking.'

'She's bought out the next-door hotel. I've just come from Sylvia Green's house and she told me all about it. Don't you think it's a coincidence that everyone who could have been in the way of Laura inheriting and spending that money is dead?'

'No. She's got the money, why shouldn't she spend it?'

'Aren't you interested in how she got Tim's money?'

'Not really. It wouldn't make a very strong story. He probably just gave it to her.'

236

'I thought maybe you'd be interested in finding out what the truth is.'

'I know the truth. The truth is that this is all over.'

'Really.'

'Yeah. You private investigators are always the same. You see so much when there really isn't anything there. It's because you have such boring lives,' he added.

'Well, I wouldn't know, since I'm not a PI.'

'Whatever.'

Tony had taken off his jacket which he had then hung over the back of his chair. I could see a small Dictaphone poking out of the right-hand pocket; a small black notebook in his left. Why wasn't he interested in getting to the bottom of this? He wasn't a nice man, but I had thought he and I might have been natural allies. Obviously Laura had got her claws into him first.

'If we worked together,' I began, 'I bet we'd get somewhere.'

'I don't see what you'd give me in return. I'm the one with all the contacts.'

All the contacts, I thought, zeroing in on his little black book.

'Look, Tony,' I said sweetly, 'I can be nice too, you know.'

'Oh, really?'

'Yeah,' I said, picking up my bag. 'Let me buy you a drink. Maybe we can be friends. Maybe then you'll want to work with me.'

'Friends? Convince me.'

'Okay.'

I stood up and crossed the small space between his chair and mine. Leaning down, I took him by surprise as I pressed my mouth to his and placed my hand firmly in his crotch. His lips opened in response to the kiss and he thrust his big dry tongue right into my mouth. It tasted sour, like he hadn't brushed his teeth for a month. But while one of my hands was in his lap, the other was fishing the black book out of his jacket and concealing it in my bag. This was too easy, I thought, pulling away from the kiss. I should have made it harder for myself. As with cheating at poker and performing card tricks, there would have been more than one way to get the book. I'd done it the easy way. But I'd wanted to be sure.

'Friends?' I said, straightening up.

'Depends how close you want to get. I don't think you're a lesbian any more, granted, but we could go out the back and you could really convince me. Christ, I might even agree to help you, after all.'

'Sorry. On second thoughts you're not my type.'

'Dyke. I thought so.'

'Maybe we'll forget about that drink,' I said.

'*She*'s very convincing,' he said, looking me up and down.

'Sorry?'

'You know, I really do want to help, but, see, if I did then I'd lose my exclusive rights with Laura, if you know what I mean. She fucking goes like a steam train, you know.'

'Exclusive,' I said slowly, turning to go. 'If that's what you want to believe.'

'What?'

'You don't really get it, do you, Tony? Some other bloke is fucking Laura right now. I even know who he is — not that I'm going to tell you because, after all, we're not sharing information, are we? And you think you've got something exclusive with her?' I laughed. 'She doesn't belong to anyone. You know, you'd probably get a much better story if you didn't think with your cock, if you don't mind me saying so.'

Tony's face fell, although he tried to conceal it. Of course, by the time I'd got into my car and driven away. I was sure he would have convinced himself that I'd lied: that whatever Laura had told him was true. He wouldn't have his black notebook but, like I'd told him, you didn't get very far thinking with your cock.

As I drove away from Torquay with Tony's black book still in my bag, I thought more about Laura. Of course she'd slept with Stan Green, probably just to prove she could. Of course she'd slept with Kurt and Tony. She would have had Jack if he'd let her. What I'd said about Ian had to be true as well. She was staying with him, and I was sure it would only have been a matter of time. It seemed that she'd fucked anyone who could be of any use to her; and then anyone else, if it would piss someone off. She was sexy and clever. She was beautiful. Even after what she'd done with Jack I found I had a grudging respect for this girl. She used what she had to get what she wanted. The only question now, of course, was: what exactly did she want? What the hell was she up to?

'One fifty.'

'A hundred and fifty grand for two hotels and the land? Get real, Mr Benson.'

The girl is on the phone now. Let's go and watch her as she smiles into the receiver; flirting with it. There is no one else in the house. Ian's gone to buy her a cheeseburger, because that's what she really wanted.

'One seven five.'

'Too low.' She sings the words, wrapping the cable around her finger.

'I'll have to think about it.'

'You've got five minutes. After that I won't sell.'

'Is that supposed to bother me?'

'No. But I have got something for you to think about.'

'*What?*'

'*Your wife, Mr Benson. Does she know you fuck teenage girls?*'

Star was still reading her documents when I returned.

'How did it go?' she asked.

'Fine,' I said. 'I think I know a few more things.'

'Like?'

'Well, Laura was knocking off the man next door — the one who killed her parents. And it also turns out that she went to visit him in prison recently. After she left he killed himself.'

'Interesting.'

'Mmm. What do you think she's up to?'

'Revenge?'

'What for? Her parents' murder?'

'Yes.'

'I thought of that, but I wondered what she'd have told Stan to make him kill himself. Apparently the wife already knew they'd been having sex, so it couldn't have been that.'

'Maybe she was blackmailing him in some other way?'

'Possibly. But you know, if she was avenging her parents' death, then where does all the stuff with Kurt, Alex and Tim fit in?' I shook my head, feeling slightly bewildered. 'You know, Jack cracked some joke the other day about how it should be Murder Central up there, up in the hotels. But all of a sudden I've realised that it really is. It *is* Murder Central, as he put it. Four murders and one dodgy suicide have taken place over the last few weeks that can be linked to the hotels. I just wonder what's actually going on.'

'Sounds like you need a coffee,' said Star.

'Thanks,' I said. 'Incidentally, has Jack phoned at all?'

She shook her head. 'Sorry. Emma called again, though.'

'She can wait. I wish I had something to tell her so I could get out of all this.'

'So where else did you go?' asked Star, putting the kettle on.

'Well, I got this,' I said, reaching in my bag and pulling out Tony's book.

Flicking through it I found names and addresses of everyone in any way connected with Laura and Alex. I was in there, and so were Cornelia, Dr Ravine and Harry from the cinema. There was a new address for the old woman and the little girl, too.

'Let's have a look,' Star said, pulling the book out of my hands. 'Ooh. This looks useful.'

'It would be if I hadn't already seen most of these people.'

'How did you get it?'

I laughed. 'I almost prostituted myself.'

'*No.* Yuck! That awful Tony Bryce?'

'Yeah. I kissed him as a diversion so I could get it out of his pocket.'

'Aha, the old sleight-of-hand stuff.'

'Mmm.'

'Here's your coffee,' she said, placing a mug in front of me on the table. I sat down and sipped at it gratefully. I lit a cigarette and Star pushed the ashtray over towards me.

'If only this all made sense,' I said.

'Have you got any other leads?'

'Only the burnt piece of paper.'

'What burnt piece of paper?'

'Didn't I tell you about it?'

'No. It sounds very intriguing.'

'Hang on and I'll go and get it.'

I'd hidden it upstairs in the bedroom in my underwear

drawer. Or, at least, I thought I had. But it didn't seem to be here. Frustrated, I shook out every pair of knickers and every bra. Nothing. In frustration, I tipped the contents of the drawer out on to the floor. It definitely wasn't there. And there was only one explanation why not.

'Laura's taken it,' I said to Star, once I was back downstairs.

'Are you sure?'

'Pretty sure. Little bitch.'

'Well, can you tell me about it anyway?'

'Yeah.' I sighed. 'But I wish I had it.'

'Did Laura write it, do you think?'

'No. The handwriting was different.'

'Did it seem like a love letter?'

'I don't know. Why would she burn it if it was?'

'Maybe it was an illicit lover.'

'All her lovers are illicit, though. Why would this one be any different?'

'Hmm. I see what you mean. What were the words?'

'Hang on.' I got a piece of paper and a pen and wrote down the words, as I remembered them looking on the scrap of paper. There they were again: *Lucky, Cornel, lipp* and that strange phrase: *she looks like the real thing.*

'Weird,' commented Star, after she'd looked at the list for a few moments.

'Aren't they? No one I've asked knows what they might be.'

'I can see why.'

'The one I have figured out,' I said, pointing to *Cornel*, 'is the beginning of the word Cornelia. But why would someone write about her in a love letter?'

'Maybe because she was important to Laura?'

'She wasn't, though, was she? Maybe it was a letter to Alex. She was the one who was close to Cornelia.'

'Maybe. What about all these other words?'

'Well, I've asked every single person I've been to see, and none of them recognise them or know what they would mean. I'm interested in *Lucky*, because of the capital letter, and because it's a complete word. I thought it could be someone's name. But no one knows of anyone called Lucky. And of course this funny phrase: *she looks like the real thing*. It almost seems a little bit familiar, but maybe that's because I've been obsessing about it for so long. I thought it might refer to one of the twins pretending to be the other, but there's no indication of which one, or in which context.'

'Hmm. What about this other one?'

'*lipp*. I just can't work out what that would be. I think it's part of a word, but I can't think what. I do crosswords, but my skills aren't helping here.'

'I suppose it would help if you had a clue, rather than just letters.'

'Exactly.'

We sat quietly for a few minutes and after a while Star went back to her documents, while I sat there thinking over all the words again. *She looks like the real thing* was still tormenting me, like a pop song I couldn't get out of my head. Knowing I wouldn't come up with anything while I was thinking like this, I decided to try to clear my head by preparing some dinner.

'Do you like pizza?' I asked, fishing around in the freezer.

'Pizza. Sure. Do you want help making the base?'

I laughed. 'I meant frozen pizza.'

'I don't think I've ever had a frozen pizza.'

'Yeah, well, I got them for Laura. It's an experience you should have at least once.'

'I can't wait. Do you want me to get a fire going?'

'Yeah. Thanks.'

Half an hour later we were settled in the sitting room eating pepperoni pizza with our fingers and drinking one of the many bottles of wine I now seemed to have in the larder. I'd stuck some baking potatoes in with the pizza and topped them with Parmesan and mozzarella.

'This pizza's nice,' said Star, tomato sauce dribbling down her chin.

'Mmm.'

'It's kind of sweet and spicy all at once. The sauce is quite, um ... unusual.'

'That's all the chemicals they put in.'

She laughed. 'I might have to get some of these when I get home.'

'I'd like to see Henri's reaction to that.' My father was known for his food and drink snobbery. He bought organic wherever possible, and he ate only fresh food. I was more or less the same, but sometimes I got a sordid thrill out of McDonald's and ready meals, rather in the same way that other people got off on pornography.

Star giggled. 'I think that would be the end of me.'

'Yeah. I wouldn't try it.'

To round off the experience nicely, *Blind Date* was playing on the TV. Three female contestants, one blonde, one dark and one black, all wearing revealing clothes, were coming up with what they thought were witty answers to the questions of the man on the other side of the partition. He was quite cute, though, and his voice was deep and hypnotic, so I reached for the remote and turned up the volume.

'What's this?' asked Star.

I smiled. '*Blind Date*, silly.'

'What's that?'

I looked at her quizzically. 'Don't tell me you don't know what *Blind Date* is.'

'No.' She shook her head. 'Tell me.'

I explained to her the way the format worked, and after about two minutes she was hooked and kept telling me to shush when I thought of other interesting *Blind Date* facts I could tell her, like that when I was at university someone from our year had been on and had won a holiday to Rome. After she'd shushed me for the third time I gave up and concentrated on the TV. I hadn't caught the question, but one of the contestants was just rounding off her answer with the words, Maybe you can let me look at your dictionary. Of course, she'd paused between the first and second syllables of the word dictionary, and the audience roared.

Star did as well.

'Is this allowed?' she said.

'You don't watch very much TV, do you?' I said.

She shook her head, still laughing.

But I had started thinking.

'Star?'

'Mmm?'

'Do you have a dictionary programme on your Powerbook?'

'I don't know,' she said. 'Probably in Microsoft Word, or something. Why?'

'Is it searchable?'

'Of course. You search for words.'

'By the first letter or something?'

'Yes.'

'What about middle bits of words?'

She shrugged. 'I don't think so. Why?'

'It's this *lipp* thing,' I said. 'I'm sure it's part of a bigger word.'

'I think so too.'

'There are just too many variables to look in a real dictionary for it, though.'

'I suppose if you don't know how many letters are either side of it ...'

I laughed. 'Yeah. This really isn't like a crossword, unfortunately.'

Star looked thoughtful.

'What's up? I asked.

'Um, just something ... Can you bear with me for a few minutes?'

'Sure. '

She got her Powerbook and switched it on. For the next five minutes she seemed to be scrolling through a document she had opened. I couldn't see what it was.

'Aha,' she said, finally.

'What?'

'Well, I'm looking through a transcript of an interview I did with one of the psychopaths. He was a computer hacker, and used to hack into people's e-mail accounts, then send them bogus messages from people they knew, arranging to meet at a certain place. But instead of the friend it would be him waiting there. He stabbed all his victims to death.'

'That is horrific,' I said, shocked. 'Can people really do that?'

'Uh-huh.'

'Are you trying to scare me for a particular reason?'

'Well, all this stuff about dictionaries made me remember a whole session where he talked about hacking passwords, about how you needed a text file of a dictionary to do it.'

'I don't understand.'

'Neither do I, really.' She laughed. 'That's why I wanted to look at the transcript again. It's very interesting. It seems that hackers have a similar problem to the one we're having. I'm not sure how to explain. The reason you can't search a computerised dictionary for middles of words is because all the words aren't in the same document. A computerised dictionary is really there to help you spell words, just like an ordinary dictionary, and it assumes you want to search according to the first letter, or letters.'

'Carry on.'

'Well, if you had every English word in a document all of its own, and you wanted to find a word, or a bit or a word in it, then you could just do a "Find" command. You use that, I take it?'

'Yeah. Find and Replace. When you want to substitute one word for another throughout a whole document. Or, I suppose, just if you want to find something in the document, although I've never used it for that.'

'Have you ever tried to find a small word, like run, or far, or something, and realised that the computer finds every single word with the small word in it? You know, like if you were looking for run, it would find runt, rung, drunk and so on.'

I smiled. 'Yeah, but you can choose whole-word search only, can't you?'

'Of course. But surely everyone makes that mistake at least once?'

'Yeah. But I still don't see what that has to do with psychotic computer hackers.'

'Well, say you wanted to find a word by typing in some of its middle letters, you could use the Find command, right?

But for that, you'd need a whole dictionary as a document.'

'Which is pretty impossible, right?'

'Not to our psychotic friend. That's why I looked him up. I remembered him spending a whole session with me talking about finding the perfect dictionary. You see, the commonest way of hacking into a password-protected document or file is to run a program that tries every word in the dictionary until it finds the right one.' She looked down at her computer and scrolled through a page or two. 'It's called the brute force method. Apparently, the key to it is finding the right dictionary to attach to the hacking software. It needs to be a text file, like I said, usually with a word on each line, but in any case, all the words in one simple – but very long – document.'

'So where do we get one?'

'Apparently they're all over the Internet and you can download them. There are specialist ones like *Star Trek* names, or film references, or place names – all kinds of different ones, depending on whose password you're trying to get.'

'What about normal English dictionaries?'

'Those too, I'm sure.'

I looked at Star's Powerbook. 'Do you have a modem for that?' I asked.

'Of course.'

'Then what are we waiting for?'

It took Star about fifteen minutes to get chatting to a computer hacker called ZaZaX whom she had found in a newsgroup then tracked down in a chat-room called the Dungeon. He gave her the address of a site with links to all sorts of dictionaries, which when we visited it turned out to include dictionaries of Klingon words, S&M terms and TeenSpeak.

Luckily it also had a choice of English dictionaries, so we chose the biggest one and downloaded it. I lit a cigarette and waited for Star to open it up in Word.

'Oh, my God,' she said, giggling.

'What?'

'Guess how many pages this is?'

I laughed. 'Shock me.'

'Almost six thousand.'

'God. A six-thousand page document. Sounds like one of my boss's management files.'

'Well, just pray it doesn't crash.'

I leaned over to see. Sure enough, it was a huge file.

'So, shall we search?' I said.

'Off you go,' she replied, passing the machine to me.

I brought up the Find command and typed in the part of word I had: *lipp*. The first word it found was *clipper*, then *clipping*. There were only six others worth noting: *flippant, Philippa, flipper, slippage, slipping and slippery.*

'What have you got?' asked Star.

I told her.

'Hmm,' she said.

'Nothing's jumping out at me,' I said.

'No. Maybe we should try the other bit you haven't worked out.'

'There isn't one, really. Just that weird phrase and the word Lucky.'

'I suppose Lucky isn't part of something else?'

'No, not with the capital letter.'

'What about this phrase, then?'

'*She looks like the real thing,*' I said, giving the words a slightly different intonation than I had before. '*She looks like the real thing.*'

Star looked at me curiously.

'Can I go back on the Internet for a second?' I asked, closing down Word on the Powerbook.

'Sure,' she said. 'I'll make some more coffee.'

The more I thought about the phrase, *she looks like the real thing*, the more I played with it in my head, the more sing-song it became. Maybe it was through over-repetition, but I thought now that maybe it was something more than that. Earlier on, the words had bothered me like a pop song would. Now I wondered if that was because they were from a pop song.

It didn't take me long to realise that identifying a lyric on the Internet was going to be harder than I'd thought. There were many song-lyrics sites out there, but they weren't searchable in the way I wanted. It was a bit like the dictionary problem all over again; you could look up any song by name and artist, but you couldn't type in a lyric and find out which song it came from.

'I don't suppose hackers use lyrics sites, do they?' I asked Star, when she brought in the coffee.

'Sorry?' she said.

I explained to her what I was trying to do.

'Don't think I've got any musical psychos, I'm afraid.'

I laughed. 'Sounds like a party game. Musical psychos.'

She laughed too. 'Mmm. When the music stops you have to kill someone.'

'I can see that catching on,' I said ironically.

I sipped at my coffee and looked back at the screen. I'd ended up on a site with Blur lyrics, which I was scrolling through mindlessly. My favourite song was 'To The End', from the album *Parklife*, and as an experiment, I tried using the browser's Find command to search for a lyric from the song in the page I was currently on. It came straight up.

'This is interesting,' I said to Star.

'What?'

'If this is a pop lyric and I could work out which group sang it, I could probably find it.'

'But isn't the whole point of this to find the group?'

'Not really. I just want to identify which song it is — if indeed it is one — and see what the line means in context, and try to work out who would want to quote it and why.'

'Sounds like a long shot to me, especially if you have to guess the band.'

'No, nothing's that much of a long shot. We've just got to think about the type of lyric it is, and make a shortlist of some bands. Then we can access their lyrics sites and search for the line. Trust me, it'll take about two minutes to rule out each band.'

'Well, I know nothing about current music, really,' she said, 'but if you think it'll work.'

Picking up the pen and paper again, I set about attempting to make a list of bands I could try. It was hard working from the line I had, though. It seemed it could equally have been sung by an ageing rocker as a new trendy indie band. Instead, I tried to think for a minute about what I already knew about the note. It had the word 'Cornelia' in it, which had made it seem as though it could be connected to Alex, somehow, although knowing that hadn't got me very far yet. *Alex*, I thought suddenly. *Alex loves Radiohead*. That's what Laura had said on the way back here that night. *They're her favourite band.*

Without thinking any more, I found a Radiohead site and called up the lyrics for their albums. With a shaking hand, I selected the Find command and typed in the words: *she looks like the real thing*. I clicked enter, and after waiting a couple of seconds, there it was. Finally, I had it.

The line was from 'Fake Plastic Trees'. The song was about being a fake: specifically a girl who was a fake. Like Laura, looking like Alex and stealing her boyfriend. Other interesting lines included the following: 'She lives with a broken man'; 'it wears her out' and 'if I could be who you wanted'. God. Alex must have written this, I was sure of it. And from the words in the song, I guessed she'd written it about Laura and Kurt.

She looks like the real thing, she tastes like the real thing, my fake plastic love.

CHAPTER TWENTY-FIVE

Cracked

———•———

Star went off to make some more coffee while I looked at the sheet of paper in front of me. On one side were the Radiohead lyrics, which, while very illuminating, didn't tell me where to go next. On the other were all the *lipp* words we had found: potentially the solution to the last piece of the puzzle that I wanted to crack. None of them made any sense, though. Most were commonplace words, and I had a feeling that either they weren't right, or even if they were, they wouldn't actually lead me any further. So what if the word was slippery? Where would that lead me?

But I was sure that wasn't it. Or any of the other nouns and adjectives there. The word I kept looking at was the name, Philippa. Had I met anyone called Philippa? I was sure I hadn't. In my head I thought through all the people I'd met or I'd heard referred to recently. Sylvia, Stan, Tony Bryce, Annabel Ravine, Harry Duckling, Cornelia, Tim, Laura, Alex, Kurt and the old woman and the little girl. What were their names? I couldn't remember.

Then like someone taking snapshots in my head, it came to me.

Flash: The little girl standing at the top of the stairs.
Flash: Those eyes.
Flash: The little girl standing at the top of the stairs.

Flash: 'My name's Philippa, but you can call me Pippa. What's your name?'

Of course. Pippa was Philippa. How the hell she figured in this I had no idea, but first thing in the morning I was going to find out. Thank God I'd stolen Tony's book. It hadn't seemed very useful earlier on, but now it was going to lead me precisely where I needed to be. I checked it again to make sure. To Torquay, to the Castle guest house, West Avenue. Wherever that was.

The next morning I was up by nine, showered and out of the door by ten. It had snowed, just as I'd thought it would, and the fields were covered with a soft white frost, like ice cream. Wherever I had to go inland it got worse, so I stuck to the coast roads, noticing how all the little puddles had iced over; strange empty spaces in the fields where no one had walked. It was like some kind of dreamworld, like living in the clouds.

In Torquay everything had already turned to grey slush. People tramped around looking pissed off, shaking the dirty ice from their feet, clapping their hands to keep warm. The wind that blew in from the sea was even icier today and made me catch my breath when I got out of the car to buy some cigarettes from the newsagent. My teeth chattering, I asked him where West Avenue was. He gave me directions and I climbed back in the car, crawling through town slowly, listening to the continual splashing, slicing sound made by cars driving through the slush on the roads.

The guest house in which Pippa and her grandmother were staying was shabbier than the Tulip Hotel and was a good three or four miles from the beach. Next door there was a dirty-looking garden centre with a special offer on potted palm trees. I walked past a line of these on my way to the front entrance of the guest house. They were all yellow, some with completely dead, brown leaves. When the cold wind blew they moved unenthusiastically, their leaves fragile and torn.

The reception area of the guest house was an off-white colour and smelt of piss. It looked like the set for a low-budget soap opera and I didn't want to touch anything in case things started falling over, like cheap chipboard props.

I also didn't want to touch anything because I was afraid of what I might catch.

The man behind the counter smelt of whisky and told me that the little girl and the old woman were in room number two, just down the hall. I'd thought he might call or buzz through for them, but he told me to go on through. Once I'd found room number two I knocked twice and waited. I heard a shuffling sound, then a click as the door was opened. There was the old woman looking at me with frightened eyes.

'Can I come in?' I asked.

CHAPTER TWENTY-SIX

Lucky

———————•———————

'Who are you?' she asked, her voice shaking.

'I'm Lily Pascale. I met you that night at the Tulip Hotel.'

'You look familiar. Are ye from the papers?'

'No.'

'You're nowt to do with that Tony Bryce, are ye?'

'No. Nothing at all.'

'So what do you want?'

'To talk to Pippa.'

'To Pippa?'

'Yes. If that's all right.'

'Hang on and I'll ask her.'

But there was no need. Pippa was suddenly at her grand-mother's side.

'Is that Lily?'

'Yes, Pippa. We've met before, do you remember?'

'Yes. At the other hotel.'

'That's right. I wanted to talk to you about Alex and Laura.'

'Okay,' she said, then, touching her grandmother's leg, 'That's all right, isn't it, Granny?'

'Aye, pet. I don't think this one's as bad as the others.'

'Which others?' I asked, entering the room.

'Tony Bryce, DC Nagy and *her*.'

'Her?'

257

'Laura Carter. Little bitch.'

'What did she want?'

'She hurt me,' said Pippa. 'She grabbed me and shook me, and asked me if I knew about *it*. I didn't know what she meant and I cried until she went away. I hate her.'

'Pippa,' I said, sitting down on a chair by the small dark window, 'do you remember that when I saw you last time a girl came up the stairs? You said it was Laura?'

'It was Laura.'

'Yes, I know that now. But you were so sure. How did you know?'

'Alex was my friend. Laura was always mean to me. *She* was mean to me so I knew it was her.'

'And Tim. What was he like?'

'I quite liked Tim. That policeman kept asking me if I'd heard him in the hotel that night that you were there. Granny told me someone had been murdered and the police wanted to take Tim away.'

'Did you hear him that night?'

The little girl blushed.

'It's all right, pet,' said the old woman. She looked at me. 'The thing is, love, that Pippa did say she had heard him that night. His wheelchair squeaked something dreadful, so you could always hear if he was about, where he was going and everything. She said she heard him just to try and impress them, I think. Maybe she knew he was going to get in trouble. She's got a funny sense of loyalty, this one, haven't ye, pet? She doesn't really understand most of what's going on to be honest. I'm just thankful that we're out of there.'

'Mmm. I can imagine.'

Her voice dropped to a whisper. 'There were some funny goings-on there, if you know what I mean.'

'Like what?'

'I shouldn't really say. But why she wanted to protect Tim I'll never know.'

'Tim and Alex were close, weren't they?' I asked, remembering what Laura had told me about Tim being obsessed with Alex.

'No, pet. It was Tim and Laura who were thick as thieves. Isn't that right, little one?'

'What, Granny?' said Pippa.

'Who was Tim friends with?' I asked her.

'Laura. He was friends with me and Alex too. But he was best friends with Laura.'

'Best friends,' said the old woman, raising her eyebrows.

'Pippa,' I said, 'can I ask you a couple of things?'

'Yes.'

'Does the name Lucky mean anything to you?'

'Lucky was my dog at our old house. He died.'

'Oh, dear. I'm sorry.'

So the note had referred to Pippa and her dead dog. How peculiar. My brain started processing this, but I couldn't come up with any answers. I struggled to think of something to ask next. The note had brought me here, to this girl, and she was obviously important in some way. I just didn't know how. But at least I was learning something from all this. Tim obviously hadn't been the violent ogre Laura had made him out to be: they had been 'best' friends, in fact.

'Would you like to see a picture of Lucky?' asked Pippa, cutting into my thoughts.

'Sure,' I said. 'I'd love to.'

'Oh, that's sweet,' said the old woman. 'No one will look at these with her. That horrible policeman and that journalist refused. Said they didn't have time. But she loves these pictures. Alex used to sit with her looking at them for hours, describing them to her. She really misses her, you know.'

'Mmm. I can imagine.'

Pippa got up and went over to a chest of drawers out of which she drew out a battered-looking photo album. We sat there for about half an hour, while I described the small terrier in great detail. In each of the pictures he was doing something cute, or bashful or naughty. I found myself wishing that Pippa could see the pictures and feeling sadder with every picture that she couldn't.

We were about half-way through the album when the old woman stood up.

'Lily, pet,' she said, 'could you sit with her for ten minutes while I go up the garage for some fags?'

'Sure,' I said.

'Only I don't like leaving her alone at the moment, with all these people about, all after her fer no apparent reason.'

'That's fine,' I said, smiling. 'I'll guard her with my life.'

'Thanks, pet,' she said, and walked out of the thin door.

'Pippa?' I said, once she had gone.

'Yes, Lily?'

'Was Alex your best friend?'

The little girl nodded and snuggled up to me. I put my arm around her and she seemed to wriggle happily beneath my touch, grinning and raising her head so I could see her smile.

'Did Alex tell you any secrets?'

She nodded a slow, sideways nod. A little-girl nod. A coy nod.

'What did she tell you?'

Pippa put a finger to her lips and giggled.

'I can't tell you,' she said. 'I promised.'

'Okay.' I could see what the old woman had meant about her sense of loyalty.

'Unless you are a ...' her face seemed to search for the word ... 'a slister.'

'A slister,' I said noncommittally. 'What if I am one?'

'Then I can show you.'

'Right,' I said, thinking, Show me what?

'Are you a slister?'

When she said the word a second time I realised she meant solicitor.

'Yes,' I said. 'I am a solicitor.'

'Wait here.'

She went over to the second twin bed and picked up a teddy-bear. It was the kind of thing that you kept pyjamas or nightdresses in: it had a little zip which you wouldn't see unless you knew it was there. With her small, fast-moving hands she unzipped it and drew out a white envelope. She brought it over to me.

'Alex said I have to give you this.'

CHAPTER TWENTY-SEVEN

Seaside

Pippa held the envelope out to me and I took it with a shaking hand. I could see that it hadn't been opened. The seal was still fresh. Of course, Pippa would have no reason to open it — she wouldn't be able to read what was inside anyway.

'Does your granny know about this?'

Pippa shook her head. 'Only me and Alex.'

'Can I open it?'

'Yes.'

I eased open the gummy flap slowly, but then Pippa said something else which stopped me dead.

'Seaside,' she said, stressing the middle A in a strange way, making the word wobble and distort as she said it. 'Seaside,' she repeated.

'Sorry?'

'Alex said she was going to commit seaside, and I had to keep this for her.'

'Suicide?' I said, shocked.

'Yes. Seaside.'

'Oh, my God,' I said, and started reading the letter.

This won't come as a surprise to any of you. I'm sorry, but I just couldn't go on any more. I can't take seeing my boyfriend with my sister. So I'm going to do what you both wanted and just go away. I just can't go on any more. I'm sick of life. So, Laura, you can finally take what I had. It's yours. Except for my third of Mum and Dad's estate. I want that to go to Philippa Miller, currently residing at the Tulip Hotel. Pippa, use the money to do something you really want. Get yourself a new puppy. Lucky can't be replaced, but I think it would be good for you. I saw Cornelia and talked to her about your dancing. She will take you on if you go and talk to her.

She looks like the real thing. She tastes like the real thing ... Look in your CD player, Laura. I was playing your song when I did it. Now you can be his fake plastic love for ever. Maybe you'll become real now I've gone. I thought I'd wear your colour and do it in your room. I was here with Kurt earlier on, and I did your voice, your giggle. He told me everything I needed to know.

For all those of you who want to blame yourselves – Kurt, for sleeping with Laura, Tim, for always taking her side, and, of course, Laura, for fucking my life up – go right ahead. I want you to all feel guilty.

Goodbye.

Alex

Looking at the note like this I could see the place where the little scrap I had picked up came from. Philippa, Lucky, Cornelia. She looks like the real thing. That was how they all fitted in. I folded the note and slipped it back in its envelope, still completely shocked by its contents. Pippa sat silently, swinging her legs on the bed. How could she have known what she had here? Her future sorted out, part of a very big mystery solved. No one had killed Alex: she had killed herself.

'Pippa,' I said, 'does anyone else know about this?'

She shook her head.

'This is very important,' I said. 'And you are a very lucky girl.'

'Am I? Is it a present?'

'Yes. A very generous one.'

The door opened and the old woman walked back in. She obviously sensed the atmosphere of surprise and astonishment coming from the room; all generated by me.

'What's gannin' on?' she asked.

'I think you'd better see this,' I said, holding out the note. 'But you'd better sit down first.'

She read it all, eyes widening as she realised the significance of the note, not just what it said but, crucially, what it was.

'So no one killed her?' she said.

'No.'

'And she's left everything to little Pippa?'

'Yes.'

'Oh, my word.'

'Look,' I said. 'We're going to have to be very careful. The only other copy of this note has been destroyed, which makes this the only record of Alex's wishes. And if Laura finds out about it she's going to try to get rid of it.'

'Why would she do that?'

'It's too complicated to go into now, but …' In my head everything started fitting into place, like I was suddenly winning the jackpot on a fruit machine. 'Look, I need to get this copied as soon as possible. Is there a photocopier in the hotel? Or a fax machine? I could fax it to myself at home, you see, and to the university where I work. I need it copied somehow, because if Laura gets hold of this then poor Pippa won't have a hope of getting any of her inheritance.'

'I doubt it, pet. Ye can ask the man at the desk if ye like, but they divn't even have kettles here. It's not very modern.'

As we spoke, Pippa still sat there, swinging her legs. All our grown-up phrases didn't mean anything to her, I was sure. Inheritance, being left everything, the whole idea of last wills and testaments. These things meant about as much to her as the notion of someone committing seaside. But when this was all sorted out we could explain to her that she could get a puppy, and somewhere nice to live, and dance lessons, just like Alex had said. That would mean something to her, for sure. We just had to get out of here and get copies of the note before Laura caught up with us. Perhaps there was no way she could know where I was, what I was doing, but I didn't want to take the chance.

'Would you mind if I took this note to be copied?' I asked.

The old woman paused. 'I do trust ye, pet, but ...'

'You don't want me to go off with the only proof of Pippa's inheritance.'

'Not really, love. How about I come too?'

'But we can't leave Pippa alone, can we?'

'She'll have to come as well, then.'

'Fine.'

We all walked out to the car, Pippa's grandmother steering her in the right direction as we went. I opened the back door for them and the old woman guided the little girl inside. I got in the driver's door and started the engine while the old woman clambered in next to me, breathing hard and heavy as she did so.

'Where are we going, Granny?' asked Pippa.

'Divn't you worry about that, pet. Just a little drive.'

'Is Lily here?'

'Yes, Pippa, I'm driving.'

'Are we in a car?'

'Yes, of course.'

'She's never been in a car before,' said the old woman. 'This'll be new to her.'

'Oh,' I said, surprised. 'I see.'

We pulled up outside some all-hours fax and print shop ten minutes later. I left Pippa and her grandmother in the car while I went inside, my heart beating fast. I handed over the note to the man at the desk and asked him to photocopy it a hundred times. Then I gave him the fax numbers for my home and work, and asked him to fax copies to these places as well. He looked bemused as he did this, the smallest smile coupled with a slight frown. When he was done I asked him to laminate one of the copies. I didn't want to take any chances.

The whole thing cost me over ten pounds. The man tried making conversation as I paid and took all my copies away, but I just smiled and mumbled some kind of non-response. I wanted to get away from there as soon as possible. For some reason I felt paranoid for Pippa. If anyone else was going to be killed, I felt sure it would be her.

Laura had seen the suicide note, and she'd burnt it because she wanted to inherit Alex's money herself. After all, somehow she'd got all the rest. And she had been quite ingenious. I hadn't yet worked out exactly how she'd done it, but somehow she had made a suicide look like murder. More: she'd set up a suicide to look like a murder that had been set up to look like a suicide. And it wasn't very often you heard of that.

But the only threat to her now was Pippa.

Presumably that was what her visit had been about, when she had shaken her and made her cry. Laura had wanted to find out whether the little girl knew about what Alex had done. But Alex had been cleverer. Of course the little girl didn't know: she couldn't read. But it had only been a matter of time before someone found the note. It was a good thing that someone had been me.

Getting in the car, my paranoia swelled up like a helium balloon. I felt magnified, like everyone could see what I was doing and read my thoughts. I looked around to see whether anyone was watching us. In the street people walked around casually, oblivious to what was going on in my head. Men carrying newspapers, women pushing buggies.

But in my mind they were all out to get us: all Laura's spies. I turned the key in the ignition and pulled away, driving at speed up the hill and around the corner

I drove to the Castle guest house as fast as I could. On the way there I learned that the old woman's name was Eva-Mary Miller and that she had been born on 5 July 1910. Which made her eighty-eight. I listened distractedly when she told me that no one knew where Pippa's parents were, that they had been poor and desperate and had left the blind little baby on her grandmother's doorstep only hours after she had been born. She and Pippa had stayed in Northumberland until their health had started to deteriorate, and now Social Services were paying for them to stay in bottom-of-the-range B-and-Bs in Torquay.

They did as I told them and rushed in to the guest house to grab what they really needed of their stuff. Then I drove them to the most expensive hotel in Torquay and paid for them to stay for a week, courtesy of Emma's first five thousand pounds. I needed them out of the way so I could get this whole thing settled, and I certainly didn't want anything to happen to Pippa when the shit hit the fan.

Eva-Mary kept fifty of the photocopies. I told her to hide each one in a different place. I also told her not to go out for a day or so; not to let anyone know where they were staying — not even the police, because I was almost certain Ian was now in Laura's pocket or, more specifically, up her skirt. Once they were settled in I got back in my car and drove home at speed. I wanted to confront Laura, and tell Ian everything I knew, but first I had to make sure of what that actually was.

CHAPTER TWENTY-EIGHT

Beyond *Noir*

When I got in, Star took one look at me and gasped. 'Lily! You're as white as a sheet. Are you okay?'

'Yeah, I'm fine. Just had a bit of a shock.'

'What happened?'

'Take a look at this,' I said, putting the laminated note down on the table in front of her. As she read it I could see her mouth slowly start to form a big disbelieving O. While she read I filled the kettle and put it on to boil, lighting a cigarette and pacing the kitchen.

'Oh, my God,' she said, when she'd finished reading.

'Yeah, exactly.'

'So she wasn't murdered after all?'

'It doesn't look like it.'

'So what happened? How come people thought there had been a murder?'

'Because someone took this note away and replaced it with another note, signed "Laura". Of course that someone has to have been Laura herself, since I saw her burning the original copy of this note.'

'But why?'

'What? Why take the original note away?'

'No, I can see why she wouldn't have wanted Pippa to inherit the money. No, I meant, why would she sign it "Laura"? It doesn't make sense.'

'No. Particularly when she then told the police she was Laura.'

'So why would she do it?'

'Possibly to make it look suspicious. When she told the police *she* was Laura, they had to think it was murder with the wrong victim. And that was what she wanted.'

'Why?'

'I imagine that she wanted to frame Tim for the murder so she wouldn't have to share Alex's money with him.'

'Hmm.'

'Except,' I said, thinking quickly, 'if she'd wanted all Alex's money, why didn't she just forge a note saying that all the money would go to her? That would have been simpler.'

'Yes, it would, wouldn't it?'

'Mmm. Also, if Alex committed suicide, why has Tim now confessed to her murder?'

Star looked serious but confused. The answer to all this wasn't as clear as I might have hoped. All of a sudden I wished Jack was here and we could do some role-play. I made coffee and sat down at the table, looking at the note.

'We are going to have to go through this logically,' I said.

Star nodded. 'Uh-huh.'

'So Laura must have discovered the body,' I said. 'We know that for sure.'

'Do we?'

'Yes, because she took the note away.'

'Could she and Tim have discovered the body together?'

'No. Or he wouldn't have thought the dead girl was Laura.'

'Okay.'

'Although, when I saw him, he said they did discover it together.'

'Which means?'

'Well, it means that Laura must have taken away the original note and planted a new one. Then she must have staged it so that she and Tim walked in there together and as far as he was concerned, there was Laura, having killed herself.'

'So there were definitely two notes.'

'No.' I shook my head. 'There must have been three.'

'Three? I don't get it.'

'Okay. The first note got destroyed by Laura. The second note was then planted by her. But the third note was in Tim's handwriting, so it must have been written by him. Also, I guess Laura's plan to frame him must have involved planting hard evidence on the scene – his fingerprints on the knife, the note in his handwriting and so on.'

'So ...'

'So she must have got him to replace the note himself, somehow.'

'How would she do that?'

'I'm not sure. She can't have let him in on anything.'

'No?'

'No. Because she'd already fooled him into thinking the dead girl was herself. So she must have wanted to con him somehow.'

'So making him forge the note was all part of her plan?'

'It would seem so. Unless he did it of his own accord, but I find that difficult to believe.'

'So why would she want him to write the new note?'

'As extra proof that he murdered Alex, I would guess. And so she wouldn't have to leave a note that she had written.'

'So how would she get him to do it?'

'I suppose, if I was Laura, I would have wanted him to come up with the idea almost by himself. And to get him to do that, she must have given him a pretty good reason for wanting to replace the note. For example, what if the note she wrote included details Tim didn't want made public? Probably she told him it would be a good idea for him to write a new one, not to get himself into trouble or anything, but just to keep his secrets out of the papers or whatever. She probably told him it would be their secret, that only they would know, or something.'

'I'm with you so far.'

'But of course she held on to what he thought was the "original"; note. And because she knew that he'd tampered with the scene of a "crime", and also whatever she'd put in the first forged note, she would have had plenty on him by that stage. Real blackmail material. Okay, now assuming she seriously wanted him out of the way, what would she do next?'

'Get him into even more trouble?'

'Exactly. She had to provide him with a reason to murder someone else, to make absolutely sure he went to prison, and to make it seem more likely that he murdered Alex. And, of course, she was already in a position where she was calling the shots. I bet she told him to murder Kurt. No wonder she went to the police and told them she'd been raped, and then made a point of telling us all that Alex was Tim's favourite sister. What a motive he would have had for killing Kurt, if any of that had been true. The interesting thing is, she admitted to me that she'd made up the rape story, but she made up such a good reason for doing so I almost believed her. But all along she was actually setting up Tim's motive. I saw her messing up her clothes on the way up to the hotel that night, and I heard her screaming and crying. That must all have been put on for the benefit of the guests, so that we could confirm how distraught she was. She must have arranged to meet Kurt at the end of the pier and then told Tim where to find him. Then she came up to the first floor just after the door slammed so we'd all know that it was Tim who had gone out. The only problem was that for a while, for whatever reason, Pippa provided him with an alibi.'

'Laura is very clever,' said Star, her face wrinkled with concentration. '*Did* Tim murder Kurt?'

'Undoubtedly. He beat him to death with a part of his wheelchair, as you know. That has to be true, because there is so much evidence, and he pretty much admitted to it straight away anyway. I bet Laura said she'd clean up the wheelchair for him, provide him with an alibi and all sorts. Then she just let him fall into her trap. Unfortunately, though, the way this is all shaping up means that Laura hasn't killed anyone, or really done anything illegal that anyone can prove – except possibly burning the original note, but now we have no proof of that.'

'And she did all this for money?'

'That's my guess. You know she had her solicitor here? I can see now what she must have been doing. She must have made Tim sign all his money over to her somehow – probably she blackmailed him – and, of course, Alex's share of the inheritance would just have been split between Tim and Laura after she died, which meant Laura would have ended up with it all. You know she's already bought Sylvia out? I bet she's going to sell up the whole lot for a massive profit and go to the States, just like she said. And the amazing thing is she did it all without killing anyone herself, or even committing any fraud – except for the second suicide note, which only Tim would have seen and which she would have denied ever existed. She left absolutely no trail to herself.'

'So why hasn't Tim told anyone about all of this? What's he got to lose?'

'That's what I need to find out.'

Star looked at me hard. 'Are you sure this makes sense, Lily?'

'I think so.'

'Let's go through it again.'

So we did, at least three times, and each time it came out the same way. After setting Tim up for the murder of her sister, Laura had manipulated him into actually murdering someone else because it was convenient for her if he was out of the picture, and because once he'd murdered someone, she had something to blackmail him with. It was convenient for this victim to be Kurt, since he might have hung around

273

causing trouble otherwise. Logically, working from the point at which Laura destroyed the suicide note, it had to have happened the way we'd worked out. She must have planted a second note, leading Tim to believe *Laura* was dead, with something in it that he didn't want seen. He must have written the third note to protect himself and from then on in he was trapped in a nightmare of Laura's making, with no way out, just getting deeper and deeper into trouble.

Remembering what Laura had told me when she was here I started to realise just how intricately she'd plotted this out. Her version actually made as much sense as mine did, and if Alex hadn't had the sense to have left a copy of her note with her only beneficiary, there would have been no way of seeing through it. Now all I had to do was talk to Tim, to verify this and to find out how Laura had managed to hook him so horrifically.

I looked at my watch. It was coming up for six o clock. I went and picked up the phone.

CHAPTER TWENTY-NINE

The Last Seduction

———————◆———————

Ian picked up the phone after two rings.

'Meet me at Sophie's coffee shop,' I said briskly.

'Lily?' His voice was uncertain. I hadn't said who I was.

'You'd better do what I say, Ian.'

'What's the matter with you? You sound ... a bit mad.'

'Did you enjoy it?'

'What?'

'Fucking Laura?'

'What's wrong with you?'

'I have the pictures.'

'What the hell are you playing at?' His voice sounded guilty.

'You know one of my best friends works for the *News of the World*?'

'The paper has the pictures?'

'Not yet. Meet me in an hour.'

'Fine.'

Star was giggling, her hand covering her mouth.

'You sounded so convincing!'

'I did, didn't I?' I said, smiling. 'Looks like I'm learning from our little friend.'

'To turn someone into a puppet all you have to do is give them strings.'

'Exactly.'

'That stuff about the *News of the World*. Are you really going to get Sarah into this?'

'I can't, she's on holiday. But I'll give her the whole story when she gets back.'

'So you were just trying to frighten him?'

'Oh, yes.' I paused and rubbed my eyes. 'I just can't believe it's actually all true.'

'What? That Laura and Ian have been …?'

'Yeah.'

'Well, if you were a man how long do you think you could go without cracking?'

'Not long, I suppose, if Laura really wanted to crack me.'

'So you've got Ian where you want him, what are you going to do next?'

'Confront him with the note, then get him to let me see Tim.'

'Couldn't you just go to Emma with what you've got now?'

'No. It's not properly resolved, and I'm still hoping I can find something to put Laura away now I know about everything she's done.'

'Are you going to see Ian, then?'

'Yep. And make sure you lock the door behind me. We don't want a repeat of last time.'

Star grinned. 'That was quite interesting, actually.'

'Star!'

'Okay. I'll lock it.'

I pulled on my coat and grabbed my bag.

'See you soon,' I said.

'Be careful,' said Star, with a twinkle in her eye.

It was completely dark as I drove down the lane and on to the small road to Torquay. The light from my headlamps glistened on fresh snow, and there were no stars in the sky. The moon was a tiny crescent tonight, providing no light. It looked as though I was driving through nothing, on my way to nowhere. Everything was swallowed in the snow and the night. White disappeared into white; black into black. The only thing that showed up was a small black sheep, standing bleating in the snow.

I wondered what Ian was thinking. He was probably thinking I was in control, which was what I wanted. What I really wanted was to show him the note, but I certainly didn't want Laura to know I had it until I was ready. As in poker, the showing of your hand had to be done right; timed to perfection. And I wanted Ian to know that I *knew* about how unprofessional and stupid he was being. He shouldn't have let himself be used and manipulated by Laura. She cut through all these people like a knife through butter, taking what she wanted and moving on. Why couldn't Ian see it? Why couldn't Tony see it? Jack had seen it but, then, he was special.

Sophie's was empty and looked like it was near to closing time. Ian was there already when I arrived. He was drinking a cup of coffee and smoking. His hair was a mess; his face unshaven. He looked as if he'd been on a three-day binge. Maybe he had. Maybe Laura really had been making it worth his while.

'What the fuck are you playing at, Lily?' he said, as I slipped into the booth and sat facing him. 'I thought we were friends.'

I smiled. 'Maybe you've got a better friend now.'

'Maybe I have. Look, why are you trying to blackmail me?'

'I'm not,' I said.

'Then what the hell ...?'

I pulled one of the copies of the note out of my pocket and placed it in front of him. As he read it his face seemed to swell with surprise and disbelief. His reaction was more intense than Star's had been because it was his fuck-up lying there on the table: he was the one who'd been investigating a murder that turned out to be suicide.

'What is this?' he hissed, his eyes narrowed. 'Where did you get it?'

'Alex left a copy of this with Pippa.'

'And who exactly is Pippa?'

'The little girl. The one you didn't think would make a credible witness.'

'Oh, shit.' Ian was shaking, his hand vibrating over the top of the note. He picked it up roughly and stood up. Grabbing my arm he pulled me to my feet.

'Come with me,' he growled. 'We're going to sort this out once and for all.'

'Ow!' I said, trying and failing to wriggle away. 'What are you doing?'

'We're going to go and ask Laura what she thinks of this.'

'Fine,' I said, defiantly. 'I can't wait to see her face.'

He eased his grip on me and I pulled my arm away, rubbing it. He obviously wasn't in the mood for messing around. I had rarely seen anyone so pissed off. Anger steamed off him all the way to his car. He drove too fast out of Torquay to his small terraced house in Marychurch, with me following behind in the Saab. When we got there, he skidded to a halt outside and virtually threw himself out of the car, shaking with rage. He could hardly get his key in the lock, he was trembling that much.

'Laura!' he called, as soon as we walked in.

She emerged dressed in a baby-doll nightdress made of what looked like white satin done up loosely with little white bows. Her gait was deeply seductive until she saw me and her body tensed. She scowled and looked from Ian to me and then back again. 'What's she doing here?' she asked.

'Never mind that,' said Ian. 'I think you've got some explaining to do.'

'Whatever she's told you she's lying,' said Laura, looking daggers at me.

Ian paced the small sitting room while I sat down on the edge of the sofa. Laura sank into one of the armchairs, pretending to look relaxed, her white knickers showing through her small flimsy nightdress. The note was still in Ian's hand; almost completely screwed up by now.

'What's that?' asked Laura, finally noticing it.

Ian dropped it in her lap. I watched with interest, to see what she would do. To her credit she remained cool and there was no sign from her face that she was feeling anything at all. She looked like anyone else who'd just been given something to look at. No one would think from watching her that she'd ever seen it before. She showed no sign of surprise or recognition; she just arranged her small features into an air of concentration and let her black eyes scan the page two or three times before looking up at us.

'Is this another forgery?' she asked, her brow wrinkled.

'Come on, Laura,' said Ian, still pacing. 'We know you've seen this before.'

'How could I? Anyway, if I'd seen it then everything would have been different, if it was real. I wouldn't have thought that someone was trying to murder me, for one thing. *Is* it real, do you think?'

'Drop the act, Laura,' I said.

'Fuck off,' she replied. 'Ian,' she said sweetly, 'where did you get this?'

'Never mind that,' he said. 'I think you're going to have to come and make statements.' He looked at me. 'Both of you.'

'I'll go and get changed,' said Laura, and taking the note with her, she flounced out of the room. When she returned Ian and I were sitting there in the silence she'd left us in. I didn't have anything to say to him, and what could he tell me?

She had obviously dressed with innocence in mind. Her

279

hair was tied back in a low ponytail, and she was wearing a long, loose white dress and no makeup.

'Where's the note?' asked Ian.

'Note? Oh, shit. What did I do with it?' She started patting her body and looking around everywhere. 'Maybe I left it upstairs ...'

I'd anticipated this, of course. I wondered where she had hidden it.

'Don't worry, Laura, I have lots of copies.'

She and Ian watched as I pulled a handful of them out of my bag.

'Oh good,' she said, trying really hard to smile.

I drove behind them on the way to the police station. There had been some kind of argument after I had revealed all the extra copies of the note. Laura had dragged Ian into the kitchen and for about five minutes I heard plenty of whining and sobbing noises. Presumably she was trying to get him on her side again, but to his credit and judging from the shouting I heard, he hadn't gone for it.

Inside the police station Ian told me to sit and wait in the entrance area. He took Laura through the thick door and off down the corridor. It was cold and lonely in the waiting area. I wondered what would happen next.

Nothing did for quite some time. I drifted in and out of the front doors, smoking, thinking. Were they charging Laura with something in there? But with what, though? She hadn't killed anyone. All she had done was to get rid of a suicide note, and she was probably in there right now telling Ian that she'd never seen it before, and acting shocked that the 'murder' had turned out to be suicide, after all. And whatever she said, it wouldn't matter: it wasn't as if they had any evidence since she'd stolen the burnt scrap I'd had.

She would say that it had been Tim going after all the

money, and that it was just fate that she'd ended up in possession of it. Maybe in a parallel universe I would give some thought to the proposition that Tim had been involved in the plan all along: a willing partner. But there was only one problem with all that: he believed that Laura was dead. He had even spoken to her at the graveyard when he thought no one else was listening. He couldn't have seen the suicide note. And if he hadn't seen it, and Laura had removed it deliberately, then it had to have happened the way Star and I had worked out. It was just a shame we didn't have the scrap of paper any more.

The only thing I wasn't sure about was why he hadn't told the police exactly how it had happened. Had there, as I'd thought, actually been three notes? And what could the second one possibly have said? Laura had something on him, but I didn't know what that could be.

Eventually Ian came back and led me through to a small interview room.

'Will I be able to see Tim?' I asked.

'Maybe afterwards. I'll have to have a word with the custody sergeant.'

'I have to see him, Ian.'

'Yeah, like I said, I'll try my best.'

'I think you should. Remember I've got pic—'

'Yes. All right,' he hissed.

I gave my statement to Ian and a chief inspector who sat in on the interview. I told them how I'd seen Laura burning the original note, and what I'd worked out from there. I told them about how she had tricked everybody; the nasty things she'd done when she'd stayed with me. But as I spoke I realised how clever she really had been. There was nothing here; nothing at all. It could all be explained, or there wasn't any evidence, and the stuff that couldn't be explained – like trying to steal my boyfriend – just wasn't a crime

'You do know she's behind all this, don't you?' I said, when Ian had read the statement back to me.

He shrugged. 'Where's the proof?'

I looked at the chief inspector. 'I think Tim knows.'

'Knows what?' he said sharply.

'I think he knows how this all fits together.'

'He still thinks she's Alex, though,' said Ian. 'He's lost it completely.'

'But he'd know what the note she wrote said,' I pointed out. 'The second one.'

'If there was, as you say, a second one,' said the chief inspector.

'And how would that help us anyway?' asked Ian. 'It's all over. One death was suicide, the other was murder. Tim committed the murder, he's admitted it. End of story. So he did it for a woman. It's the oldest motive in the world. Doesn't mean the woman's guilty. She didn't ask him to protect her.'

He looked at the chief inspector for confirmation of what he was saying, and the older man nodded.

'But I think she did,' I said emphatically.

'Did she specifically ask him to go and bash Kurt's brains in with his footrest? I can't see it. And even if she did, we can't prove it. Incitement isn't going to work here, because there's just no evidence. And I doubt Tim's going to back any of this up since he's said nothing so far. You say you heard her screaming and crying in the hotel that night, but she would be like that if she'd just been raped.'

'But she wasn't raped.'

'You say. But I doubt she'd admit that to us if we asked her. And, as you know, there was plenty of evidence at the time, and Kurt's not around any more to defend himself. I can see exactly how it happened. Tim, the over-protective brother, went out to avenge what had happened to his sister. I probably would have done the same if it had been my sister. Maybe she told him to do it, but who'd know? She could say she begged him not to, and no one could disagree with her. She could say she was tucked up in bed and never even knew he went out.'

'What if Tim said she told him to do it?'

'But he hasn't said that.'

'Well, try asking him again!'

The chief inspector looked from Ian to me.

'Well, come on,' he said. 'It's worth a try, isn't it?'

'But why?' said Ian. 'It's not going to prove he's innocent.'

'But it might prove something about the girl,' said the chief inspector. 'Come on Ian, we can't be seen to be cutting corners here. If the girl was an accomplice of some sort then let's put her away if we can. Christ, it sounds like she deserves it.'

'Maybe it's worth a try,' Ian said, looking at the floor.

'I don't want to interfere,' I began.

The chief inspector smiled. 'Go on,' he said.

'Well, perhaps I could have a word with Tim. I've met him before, you know, and we got on well. I could pretend to be a visitor and maybe he'd let something slip.'

'I've tried to tell her,' said Ian. 'The custody sergeant's not going to go for that.'

'We'll see,' said the chief inspector, and gestured for me to follow him out of the room.

CHAPTER THIRTY

Confession Box

Tim was sitting in his small cell facing the wall.

I noticed that his wheelchair looked different, even older, even shabbier than the original one, which had probably been submitted as evidence. Even though I knew that this was a man who had taken another man's life, I somehow still felt sorry for him.

'I'll be just here,' said the chief inspector, standing outside. 'And I have to remind you that this is very irregular. You step out of line one little bit and you could have his solicitor throw the case out. So just ask what you've got to ask and then leave. No giving him anything, no physical contact or anything at all.'

'Can I show him the note?'

The chief inspector frowned. 'I don't think that would be a very good idea. Can you do without?'

'Yeah. I suppose so.'

He unlocked the door and I stepped carefully into the cell, immediately gagging on the heat and the smell: body odour, urine and stale smoke. Tim's posture was guilty and weak; he looked like he just wanted to disappear into his wheelchair. His hands gripped the armrests hard; all white and drained of blood. He didn't turn to face me, he just sat, unmoving, still staring at the wall.

'Tim?' I said, tentatively. He didn't move. 'Tim it's me, from the cemetery.'

He turned slowly. 'How did you know I was ...?'

'Because I lied to you at the cemetery. I was investigating this all along.'

'Are you a detective?'

'No. I'm working for someone. You don't know her.'

'I'm not going to say anything, you know. Never.'

'Because you're scared of what Laura might say if you do?'

He blushed. 'Laura's dead.'

'Do you really believe that?'

'Yes. I found her there.'

'That was Alex, Tim.'

'No.'

'Yes. We have proof. It was definitely Alex.'

'But Laura wouldn't—'

'Wouldn't what? Blackmail you?'

He shivered. 'I'm not saying anything.'

'Well, just listen, then. Look, we found the original suicide note, from Alex. It said that she was leaving her share of your parents' estate to the little girl, Pippa. Laura saw the note and removed it. Then she wrote a new one. When you discovered the body together you were really walking into a set-up. She made you touch the knife, didn't she? Then you wrote the new note. Why did you do that, Tim?'

He didn't answer.

'Was it your idea? Or was it hers? I don't know why you're protecting her. After all, she set you up for a murder that wasn't even a murder. But that wasn't enough. She wanted to make sure you went away for good. Remember at the graveyard you told me that you wanted to sell up but she opposed it? Well, she's selling up now. She just wanted to stall you. From what I can make out she's bought Sylvia out and is planning to sell both hotels for a massive profit. She's going to America, she says.'

'It's not true.'

'Come on, Tim. What's she got on you?'

'Nothing. I did it all. It was all my idea.'

'Did she tell you to say that?'

'No!'

The small flap on the door of the cell opened and the chief inspector peered in. 'Everything okay?' he asked.

'Yes,' I said.

'You've got five more minutes, okay?'

'Fine.' I turned back to Tim. 'Come on, Tim, this isn't getting us anywhere.'

'I didn't ask you to come here.'

'Why did Stan kill himself, Tim?'

'He killed himself?'

'Yep. Right after Laura went to visit him.'

'Are you sure it *is* Laura?'

'Yes.'

'She said she was Alex.'

'Yeah.'

'And the note said "Laura".'

'She wrote it.'

'Oh, fuck.' He put his head in his hands. 'That's how she knew.'

'Knew what, Tim?'

'Nothing.'

'Tim?'

He put his head in his hands. 'Shit. Stan really killed himself?'

'Yeah. Like I said.'

'Oh, God. She's gone too far now.'

'So talk, then, before I get thrown out of here.'

'Okay. Look, I don't know what she did to him, but there was something going on. I remember when he was arrested, he winked at her. It was bizarre, because we were all in a state about our parents. I thought he was maybe just being spiteful at the time, but why would he? After all, he was doing it for the money, not out of hate, or anything. It was like they were in it together, or something.'

'What do you think she did to him?'

'I'm not sure. But I've been thinking about it, and I reckon she fitted him up.'

'Just like she did to you?'

'No comment.'

'What has she got on you? It can't be that bad.'

'I said no comment.'

I thought about what Eva-Mary had said. *Best* friends. 'Did you sleep with her?'

Silence. But he started to flush.

'You did, didn't you?'

Tim nodded and put his head in his hands. 'My own sister.'

'Laura?'

'Yes. That's what the note was all about. It said she'd killed herself because she couldn't go on having a relationship with me. It was all about how she'd had a pregnancy scare and she couldn't face the thought of some kind of incestuous child being born. It was awful. That's why I wrote the other note. To protect my fiancée, Christine, from the truth.'

'But I don't understand.'

'There's not much to understand. Incest? It's a crime you know.'

'But she isn't your real sister, though.'

The expression on his face changed dramatically. He looked like he was about to throw up.

'Oh, God,' I said slowly, drawing my breath out behind the words. 'You never knew.'

'Not my real sister?' he said in a stammer.

'They were adopted. Don't tell me your parents never told you?'

He shook his head.

'And you thought you were sleeping with your sister? God.'

'I was nine when they were born,' he said, developing a faraway look. 'I'd been to stay with my gran up in Manchester for the whole summer holidays, and when I got back Mum said she had a surprise for me, and there they were, these matching babies.' He banged his fists on the armrests of the wheelchair. 'Christ. It's so fucking obvious. You must think I'm so stupid.'

'No, I don't.'

'So all this was for nothing?'

'I'm so sorry.

'Alex – well, I suppose it was Laura – said she'd clean the wheelchair and give me an alibi for Kurt's murder. That's why I couldn't understand it when I got charged. Of course, I deserved it – I did kill him, after all. But I thought I could protect her. After all, I'd let my other sister down so badly she'd killed herself. I wasn't thinking straight. She said it would be okay. But it isn't.'

'Time's up, Lily,' came the chief inspector's voice from beyond the small hatch.

'She raped me, Lily,' Tim said urgently.

'She what?'

'Alex. Or should I say, Laura. After the suicide and everything. She trapped me in a corner and I can't say what she did. She made me call her a bitch, and pretended to be Laura. Although I suppose she was Laura all along. Later I found out that she'd taped it. That's when she took the money.'

'What money?'

'All of it. My inheritance. She made me sign something she'd written to say that I was passing all the money and all the decisions over to her. She said if I signed then she wouldn't tell anyone about the note I wrote, and that she wouldn't show anyone the tape or say anything about Kurt. That was when I realised that I couldn't escape. I did everything she said.'

The door opened and the chief inspector walked in.

289

'Okay?' he said.

I nodded, and touched Tim's arm. 'I wish I could say everything will be all right.'

'It's all my own stupid fault,' he said.

'Tell your solicitor everything.'

He shook his head. 'I can't. Christine would never forgive me.'

'I suppose not.'

'And don't you say anything either.'

'No.'

'What was all that about?' asked the chief inspector; once we were out of earshot. 'Nothing,' I said quietly.

'So you didn't get anything from him?'

'No.'

I left the building and walked slowly to my car, shivery and cold. There was no way I could tell the police what Tim had said. Laura had him over a barrel. If there had just been the suicide, then he might have had a hope but, like he'd said, he had murdered someone, and taking Laura down wasn't going to help him. At least with the way things stood he still had Christine to visit him in prison. But who was I kidding? No one was taking Laura down anywhere, even if they wanted to. She was just too damn clever.

If only there was one thing, something that would prove she was guilty. Because she was so guilty. Of course she'd stitched Stan up. I could see her making a pact with him, telling him she'd give him an alibi if he killed her parents. He wanted their hotel. Perhaps Laura had told him she'd sell to him if he helped her out. But her motive all along had been the money. She had eliminated her entire family for one end: *money*. Of course, by rights Alex had eliminated herself, but Laura had created all the reasons for her to commit suicide. She'd slept with her boyfriend, arranged for her parents to be killed and more or less fucked up everything she had. She was even a better dancer, the black swan spinning around so fast no one could keep up.

Once Laura had set up Stan as the fall guy for her parents' murders, and Alex had helpfully killed herself, all she'd had to do was engineer a way of getting hold of all their money and property. And for that she had to remove Tim. There was no one left to take the rap for killing him, so instead she'd blackmailed him for his money, then set him up as a murderer to make sure he was out of the picture. But then she had spun again, buying out Sylvia and taking the hotel profits herself. Now I knew what she must have told Stan. She'd told him the truth: that he was never getting her hotel and that she would not be providing him with any kind of alibi. Poor, stupid Stan had actually thought she would sell to him so he could make a bigger profit. As I thought through all this all I could see was an image of her on that rock. Her *fouettés* were like her plans: too quick, too many and just too good.

CHAPTER THIRTY-ONE

Answers

When I got in Star was asleep. I didn't want to wake her to tell her the bad news. Instead I sat up by myself, drinking the last of the Scotch and watching for Laura. The police had a copy of the note now so she would have nothing to gain from coming here to try to remove it once and for all, especially since she already had the important bit: the original. But I thought she might come out of spite. But what would she gain from that? She'd got away with it all, and I doubted that she would risk messing it all up now. So she would have to give some of her money to Pippa? Big deal. She still had the profit from the hotel sale and two-thirds of everything else.

But still I sat and watched and waited, at the kitchen table. In the silence I thought through everything: not just Laura but my job and Jack. It seemed that there had been no satisfactory resolution to anything. It had been a dark week, I concluded. A dark week with no dawn.

At about five I went to sit on the beach. The sun came up uncertainly, the sky looking as though it might turn back to night at any moment and just not bother with the day. A single seagull screamed over the cliffs and small waves broke rhythmically on the sand. I felt a strange kind of loss knowing there would be no more investigative strolls down Torquay pier with or without Jack; no more riddles. Was I getting too used to doing this? It was all very confusing.

It was almost six. The university would probably be open again today and I would be expected in. But I would be phoning David to tell him I had flu. I had to see Emma and after that I had a lot of thinking to do. It was time I made a choice: I should either apply for the senior lecturer position or get the hell out of that place.

By the time I went back inside Star was up.

'Lily?' she said tentatively, when I walked into the kitchen.

'It's all over,' I said wearily, sitting down.

'What? They've arrested Laura?'

'Nope.'

'Then how can it all be over?'

I explained to her everything that had happened at Ian's and at the police station. I also told her what I'd worked out about Stan. There was no way it could be proven, of course, but I was sure that was what had happened.

'It's so bizarre,' she said, when I'd finished. 'How could she have plotted it all so intricately?'

'She obviously got that from her mother,' I said wryly, thinking of Emma Winter and her famous twists in the tale.

'Is there no way of proving anything?'

'No. I'm going to see Emma once I've dropped you off at the station.'

'Well, good luck,' said Star.

'Thanks. I don't know what her reaction will be.'

'No.'

Star busied herself showering and getting ready. I splashed my face with cold water and touched up the makeup I still had on from yesterday. I changed my clothes while Star packed her things. I needed waking up: sleep was just starting to try to make a play for me.

*

Emma looked brighter when she answered the door today. 'Lily,' she said. 'Have we got things all wrapped up?'

'Yeah.'

'Well, sound a bit happier about it.'

'It's not very happy news, I'm afraid.'

'You'd better come in.'

She offered me gin again but the thought made me feel a bit sick so I asked for black coffee instead. We sat in her sitting room on the sofa, with the two dogs at our feet and sunlight streaming in through the large window.

'Alex is dead,' I said.

Emma frowned. 'Are you sure?'

'Yep. But Laura didn't kill her.'

'Who did?'

'No one. It was suicide.' I took a piece of paper out of my bag and handed it to her. 'Here's a copy of the suicide note. Laura removed the original and burnt it, because she didn't want Pippa to inherit Alex's money. Then she set Tim up so she would have something on him and made him play fall-guy for her. He murdered Kurt and will almost certainly go to prison for that. Laura was sleeping with him and apparently taped them doing it as part of her whole blackmail routine.'

'Inventive.'

'Yeah. All the more so because he thought he was sleeping with his real sister.'

'The parents never told him the twins were adopted?'

'No. I guess they wanted him to accept them.'

'Oh dear.'

'Mmm.'

Suddenly my insides went sour and I felt sick. 'Can I use your loo?' I asked.

'Sure. Upstairs first right.'

'Thanks.'

The stairs creaked under my feet as I walked to the top. Being on my feet made me feel a bit better and the sour feeling had almost gone by the time I reached the upstairs hallway. The bathroom door was the first on the right, as Emma had said, but I found myself drawn by the smallest noise further down the corridor to where a door stood ajar. This is what I could hear: 'We will go to Mummy's house, Odette, and stay there for ever. Would you like that? Shh. There's someone coming, we'll have to get out of here quick. Who do you think it is? Is it Tony or Lily? Perhaps it's Tim, the evil sorcerer. He is evil, Odette, and I took care of him for us. He won't bother us any more.'

Approaching the door slowly, I strained to hear as the small female voice dropped to a whisper. Surely it couldn't be her? But when I peeked inside the room, there was Laura, dressed in a black tutu, sitting cross-legged on the floor, playing with a small doll. This doll was whom she was referring to as Odette. She didn't appear to see me, just kept playing with the doll, seeming infantilised and awkward, the doll bobbing jerkily in an arc in front of her as she moved it around.

The room was obviously intended for a child: specifically, two children; two girls. Identical bunk beds stood by the far wall, both covered in pink duvets with little white ballerinas all over them. There were toys scattered all over the floor. A small gingham rag-doll, a headless Sindy doll and a faded teddy bear lying there as if they had just been flung out of a toybox. My eye didn't catch the jack-in-the-box until it erupted, sinister and sudden, to greet me with a 'ha ha ha ha.' The disembodied head danced maniacally on the bare silver spring and I gulped and jumped backwards.

Then Laura turned and stared at me with her black eyes. She was totally expressionless, the way a ghost or a dead person might look. There was no flicker of recognition; nothing. It looked as though she had gone quite mad. Did she remember me at all? Wanting to escape from that dead glare I turned and walked back downstairs, forgetting all about going to the loo.

Emma was sitting on the sofa, still, flicking through a pile of handwritten papers.

'Did you find it okay?' she said.

'Um, yes ... Emma, what's going on?'

'Sorry?'

'Laura's up there. What's the story?'

'She's staying here while she gets her head together.'

'What do you mean?'

'Did you see her?'

'Yes. She seemed ...'

'Completely mad? She is. I think all this has just sent her spinning.'

'You mean she's actually insane?'

'Yes. I've spoken to my psychiatrist. From what I've told him he thinks it's some form of schizophrenia. He's coming to see her tomorrow.'

'She seemed to think she was speaking to someone called Odette. Isn't that a character from *Swan Lake*?'

'Yes. It's the White Swan. From what I can gather, she thinks she has actually become Odile, the Black Swan.'

'Weird.'

'Yes. It's because she's lost her twin, I think. She seems to talk as if there is someone else with her all the time. It's all *we* this and *we* that. I think being on her own after being part of a pair for so long ... This hasn't been easy for her.'

'But all the things she did ...'

'All part of the descent into madness. And, like you say, she's innocent, really. When she destroyed the note, it was because she thought it had been planted by the evil sorcerer. But we'll get her better and sorted out.'

'But if you knew all this, why didn't you say something earlier on?'

'I wanted all the facts and you've given them to me.' She

reached for her chequebook and tore off a cheque she'd already filled out. 'Here's the rest of what I owe you.'

'Thanks,' I said, taking it.

'Do you want to see something interesting?'

'Sure.'

'Well, since Laura has been here, she's been rambling. Apparently schizophrenics do that. As you saw, it's as if she's having a conversation with someone all the time.'

'Odette.'

'Yes, or whoever. Anyway, last night I started transcribing everything, and it all makes a remarkable amount of sense. It tells how all the events of the past two weeks have happened, from her point of view.'

'Can I see?'

'Of course,' said Emma, handing me the stack of papers she'd been holding before.

I read out loud from the top sheet.

'The room is at the end of the corridor; small and dark. At night there are tangerine shadows, cast by the single street-lamp outside. It's dark in there now. Do you want to come in? If you come with me I can show you what's in there. It's white. That was her colour. It's white. The wardrobe, the curtains and the walls. The carpet is white too. But wait. Here, next to the bed we can see that the carpet is red. And there, on the other side. Red.'

Emma looked at me expectantly.

'Did she say all this?' I asked.

'More or less. She said orange. I put tangerine. I've made minor changes.'

'What for?'

'The book. When I told you I was writing a novel about the twins I wasn't lying.'

'But doesn't it bother you?'

'What?'

'Everything that's happened. Five people are dead

298

and one is in prison as a direct result of what Laura's done.'

'They all made their own choices, Lily. Stan decided to try and kill his neighbours and later decided to kill himself. Mr Carter didn't have to drink until he was too over the limit to realise that his brakes were failing. If he'd been sober he and his wife might still be here. Alex chose to kill herself, and Kurt – well, he chose to go and stand at the end of a dark, deserted pier in the middle of the night.'

'I don't see that any of them deserved to die.'

'Not *deserved*, no. But Laura isn't wholly to blame. If all these people hadn't let themselves be manipulated by her ... She's just a kid, after all.'

'Do you really believe that?'

She shrugged. 'I have to. She's my daughter.'

CHAPTER THIRTY-TWO

Fouetté 32

———◆———

Back at home I slept for the rest of the morning then got up in the afternoon to go and bank Emma's second cheque. On the way back I checked in to see how Pippa and Eva-Mary Miller were doing, but they were out. At least they would have nothing to worry about now.

Back at work the next day it was still freezing cold, but legally so, which meant there was no chance of being sent home again. Just after lunch a package appeared in my pigeon-hole. It was from David: the application form for the senior lecturer position and a note asking me to attend Fenn Baker's leaving party. My phone extension rang just after I'd taken in the note. It was David.

'So,' he said. 'Looks like you won't have much competition, then?'

'I didn't know Fenn was leaving.'

'No, neither did I until last week. He's off to Canada.'

'Canada?'

'Yep. So it looks like it's just going to be a one-horse race.'

'If I apply.'

'You will.'

Back at home I felt restless. The house felt empty. No Jack, no Star. Even Laura would have livened the place up a bit. Had

301

she gone mad? Emma had given me photocopies of the material she'd transcribed and I'd read through them last night. What had struck me about all the material was that Laura still came over as innocent: her ramblings didn't include taking responsibility for anything that had happened. And they weren't even ramblings, really. It could have been her statement to the police, told in a more enigmatic style.

But what did I know?

It was almost ten when the phone rang. It was Jack.

'Lily,' he said uncertainly.

'Jack?'

'I'm on my way back.'

'From?'

He laughed nervously. 'The edge. Well, Totnes, actually. Can I come over?'

'So we can play more of this game?'

'What game?'

'This get-close-then-run-away thing you seem so fond of.'

'Please. I have to explain.'

'Explain what?'

'All that stuff you read in my journal.'

'I'm really sorry about that. I should never have read it.'

'But I'm glad you did. Please? I've got you a present.'

My tone softened. 'What kind of present?'

'Aha. You'll have to wait and see.'

I laughed. 'This had better be good.'

'See you in about fifteen minutes.'

'Sure.'

Fifteen minutes? My heart beating wildly, I ran upstairs to the bathroom and stepped into a hot shower. I washed my hair in record time, then dried it while smoking a cigarette and trying to get dressed. I kept checking my watch. Ten minutes to go: hair dry, dressed. Five minutes to go: makeup on, hair up. Three minutes to go: wine open, stereo on. One minute to go: sitting casually on the sofa, looking as though I hadn't moved since he phoned, pretending that this black satin shirt was just something I'd been wearing anyway.

Ten minutes later he still hadn't appeared. I drank one glass of wine, then two. I smoked about five cigarettes. He couldn't have let me down again, could he? The fire crackled and hissed and Maude appeared at my feet, chirruping. Fifteen minutes later I heard a car pull up outside. Then there was a knock at the door.

When I opened it and found Jack standing there looking slightly tousled and sheepish, I almost forgot I was pissed off with him. He was carrying a bottle of champagne and a bunch of red roses, which he offered to me. I smiled and took the flowers, deciding not to tell him off for being late. He may have broken down, had a puncture or even got lost. After all, he was still new to the area.

He came into the sitting room and sat down. He was grinning, as if someone had just told him a joke and he was working himself up to sharing it with me. I poured him a glass of wine and lit a cigarette.

'So come on, what are you so pleased about?'

'Seeing you.'

'And?'

'Well, I've just had the strangest experience.'

'Go on.'

'There I was, driving through Tuckenhay, and you'll never guess who I found standing by the side of the road, trying to hitch a ride?'

'I can't guess.'

'Our little friend Laura.'

'Laura?'

'Yep. On her way to America, finally. I gave her a lift into Totnes. She'll be on the train by now.'

'But she's gone mad. Emma was looking after her.'

'Yeah, so she was telling me. She even performed a bit of her mad self for me.'

'Performed?'

'Yeah. She called it the Dance of the Mad Swan.'

Without meaning to I burst into laughter. Jack joined in.

'The final twist,' I said.

'She's a real little psychopath,' said Jack.

Suddenly there were noises outside. Two car engines; squeals of brakes then slamming doors.

'What the ...?' said Jack, starting to get up.

There was no need. Without even knocking Emma swept in, closely followed by Tony Bryce.

'Have you seen her?' demanded Emma.

'Who?' I said innocently.

'Laura.'

'No. Jack?'

He shook his head. 'I've only just got back into town.'

'That little slut,' said Tony.

'Calm down,' I said. 'What's the problem?'

'She's disappeared,' began Emma.

'With twenty grand of my newspaper's money,' said Tony.

'And the contents of my savings account,' said Emma.

'Oh dear,' I said sweetly. 'So you won't get your story, then, Tony? How sad. Do you think you might lose your job?'

'Fuck you,' he said.

'Can you think of somewhere she might have gone?' asked Emma, urgently.

'Why do you want to find her so much?' asked Jack.

'She's taken all my money!' said Emma furiously.

'And you're not a bit concerned about how she is?' he said.

'Well, yes, of course I am ...' said Emma.

'And is this for your book, or because you actually care about her?' I said.

Emma raised a single pink fingernail. 'Don't get sanctimonious with me, Lily. You've got to find her.'

'No way.'

'I'm rehiring you.'

'Lily's not for hire,' said Jack, putting his hand on my shoulder.

'He's right,' I said. 'Sorry, Emma.'

'But what am I going to do?' she said in a small voice as Jack ushered her and Tony towards the door.

'Go get some therapy,' said Jack. 'Deal with it, get over it and move on.'

The door slammed and they were gone.

EPILOGUE

The night that it all ended was one of those nights you never forget. After Emma and Tony left, Jack and I settled down to talk seriously about our future. The next day he moved in with me. It seemed like a sensible thing to do.

We didn't discuss him going back to America. I knew it would have to happen at some point, but we were so in love that details like that didn't seem to matter. He would be here until June at least, anyway, and that seemed so far into the future that I just didn't worry. Instead we made all those adjustments you have to make. He learnt to cook my favourite meals, to bring me hot chocolate in the mornings and never to speak to me until I'd had my first cigarette of the morning. He met my mother and father, and got to work properly on his next film.

The application form for senior lecturer sat untouched on the windowsill in the kitchen for a long time. We tidied up around it, watered the plant next to it, but we never actually discussed it. And I didn't give it too much thought. I knew I didn't want to apply, but unless I had another great idea soon, I was going to have to.

Emma never got in touch again, but Jack and I got a postcard from Laura about two weeks after she left. In it she apologised for any 'trouble' she had caused and asked us to give her best wishes to her mother. We never heard from her again. I imagined what she would be doing in America; which poor suckers were going to take part in her next scam. Pippa and Eva-Mary settled in Paignton. Alex's share of the estate, once it had all been calculated, came to just over a hundred thousand pounds, so Pippa was a very rich little girl. I'd thought that Laura might contest the 'will' that her sister had left, but she probably realised that she'd have a lot to lose if she did. If I was her, I wouldn't have wanted to bring up all those details again.

Jack seemed to get better every day. By the middle of December he was sleeping right through the night, and the shakes had almost completely vanished. I realised what true love really was in those few weeks. I'd never met anyone like Jack. We had great fun role-playing some scenes for his new film, and he always marked half my essays for me.

I would never forget the Monday he did a talk to my crime-fiction students about *film noir*. He winked at me when he talked about *femmes fatales* and in my head I saw Laura, twisting her body around on that rock that day. Of course she was a bad person, but sometimes, if I was feeling weak or if I was in a sticky situation, I thought of her and tried to do what she would do.

As Jack and I left the university after he had done his talk one of these situations arose. We bumped into David, walking briskly across the car park.

'Lily,' he said, 'you were late this morning.'

'No,' I said sweetly, 'you must have made a mistake.'

Jack dug me in the ribs, and I tried not to laugh. Of course I'd been late this morning, and Jack knew what I'd been doing, since I'd been doing it to him. He kissed me and walked over to unlock the car, leaving me with horrible David.

'Have you done your form yet?' he asked me.

'Form?'

'Come on, Lily.' He sighed. 'The application form?'

'Oh, that. I'm still thinking about it.'

'Well, think quickly. The deadline's tomorrow, remember.'

*

Jack found me at one o'clock in the morning at my desk in my small study, hunched over the form. It was filled in, but not very well, and I still didn't know if I even wanted to apply.

'What are you doing?' he asked, sticking his head around the door.

'A stupid application form.'

'Uh-huh. For?'

'A job.'

'A job. Have I just missed the last two episodes in this soap opera?'

'Sorry?'

'Your life, Lily. Have I missed something?'

'I don't think so.'

'So how come I don't know you're applying for a job?'

'Because I haven't decided if I am yet.'

'You seem to be filling out the form.'

'I'm just keeping my options open. I may not even give it in.'

'And the job is?'

'Just senior lecturer at the university.'

'So it's not a big deal, then?'

'I don't know. It would mean going full-time.'

He came in and sat down. 'Do you want to do that?'

'No.'

'So why are you filling out the form?'

I held out my hands. 'I don't know. God, Jack, I'm twenty-six and I still don't know what I want to do. It's all right for you, you've got an exciting career as a screenwriter. What am I? A literature lecturer. Very exciting.'

'Yeah, but you've still managed to do more amazing things than I'd ever do.'

'Like?'

'Lily, you've recently solved three murder cases. That makes you pretty special.'

I looked down. 'I was thinking maybe I should do that for a living.'

'It sure would beat sitting at a desk all day.'

'You wouldn't mind?'

'It would give me lots of new material.' He laughed.

'This is serious.'

'I am serious. I just want you to be happy.'

'Really?'

'Yes. Would you be happy doing this?' He pointed at the form on my desk.

'No.'

'So give it up.'

'But I like my students.'

'Can't you do both?'

'I could just stay part-time and maybe try taking on cases less haphazardly.'

He smiled. 'Exactly.'

'So I guess I should bin this,' I said, picking up the form and tearing it in two.

'That's the Lily I know,' he said.

'I can't believe I've actually made a decision at last.'

'It's not hard when you try.'

'No.'

'Now you've only got one more decision to make.'

'Have I? What?'

'Whether you're going to marry me or not.'

'What?'

'You heard. But I'll give you a while to think about that one.'

'Uh ...' I was lost for words.

Jack grinned. 'So how about some coffee?'

And without saying another word he left the room and went to the kitchen, leaving me wondering whether or not I'd just imagined all that. Had he really asked me to marry him? Oh, God.